WHEN ALEC met EVIE

WHEN ALEC met EVIE

A SWEET HOCKEY ROMCOM

JENNY PROCTOR

ISBN: 979-8-9920796-9-2

This one is for the moms. The single moms. The tired moms. The "what happened to my body" moms and the "what did I sign up for" moms. I see you. You're doing great.

A NOTE FROM THE AUTHOR

The Appies are a very special hockey team. While I don't pretend to know everything about the sport, I know enough to acknowledge that the Appies fictional world contains minor elements surrounding the team and players and their positioning in the league that is unique. If I've gotten something wrong, it is either a human error (forgive me) or an intentional choice to fit the needs of the story, the characters, or the Appies world. While I tried very hard to stay true to the integrity of hockey as a sport, to honor the hard work and dedication of the athletes who play, this is a work of fiction, which means I get to make stuff up. Though hockey is the backdrop to this story, the romance, as always, is the true star, and I hope you find it both satisfying and enjoyable.

This story contains themes of divorce and single parenthood; it includes a narcissistic ex-husband, mentions of past emotional abuse, and candid conversations about pregnancy and breastfeeding. Also, there's kissing. Lots and lots of kissing. I hope you enjoy!

CHAPTER 1

ALEC

DON'T GET ME WRONG—MY teammates deserve to be happy. But seeing the ones I'm closest to suddenly coupled off, three guys married and two in serious relationships—I have to admit. I didn't see this one coming.

I'm the Appies *captain*. And I'm spending my Friday night with the rookies because all of *my* friends are at some sort of couples' party.

They invited me.

They aren't jerks.

But I'm not enough of a masochist to go to something like that on my own. Even sitting at Mulligan's with a pair of eighteen-year-old defensemen is better than watching my friends pretend I'm as interesting as the women in their lives.

Across the table, Carter, one of the newest Appies, laughs and Coke comes out of his nose. His twin brother, Theo—

they were recruited together because of how well they read each other on the ice—smacks him on the back and they both start to laugh.

I twitch as my jaw tenses.

I take it back. This isn't better.

I should have just stayed home. There's a new episode of *The Voice* I still haven't watched, and there's leftover lasagna in the fridge from the team dinner Felix hosted last night. Nobody makes lasagna like our goalie and...*man,* I sound old.

But these guys are barely out of high school. I'm practically babysitting. Especially since we're in a bar, and they aren't old enough to drink. Even if Mulligan's won't serve them—and they won't—the twins are both wearing Appies gear. I can't be sure an enthusiastic fan won't buy them a round if I'm not watching.

"Dude, she's checking you out," Carter says, tilting his head toward the bar.

I glance over my shoulder and recognize a blond woman I've talked to before. Jessica? Jasmine? Jennifer? We make eye contact, and she lifts her fingers in a fluttery wave.

Last season, I might have invited her over. Bought her a drink. Charmed her like I know I can. But in my current mood, I can't bring myself to care.

"Who's checking who out?" Tucker says as he rejoins the table, fresh beer in hand. He was the one who convinced me to come to Mulligan's in the first place—something about camaraderie and helping the rookies feel like they're part of the team. That used to be me. Looking out for people, making sure we're united on the ice and off. But Tucker has been stepping up lately. It's a good thing, but I have to wonder what happened to the player I was last season and if he'll ever make an appearance again.

Theo tilts his head toward the woman. "She is. Been staring at Captain all night."

Tucker looks over his shoulder. "You know her, right? I can't remember her name."

"Doesn't matter," I say before draining the last of my drink. "I'm not interested."

"That's right. You're still seeing that woman in Chicago. Riley somebody?"

I should probably correct him because I'm not seeing Riley. Not anymore.

I met her last spring when I was in Chicago doing a brand deal with the company she works for. We saw each other a few times over the summer, once when I went back to Chicago to visit, and two more times when she happened to be on the east coast for a wedding and then again visiting her family. She's nice enough. But she's busy and I'm busy, and whatever we had never felt special enough to do the extra work the distance created. She still texts every once in a while, and if she showed up in Harvest Hollow, I'd probably want to see her. But I think we both know nothing will ever happen between us.

But I don't feel like explaining all that to Tucker. And it won't change my level of interest in the woman at the bar. I glance at my watch.

"All right, I'm out," I say.

"Already?" Theo asks.

"Already," I repeat. "And you guys shouldn't be far behind me. You'll probably be on the ice a lot tomorrow." Rookies usually are in preseason games, so I fully expect Coach Davis to start these two over me and Nathan, even though we usually defend with the first line. I hold up a warning finger. "That means no drinking. Even if someone offers."

Theo and Carter nod in unison, their faces looking more similar than ever. "Right. Yes. Understood," Carter says.

I glance over at Tucker. "Sorry to bail early."

He waves a dismissive hand. "You already stayed longer than I thought you would."

I tilt my head toward the pair of rookies. "Keep an eye on them?"

"You know I will." Tucker cocks an eyebrow and smirks. "I know you older guys need more sleep than the rest of us."

I clamp a hand down on his shoulder and squeeze a little too hard. "Do you think it's my age or my sleep that makes me faster than you?"

Carter and Theo let out identical *oooohs*, but Tucker only chuckles.

"Yeah, yeah. Get out of here, old man."

I leave the bar, ignoring the ache in my right knee. Considering how I've been feeling lately, *old man* isn't that far off. At thirty-two, I'm one of the oldest guys on the team, maybe even in the league. And my body seems to be taking every opportunity to let me know.

Even after an off-season of careful training and intentional rest, I'm already feeling my time on the ice, and we haven't even played a game yet. After an ACL injury my last season of college, and two more once I went pro, impacting both my ACL and MCL, I've gotten used to my knee giving me trouble. But there's a new depth to the pain I definitely need to talk over with one of the Appies trainers. They've been telling me this might happen. That at some point, I'll have to weigh my desire to keep playing against my desire to have general mobility once I retire—walking, running, hiking. Regular life stuff.

Hard to think about a life that doesn't include pro hockey, but I get it.

4

The late September air is cool when I step into the parking lot, fall leaves crunching under my feet. I take a deep breath of mountain air. I used to think I'd move back to New York as soon as I could, but I'm not so sure anymore. It'd be nice to be closer to family, but there's something about these mountains that makes me think I could live here too. Even when I no longer have to.

I'm halfway home when my phone buzzes with a call, and I answer it through my car's sound system. "Hey, Meg," I say.

"Hey!" My younger sister's voice comes through with all the enthusiasm I've grown to expect. "I didn't think you'd answer."

"No?"

"Well, I mean, it's Friday night, and you're you. You aren't out? On a date?"

"On my way home," I say. "Got a game tomorrow."

"Ohhh, that's right. I've seen the news talking about it. Everyone's out to take down the Calder Cup champions. Did you read the Sports News Daily article?" she asks. "They were not nice to you."

The article Megan is referencing *wasn't* nice to me. Well, it was *sort of* nice to me, but in a backhanded way. The point of the article was to identify all the players on the Appies hockey team who *should* be playing in the NHL, listing most of our first and second lines, as well as me and Nathan, who I usually play with as a defensive partner.

It's not entirely untrue. Most AHL contracts are signed through the team's NHL affiliate so players can easily shift from one organization to the other, according to what's needed and where.

But the Appies aren't typical. With our social media presence and huge fan following, there's a lot of money in this

5

team, even though it's technically minor league. The Appies offer specific perks that give guys reasons to play here instead of aiming for the NHL. Which just means there's a lot of talent on the Appies' ice, and we're hard to beat.

Logan, our first-line left winger, has the most NHL experience and will likely be recalled sooner than later. A few others play with the same possibility, knowing they could shift teams any minute. But a lot of us signed AHL-only contracts that aren't up for renegotiation for another year or two. That means we're likely to keep dominating, which is starting to piss off the other teams in our league.

My name was mentioned a few times in the article, including one memorable line that called me a "very talented idiot who should give up online dance trends and stick to hockey where he actually belongs."

Flattering, I know.

What the article *didn't* mention is that my reason for staying with the Appies has a lot less to do with the dancing (though I don't really mind it) and a lot more to do with my knee.

It throbs as I shift my leg, easing off the gas to make a left turn.

I'm doing everything I can to make sure this isn't my last season of professional hockey, but if it is, I'd rather finish proud with the teammates who have come to feel more like brothers than play for someone else just because some stupid article says I should. The Appies have been good to me. It's not like I need the money.

"It's fine," I say to Megan. "You know I don't care what they say."

She makes a grumbling sound of complaint. "But you aren't an idiot."

"And Sports News Daily calling me one doesn't make that

6

any less true," I say. "What's up with you? How are Mom and Dad?"

"They just won a pickleball tournament in the over-seventy-five category," Megan says.

Technically, Mom and Dad are actually Grandma and Grandpa, but they've been raising us since three days after Megan was born when our actual mother—their only daughter—walked out on all of us.

We didn't see her for ten years, not until she showed up one random afternoon two weeks before I headed to Cornell for my freshman year of college. She was finally clean and sober and had a new husband, two stepchildren, and a brand new baby in her arms.

I barely recognized her, and Megan didn't at all, so when she told her toddler-aged stepchildren we were their aunt and uncle, we went along with it. We'd already been calling our grandparents Mom and Dad for years anyway. From then on, we called our actual mom Stacy and thought of her kids, including our half-brother, as our nieces and nephews.

"Dad played pickleball?"

"And he really liked it," Megan says.

I spent the last few weeks of my off-season up in New York with Megan, getting our parents moved out of the house in White Plains where they raised Megan and me and into a condo in a retirement community just down the road. No one was more surprised than me that they decided to move, but I do like knowing the change means they can get more help if they need it, especially since I'm so far away and Megan is still in school in the city.

Their neighborhood has several tiers of support for their residents, everything from meal delivery and daily check-ins with medical professionals to social gatherings and pickleball tournaments. Mom and Dad don't need any of the more intense care yet and probably won't for years. In a perfect world, they'll be living with me or Megan before they do. But I'm happy they're happy for now. That's what matters most.

"He has these little white shorts and a visor, and you'd die if you saw him," Megan says. "It's so cute."

"Send me a picture next time," I say as I turn into my neighborhood, waiting for the security gate to open before passing one perfectly manicured lawn after another. "What else is up?"

"Actually, something pretty big," Megan says. "I have a favor to ask of you."

I ease the truck up my driveway and open the garage door, then slowly pull inside. I turn off the engine but keep my phone connected so I don't lose Megan's call. The house I bought in the off season is stupidly big for one person, but it came fully furnished, which seemed easy, and I liked the idea of a security gate. The Appies are only getting more popular, so anything that puts a little distance between me and curious fans is a good thing.

"Whatever you need," I say to Megan without even having to think about it. I'd do anything for my little sister, and she knows it.

"So, you remember my best friend Evie?"

"Sure." When I was in college at Cornell, home was only a few hours away, and even though hockey kept me busy, I still made it home enough to keep up with Megan's life. Evie was around all the time. She was a pretty mellow kid. Funny like Megan, when she wanted to be, but never as giggly or silly as my sister.

"So, she just got this really incredible apprenticeship with a luthier in North Carolina," Megan says.

"A what? What's a luthier?"

"It's someone who makes stringed instruments. Or

maybe just repairs them? Actually, I think it's both. Evie has always played the violin, but I'm with you. I had no idea this was even a thing until she called to tell me about it. Anyway, apparently it's this really big deal that she was chosen because she'll be learning from one of the best in the business. It just means she has to move to Harvest Hollow."

"Ah," I say, suddenly sensing where this conversation is headed. I shouldn't be surprised. This is generally how Megan operates. If she loves someone, she'll do anything for them and, by extension, expect *me* to do anything for them too.

The only problem is, Megan loves *everyone*. Even strangers. She once gave my phone number to a couple of Appies fans she sat with on an airplane, promising them I'd be happy to get them tickets.

That only happened once because while her love knows no bounds, mine does. And it's firmly on the side of protecting my privacy.

"So I'm guessing you're asking me to help her move?"

"That would be amazing," Megan says. "I know I'm always doing this, but this time, Evie really needs the help. She doesn't know anyone in North Carolina. And she's basically like a sister to you, so you really have to say yes."

She's not quite like a sister, seeing as how I haven't seen or spoken to her in years. And my season is just about to start. I'm not exactly rolling around in free time. "You know I would, Meg, but I'm gone more than I'm not."

"No, I know," Megan says. "But we actually checked your game schedule and picked a timeframe that won't conflict. You shouldn't be traveling at all when she gets into town."

It's the most Megan thing I've ever heard. Of course she would check my game schedule before checking with me. Still, it's hard to be annoyed because Megan is the kind of sister who would get on a flight tomorrow if she thought I needed a hug. I've been on the receiving end of her devotion way more times than she's roped me into helping someone else, which is both amazing and frustrating.

Because it means I won't say no, and Megan knows it.

"Did she for real base her move on when I'll be in town?"

"She has to be there when her apprenticeship starts no matter what," Megan says. "But she wants to get into town a couple of weeks early so she has time to get settled with Juno and figure out childcare. She literally has no one else who can help. Please? I promised her you'd be willing. She's already going to feel so overwhelmed because Juno is only four months old."

"Juno?"

"Her daughter."

I groan. "Megan. Evie has a kid?" I don't know a lot about kids, but I'm guessing they make everything more complicated. Especially moving.

"A very small one," Megan says. "She won't get in the way at all."

I huff out a laugh. "I highly doubt that's true."

"Probably not," Megan says. "But if you can't help, I'm going to have to miss a week of class to do it myself, and that will probably mean failing at least two of my classes, which would set me back—"

"Fine. Fine!" I say, cutting her off. "I'll help her."

I hear the smile in Megan's voice when she says, "Thank you. You're the best brother ever."

I lean back in my seat. "I can't believe Evie has a kid. Is she even old enough for that?"

"She's twenty-three," Megan says. "Three months older than me."

"Is she married?"

10

"Alec. I was *in* her wedding. You saw all the pictures."

A few vague memories of Evie's wedding pop into my mind. Or more just memories of thinking she was way too young to be getting married. "Oh, that's right. I do remember. But if she's married, why does she need help moving?"

"Because she's divorced," Megan says. "And don't even get me started on her jerk of an ex-husband."

A surge of protectiveness pushes through me. She's *divorced* with a four-month-old baby? What kind of a loser husband did she have?

Maybe it's the similarity to my own situation—I'm no stranger to dads cutting out on their kids—but the thought makes me want to punch something. Who would do that?

"That really sucks."

"It does. But she's tough. Just not tough enough to unload her moving pod by herself with a baby strapped to her chest. Think you could take over some teammates to help?"

"Anything else I can do? Stock her pantry? Mow the lawn before she gets into town?"

"Stop being snarky," Megan says. "Did I catch you in a grumpy mood or something?"

Or something.

"Evie is literally the least demanding person ever," Megan continues. "Once you get her stuff unloaded, you'll probably never even hear from her again. I practically had to coerce her into letting me call you in the first place, and I know the only reason she caved is because her finances are really tight and she can't afford to pay for movers."

The note of genuine concern in Megan's voice softens the last bit of my resistance. Honestly, I'm not even sure why I've been hesitating. A year ago, this is the kind of thing I would have agreed to in a second. But everything has felt harder lately. Hockey stuff. Social stuff. Just general *life* stuff. I

11

haven't truly been myself since training started back up. But that's not an excuse to be a jerk. To Megan *or* Evie.

"It's fine. I'm sorry. I'll take some guys over, and we'll take care of it."

"Perfect. Thank you."

"Do you know where she's moving?" I ask.

"I can text you the address," Megan says. "It's a house on this cute street with tons of trees. It looked totally adorable in the pictures."

"She hasn't seen it in person?"

"It's just a rental, and of course she hasn't. She just had a baby. It's not like she's had time to hop on down to North Carolina to check things out."

I finally climb out of my truck, switching Megan's call back onto my phone and turning on the speaker. "If you send me the address soon, I'll drive over and check it out. Make sure it's in an okay part of town." This concession at least makes me feel better about my initially grumpy response.

"That would be awesome. See? I told her you'd be willing to help. She'll be so happy to have a friend in town."

"I'll do what I can," I say. "But remind her how much I'm gone. And I will be useless when it comes to the baby. I don't do babies."

Megan scoffs as I let myself inside. "What does that even mean? You don't do babies?"

"It means exactly what it means. I'm not a babysitter."

"I would *not* have asked you to babysit."

"You just had someone plan an entire move around my schedule without asking me first. Would babysitting really be that much of a stretch?"

"Okay. That's fair," Megan says. "Juno *is* a cute baby, though."

"She could be the cutest baby in the world and it

wouldn't matter. I've only ever held one, and it was our nephew. Half-brother. Whatever Stacy's kid is to us. The point is, he's eleven now. That was a long time ago."

"That's the thing. Most people have never held a baby until they have one. Pretty sure it's one of those things you just figure out." She yawns. "Okay. I gotta get back to studying. Thanks for helping Evie. Can I just give her your number?"

"Sure."

"K, I will. But Alec—"

Her words cut off, and I wait as I toss my keys onto the kitchen counter and toe off my shoes. "What?" I finally prompt.

She takes a breath, then hesitates before finally saying, "I'm just trying to decide if I need to say what I was thinking out loud."

"Just say it."

"It's just that Evie has really been through something. She needs your help, but she doesn't need you to be handsome and charming."

"What does *that* mean?"

"It means that you're *you*, and women love you."

"Megan. She's, what, nine years younger than I am? I promise I'm capable of helping a woman without asking her out."

"I know. I know! That's not even what I'm saying because honestly, I wouldn't hate it if you did ask her out. I just mean maybe not right now, okay? She's fragile."

"The thought has never occurred to me. She's *your age*. I'm way too old for her."

Megan is quiet for a beat before she says, "You might feel differently when you see her. She's changed a lot since high school."

"Unless she miraculously aged five years, I doubt it."

"Okay, okay," my sister says. "I believe you. But the warning still stands. Be careful with Evie."

We chat for a few more minutes before I end the call, but even after I hang up, I can't quite shake Megan's words or the knowing tone she used when she said them.

You might feel differently when you see her.

CHAPTER 2

EVIE

ONCE UPON A TIME, I used to love road trips. The snacks, the music, the endless stretch of road ahead of me.

But that was *before* I drove seven hundred miles with one arm stretched into the backseat, hooked over the edge of Juno's rear-facing car seat so she could hold onto my fingers. Or so I could retrieve her pacifier or stroke her forehead or tickle her shoulder in what were mostly fruitless attempts to calm her fussing.

Not to mention the fifteen billion times we stopped at rest stops to nurse or change diapers or question every decision I've ever made in my life.

Now that I'm finally standing outside my new home in Harvest Hollow, I'm pretty sure I never need another road trip for as long as I live.

All things considered, it probably could have been worse. Juno slept a lot more than I expected, and we had good weather the entire way. So I said a few more swear words

15

than I should have when I stopped to change Juno's diaper in rural Virginia. It's fine! We survived! Plus, she *did* shoot poop all the way up to her shoulder blades, so I kinda feel like at least sixty percent of those swear words were justified.

And now we're finally here in Harvest Hollow—a town I'd never even heard of until I stumbled across the listing for an apprenticeship that triggered my move. When I was researching the city, the internet told me it's a top destination in the fall both because of the fall leaves covering the Appalachian mountains, which are admittedly gorgeous, and because Harvest Hollow goes *all in* on celebrating the season. I drove down Maple Street on my way in, which appears to be the town's main thoroughfare, and quickly concluded that the internet doesn't lie. Pumpkins and hay bales on every street corner, fall leaves in every window display, twinkle lights overhead. If I hadn't seen it with my own eyes, I might not believe a place like this actually exists. It's picturesque to the point of seeming like it could only exist in a Hallmark movie.

And yet, here it is.

As long as my family is in White Plains, a part of my heart will always be in New York. But I'm liking the change and challenge of being out on my own. If only because I'm more ready than ever for a fresh start.

Or, fresh-*ish*? I can't completely start over when I'm financially dependent on my mother-in-law. *Ex*-mother-in-law now, I guess. But I wouldn't be here without her, and honestly, I'm lucky she still wants to be involved at all.

After her son basically signed over his parental rights in the divorce, giving me full custody of Juno, not every mother-in-law would want to be.

Devon is the youngest in his family, a surprise baby ten years younger than his closest sibling. His dad passed away a few years back, but his mom, Karen, is an active, busy grandma. Her three daughters are all married, all living in the same coastal Oregon town where they grew up, and they've given Karen seven grandkids that she sees all the time. But she still flew out to see me right after Juno was born, still talked to me like I was as much a part of her family as I was before the divorce. Best of all, she apologized profusely for her son's ridiculous behavior and promised she would help me financially for as long as I needed it.

It killed me to take her up on the offer. My identity is rooted firmly in self-sufficiency, and having someone send money every month simply because I believed all the lies her son told me feels wrong. Like I'm taking advantage.

If I only had to think about myself, I probably would have declined. But I'll swallow any amount of discomfort for Juno.

Besides. I can't make this apprenticeship work without her help, and I *really* want it to work.

First order of business?

Make the house in front of me look as cute as it did in the rental listing. It's *mostly* what I saw in the pictures. Same front porch, same bright blue shutters. But the overflowing flowerpots are nowhere to be found. Same with the porch swing and the neatly manicured front lawn.

I was excited about that porch swing. I thought it might be a nice place to sit with Juno.

I take a deep breath and look back at the car.

It's going to be fine.

It *has* to be fine, because I'm here, and I'm definitely not driving back to White Plains.

And really, I shouldn't be so critical of the house. I just need to warm it up a little. I can't exactly expect spring flowers in the middle of fall. But if I add a few of those pumpkins I saw all over Maple Street and some brightly

17

colored mums, the house will be halfway to what I expected, just like that.

I move back to my Honda and pull Juno's carrier out of the back seat. She was asleep when I pulled up, but she's awake now, staring up at me with wide blue eyes. She smiles when she sees me and kicks her pajama-clad feet.

Just looking at her stills some of the panic creeping into my heart. Nothing calms me faster than knowing I have to be calm for *her*.

With Juno's carrier looped over one arm, I step back up to the front seat and grab my violin—the only other thing I won't leave in the car—then head up the sidewalk to my new porch. I pass the enormous moving pod sitting in the driveway, ignoring the sense of overwhelm that creeps in whenever I think about unpacking it by myself. I'll at least have help moving it all inside, but after that, I'll have to come up with some sort of system. Unpack a box, feed the baby. Unpack another box...feed the baby *again*.

When I reach the porch, the boards on the bottom step look like they've been recently replaced, which makes me feel a little better about the empty flower beds and leaf-strewn lawn.

And the street looks nice too. All the Craftsman-style houses are small, including mine, but they look loved and well maintained, with wide sidewalks on either side and a line of maple trees with bright yellow leaves shading the pavement.

The front door has a coded entry, so I pull up the latest email from my landlord to retrieve the code. I read over his message one more time.

Hi Evie, I hope you find all in order once you arrive. The code is the same for the front door and the garage. There's a key in the kitchen drawer that will open the back door in case you ever need it. The back

door sticks when it rains, so you might have to pull extra hard on those days. Also, watch out for the bottom step on the front porch. I didn't notice it was rotten until I was on my way out of town, but I'll fix it next month as soon as I return. I'm backpacking in Yosemite until October 20th, so I'll have limited access to cell service, but I'll check messages as often as I can. The code for the door is 7412. Cheers
—John

I look back at the step, which is definitely *not* rotten, and frown. If John didn't do it, who did?

"Hello?"

I spin around to see an elderly woman with deep brown skin and striking gray hair making her way up the front walk. She's carrying a tinfoil-covered pie plate in her hands, and she smiles wide when we make eye contact.

"You must be Evie," she says.

"Um, yes?"

She climbs the steps and stops in front of me. "I'm Ruth. I live a few houses down."

"Oh. Hi. Nice to meet you."

She looks down at Juno's carrier and smiles. "And this must be Juno."

There is nothing even a little bit creepy or uncomfortable about this woman. Everything about her vibe is friendly and kind, but it still feels a little weird that she knows my name *and* Juno's name.

"I'm sorry, do we—was it the landlord who told you about me?"

Her eyes widen like she's just remembered something very important. "Oh! I skipped right over that part, didn't I? Look at me, walking up here like we're already friends when I'm nothing but a stranger to you."

"No, I'm so happy to meet you. Just a little confused."

Ruth smiles. "We have friends in common. My nephew,

19

Malik, he's the manager of the Appies hockey team. He told me one of his players had a friend moving in who might be looking for a little bit of help with the baby."

My heart speeds the slightest bit at the thought. "Alec?"

She nods. "That's the one. I met him when he was here fixing your steps the other day. I tell you what. He's just as handsome in person as he is on television."

Alec.

As soon as my best friend Megan learned I was moving to North Carolina, she all but coerced me into letting her older brother, who's the captain of the pro hockey team based in Harvest Hollow, help me move in. I clearly need it—it's not like Juno can help me move a couch—but it's still trippy to think about seeing Alec again.

We've texted twice since Megan gave me his number, just enough to confirm what time I would arrive. But we haven't talked at all, and I haven't seen him in years. Not since I was eighteen and he watched Megan and me walk across our high school graduation stage.

Back then, I thought the sun rose and set on Alec Sheridan. He was nine years older than me—too old for my crush to ever be anything but a silly fantasy.

But here lately, even before I decided to move, he's been on my mind all over again.

I've always followed his career, watched as his hockey star rose higher and higher and his online presence grew larger and larger. But then, when Juno was three weeks old, cranky and colicky, I was up in the middle of the night, pacing through my parents' living room trying to soothe her, mindlessly scrolling Instagram reels to keep myself awake. A video of Alec popped up, an interview in which he talked about his favorite parts of the game.

It was only four minutes long, but something about the

tone of his deep voice must have soothed Juno because she settled as soon as it started and stayed quiet until it ended. When I scrolled onto the next video, she started fussing again, so we went back to Alec.

It worked like magic.

Three and a half months later, I've listened to that four-minute video no less than a hundred times.

Me and a million other fans, apparently. It's one of his most popular videos.

Alec's Instagram account isn't the biggest of the Appies, but he still has over five hundred thousand followers. That's a lot of people.

But I knew him *before.*

I know how much he loves his sister. How good and kind and protective he is.

I was there when he got the phone call about his hockey scholarship to Cornell, and I went to countless college games with Megan, the two of us wearing matching jerseys, Alec's name and number printed on the back. I heard about him signing with the Appies the same day it happened, when Megan called to tell me the good news, and I was there when he graduated from college.

In my mind, Alec was larger than life. Perfect in all the ways a man should be perfect.

It's nothing short of surreal to think of him coming over here early, checking on my house and fixing my steps.

Apparently, imagining Alec wielding a hammer is more than enough to reignite my long-dormant feelings, because a twinge of something familiar pushes against my ribcage, making my chest flush with heat and my skin tingle with awareness.

Except...*no.* Those are not feelings I need. I can feel grati-tude, maybe even hints of admiration. But now is not the time for a crush, and not just because he's my best friend's older brother. Barely a year out from my divorce, I'm not even sure I'm capable of the emotions a relationship would require.

Not that I would actually expect the internet's favorite hockey captain to ever be interested in me. I'm just saying if he was, I don't think it would matter. Sometimes I feel like my divorce acted like a factory reset, and I'm having to learn how to love and trust all over again.

The only exception to the very depressing condition of my heart is Juno. Loving her is the easiest thing I've ever done. Most of the time, I have no idea how to mother her or teach her or raise her into a capable human. But loving her—that's like breathing.

In the carrier at my feet, Juno starts to fuss, and I pick it up, swinging it back and forth. She's going to need to eat soon and probably needs her diaper changed.

"Alec is my best friend Megan's older brother," I say to Ruth. "That's why he's helping out. I've known him since I was a kid."

"Is that right?" Ruth says. "Well, it's wonderful he's here and willing to help. Now, I know we've just met and you're under no obligation to be my friend, but I retired last year, after teaching for thirty-seven years. My kids are off living their lives and haven't given me any grandchildren yet, and my husband passed six months ago, leaving me all alone in a house that's too empty, too big for just me."

My heart squeezes at the mention of her husband's passing, but Ruth blazes on, her expression shuttering just enough for me to sense she'd rather not dwell on it.

"I've got a knack for babies," she continues, "so if you need a helping hand, I hope you'll call me." She holds up the pie plate and looks at the bottom. "I taped my phone number to the bottom of the pie plate. Chicken pot pie. Figured you'd need food more than you'd need dessert, what with a baby to care for."

"I don't know what to say." Juno's crying escalates, so I put her carrier down long enough to check my landlord's note one more time and type the code into the front door lock.

Ruth sets the pie down on the porch railing behind her and picks up the carrier, swinging Juno just like I was. "Beautiful baby," she says. "Look at those big eyes."

Juno quiets at the sound of Ruth's voice as I push open my front door. It creaks as it swings inward, and a wave of musty, damp air washes over my face. Frowning, I take one step into the living room, and the carpet squishes under my foot, water seeping up on either side of my sneaker.

So...that's fun.

There's a lake in my new living room.

CHAPTER 3

EVIE

I FIGHT to steady my breathing as I survey the damage in my new house. Every inch of carpet that I can see from the door looks wet, and from what I can see of the kitchen, just visible around the corner, there's standing water there as well.

"Uh-oh," Ruth says from behind me. "That doesn't look good."

Emotion pinches my chest, and tears rush to my eyes. My logical brain knows this isn't the end of the world. That whatever randomly flooded my house, my landlord, who has so far proven to be both helpful *and* kind, will very likely fix it. But my logical brain checked out somewhere along I-85. Dreaming of this house, this cute little cottage where Juno and I can start over, has been a big motivator through all the stress and emotion of the past few months.

I imagined Juno's room, crib set up next to the big window I saw in the rental listing, a fall breeze fluttering the curtains. I imagined my tiny couch and overstuffed chair positioned in the living room, full of fluffy blankets and throw pillows, warm lamplight casting the room in a cozy glow.

That feels so impossibly far from where I am now. I swallowed the missing porch swing. But a flood? I just don't have it in me.

As if to punctuate the hopelessness of the moment with an exclamation point, Juno lets out an extra loud wail, and my milk lets down, seeping through my bra and soaking the thin cotton of my t-shirt. I look down at my leaky, too-large boobs and sigh.

"Now, now," Ruth says quietly beside me, her hand squeezing my shoulder. "You wipe those tears away." Her words are soft and lilting, her Southern accent touching the edges of every syllable. "We'll get your landlord on the phone and sort this out in no time."

We can't, actually, sort anything out. At least not anytime soon.

Ruth manages to trace the flood to the still-leaking water heater and turns off the water to the whole house, but that doesn't do anything to help the inches of water already pooling on the floor. The carpet is soaked, the wood floors in the kitchen are warped, the baseboards and several inches of drywall are completely waterlogged.

And I can't get my landlord to answer his phone.

Though I'm not sure how much help he'll be until he's home from his backpacking trip, even if he does answer. I don't know a lot about water damage, but I'm guessing this is going to take days, maybe even weeks to fix.

Which means Juno and I are essentially homeless.

It's too cold to sleep in my car, which means...I can get a hotel, maybe? Or...I guess that's my only option. A hotel.

A wave of nausea makes my skin feel clammy, and a cold sweat breaks out on my forehead.

I can't afford a hotel. I was basically scraping the bottom of the barrel to pay for the move and get myself down here. I'll get another deposit from my ex-inlaws at the first of next month, and I have savings. But there isn't an ounce of wiggle room in the spreadsheet I made for myself, in the meticulous calculations I did to make sure those savings will stretch and supplement my income for the entire nine months of my apprenticeship.

There's no way I'll make it if I have to spend a week—maybe longer—in a hotel room.

Ruth eventually coaxes me away from the porch and down the sidewalk to her house where I finally sit down to feed Juno. She disappears into the kitchen, returning moments later with a huge helping of chicken pot pie. She sets it on the coffee table in front of me. "I know this won't help us solve the problem," she says as she hands me a fork, "but it won't hurt either."

My chest tightens, and another round of tears threatens to spill over.

I have never liked being a burden to other people. I'm a middle child, the only daughter in between two brothers. An older one, Charlie, who spent his teenage years challenging my parents at every turn, and a younger one, Brady, who was diagnosed with leukemia the week before his fifth birthday and spent the next seven years in and out of the hospital. He's completely healthy now—a senior in high school, a state champion swimmer, and cancer free going on five years.

But there's no undoing the way his illness impacted my childhood. I know my parents loved me—they still love me—but they had their hands full. I quickly learned the best thing I could do to help was stay quiet and out of the way.

It's why I spent so much time with Megan. She lived two houses down, and it was always easier at her place. I still hated it—hated realizing how many gaps Megan's mom had to fill because mine had too much going on. Having Ruth talk like this is a problem we'll solve together is almost enough to unravel me.

"Thank you for being so kind," I say to Ruth. "But I don't want to put you out. Once I eat, I'm sure I can..."

"You can what? Look a lonely old lady in the eye and tell her you don't want her help? As long as you let me hold that baby when she's finished her meal, you can stay here all afternoon." She sits down across from me. "Have you heard from Alec?"

"I sent him a message and told him where I am," I say, "but he hasn't responded yet."

I almost told Alec not to come—it's not like we can move anything into the house—but the moving pod that was delivered just over a week ago is supposed to be picked up tomorrow, and I'd rather not pay to keep it for another month. Especially if my already stretched bank account is going to pay for a hotel. So my hope is that instead of moving everything inside, we can move it all into the garage.

"I'm sure he'll find you," Ruth says. "Now, eat. I promise it's delicious."

Forty-five minutes later, Juno is fed and down for a nap in the portable crib I retrieved from my car, my belly is full of the best chicken pot pie I've ever had, and Ruth is entertaining me with stories about her children, a daughter and a son who are, respectively, studying medicine at Harvard and serving as an officer in the Marine Corps.

"Your kids sound amazing," I say.

She stands and moves into the small kitchen just off the

28

living room, dishes clinking together as she says, "They've made their mamma proud."

When she returns, she hands me a second plate, this one holding some sort of apple dessert.

"It's a crumble," she says. "And you might like it more than the pot pie."

"Hard to imagine how." I take the plate and scoop up a generous bite. "Oh man, Ruth. This is unbelievable."

She beams, and I get the sense it really does bring her joy to feed people. Which, I'm just saying, there are worse qualities for neighbors to have.

I've just finished the last of my crumble and am debating the merits of licking the plate clean when a knock sounds on the front door.

Ruth stands and smiles. "That's probably your hockey player."

Ha! *My hockey player.* That's a pipe dream if ever there was one.

I press a hand to my stomach, a vain attempt to quell the nerves fluttering in my belly. I'm already tense from the emotional upheaval of the last hour, so the thought of seeing Alec again has me dangerously close to throwing up.

I take several deep breaths, in through my nose and out through my mouth, finishing just in time for Alec to walk into the living room, flanked by three broad-shouldered men I immediately recognize as his teammates. There's something to be said about seeing four professional athletes in one very small living room, especially when they're as handsome as this group.

Though, to be honest, it's hard to peel my eyes off Alec to even notice the other guys.

He was handsome when I was a kid. And I've seen him online enough to know he's *still* handsome. But seeing him in

29

person is something else entirely. He isn't quite as broad or as bulky as his teammates, but that's hardly a fair comparison because two of the guys behind him have to be close to six-foot-five.

Alec still looks every inch the athlete, well-muscled and fit. His hair is longer than I remember, and he's got a faint five o'clock shadow dusting his jawline.

I quickly stand, and his eyes move over me before catching and holding my gaze.

I bite my lip, wondering what he's noticing. What he thinks of me.

Annnd then I think about the milk stains on my t-shirt and the baby barf on my shoulder.

Nothing like a little bodily fluid to ground me back in reality.

Alec Sheridan is not here for me to ogle him, and he definitely isn't ogling me.

Stretch marks for miles, boobs that turn into milk-filled cantaloupes at least five times a day. I am so far from sexy right now, I'm not deluded enough to think I'm turning any heads.

That means if I'm going to get through the rest of this day with any dignity at all, I need to shelve any and all thoughts about Alec and his sexy man stubble in the very back of my mind.

Alec smiles, his lips lifting a little more on the left than the right, just like they always did. "Hey, nerd."

His voice is a low and delicious rumble, sending a wave of goosebumps skittering across my skin. It's not a wonder Juno loves it so much.

Then it registers that Alec just called me *nerd*.

It's a nickname I earned my freshman year of high school when I took a history textbook to one of Alec's hockey

30

games. Hearing it now brings an unexpected sense of home to an afternoon that, so far, has pushed me completely out of my comfort zone. I'm a stranger to North Carolina, even to Ruth, as kind as she's being. But I'm not a stranger to Alec.

I grin with relief, emotion making my eyes sting with moisture. I had no idea how much I needed to see a familiar face until he walked in.

I'm still so scared. Completely overwhelmed.

But for the first time today, I'm feeling a little more certain that things are going to be okay.

CHAPTER 4

ALEC

THE WOMAN STANDING in front of me can't be Evie Thomas.

She's got the same blue eyes, the same wavy hair falling over her shoulders. But everything else I'm noticing—it's breaking my brain.

Dark lashes, full, pink lips, creamy skin, subtle curves.

Logically, I know I shouldn't be surprised. Megan warned me. Reminded me that Evie is in her twenties now. She's been married, had a baby, experienced parts of life I haven't even started to think about. But in my head, she's always been my kid sister's best friend, cheering from the stands at my college hockey games. This version of Evie doesn't fit in that box.

She's all grown up, and she's *gorgeous*.

Still Megan's best friend, and still too young for me. But gorgeous.

Beside me, Camden digs an elbow into my ribs, and I

33

realize I've been staring. I said hello, called Evie a nerd, then she smiled, and I apparently lost my ability to speak.

Luckily, Evie fills the silence for me. "I am *never* going to live that down, am I? It was *one* game."

I glance over my shoulder at my teammates. "She brought a textbook to one of my college playoff games."

"I had a really important history exam," she counters.

"Sounds like a logical choice to me," Felix says from just over my right shoulder.

"Especially if the alternative was watching *you* play," Nathan adds.

The insult doesn't hold an ounce of water coming from Nathan, who has been my defensive partner for the past four seasons. We're rarely on the ice without the other, so if I play well, he usually does too, and vice versa.

But then Camden adds, "Without Nathan next to you to make you look good, watching had to be painful."

My teammates chuckle, and Evie's eyes dance as she looks us over, like she finds them dogging on me highly entertaining.

I roll my eyes and step to the side, waving a hand toward my friends. "If it wasn't obvious, these idiots are a few of my teammates, and they've clearly forgotten how to respect their captain. Evie, meet Nathan, Camden, and Felix."

I introduce Evie and Malik's aunt, whom I met the other day when I was fixing Evie's front step, and the guys take turns stepping forward to shake hands with them both. When they finish, I look at Evie. "Want to point us in the right direction? It shouldn't take long with all four of us working."

Despite their teasing, considering what Megan told me about Evie, I'm glad it's these three teammates who are with me. Camden is the only one who is single, but he's still hung up on a woman he met over the summer while visiting his family in Savannah. He hasn't said much about it, but he's clearly still licking his wounds over what happened when he left. Felix got married at the end of the off-season, and Nathan is in a committed relationship. Even if they weren't, I'd trust all three of these guys to be respectful in any circumstance, but it feels particularly important this time.

If Evie's ex-husband walked out on her, leaving her pregnant and alone, she probably doesn't have the highest opinion of men. Maybe that's what Megan meant when she said Evie was fragile.

"Yes. Definitely," Evie says, a beat of worry crossing over her expression. "But there's been a slight change of plans."

After Ruth agrees to keep an eye on Juno, who must be sleeping somewhere, Evie leads the way, and we head down the sidewalk to her house. As we walk, she explains the flooding she found when she first opened her front door, then details her desire to just move everything into the garage instead. I hear and process her words, but I'm admittedly distracted by this more mature version of Evie's voice, by the way she moves her hands as she talks as if to punctuate her words.

Did she do that before? I can't remember, but I like that she does it now.

"And you still haven't gotten through to your landlord?" I ask as we turn and head up her driveway.

"Not yet. But he did warn me he'd be hard to reach for the next week or so. He's backpacking in Yosemite. Either way, there's no way I can sleep here tonight, so moving stuff into the garage will have to do."

I frown. "If you aren't going to sleep here, where are you going to go?"

She shrugs. "A hotel, probably."

Felix, who is a landlord himself, moves to Evie's other side and starts asking questions about her lease.

Meanwhile, all I can think about is the enormous house I'm living in all by myself.

If Megan were here, she wouldn't want Evie paying for a hotel. But...Evie has a *baby*. Do I really want a baby staying in my house? Would Evie even feel comfortable staying with me? After Sunday's final preseason game, we'll be on the road for close to a week. She'd basically have the whole place to herself.

"I just went through this last year," Felix is saying, "and I've got a great disaster repair company we can call. Even if your landlord doesn't get back to you right away, if you go with a company that's licensed and insured, considering the circumstances, I doubt he'll protest you moving forward with the repairs."

"He's been really easy to work with so far," Evie says. "But I'm not sure I could afford to start if he's not footing the bill."

I watch Felix's expression soften. He's got the resources and the connections, and I know he'd take care of this for Evie without batting an eye. But something deep in my gut doesn't want Felix to be the one who solves this problem for her.

"That shouldn't—"

I take a step forward and turn to face Evie. "Let's just get through today and see if we hear from your landlord," I say, cutting off Felix's words. "We can figure out next steps once we get everything unloaded."

"Yes. Good plan," Evie says, but Felix shoots me a knowing look, one eyebrow raised like he understands exactly what's going through my mind.

If he does, then he's a few steps ahead of me, because I

can't make sense of it at all. I just know that despite the grumbling I did about Megan volunteering me to help, Felix shouldn't be the one who solves Evie's problem.

It should be me. I *want* it to be me.

Besides, Megan would never let me forget it if I didn't step up, and I'm sure Evie is going to tell her what happened, if she hasn't already. My hands are basically tied here.

It isn't going to take long to stash everything in the garage because Evie doesn't have that much stuff. A couch, a couple of chairs, a bed, a single dresser. There's more furniture for the baby than there is for her.

After ten minutes of the five of us working in relative silence, I carry an open crate full of what looks like music books into the garage and set it down on top of a dresser that Nathan and Felix just brought in. Evie is standing beside it, adjusting the shade on a floor lamp that looks like it was bent in the move.

"You play violin, right?" I say, shifting the box forward.

She glances at the music books and smiles. "I'm surprised you have to ask. I practiced at your house almost as much as mine."

A memory pops into my head of Evie playing the same simple song over and over again while I was home on break from college, trying to watch a movie with friends. She must have been in middle school at the time and had seemed upset when she crossed through the living room to Megan's room, instrument case in hand.

She'd sounded terrible—cracked and squeaky—nowhere near like actual music. But I'd refused to ask her to stop even when my friends complained. There had to be a reason she wasn't practicing at home, and if the tears I noticed when she passed through were any indication, it probably had something to do with her brother, who'd been sick as long as I could remember.

I must be frowning because Evie starts to laugh. "I know. I sounded terrible back then."

"No, no, that's not what I was—"

She lifts an eyebrow, cutting off my protests, because I *was* thinking about how bad she sounded. But that wasn't why I frowned.

"I was just thinking about your brother," I explain. "He was why you practiced at our place, wasn't he? Brady, right? How's he doing?"

Her expression brightens. "He's great. Totally cancer free. He's a senior this year."

"Really? Wasn't he just a few years younger than you? He's still in high school?"

"Five years younger," she says easily. "It's freaking my parents out that they're so close to having an empty nest."

The fact that Brady is only five years younger than Evie and he's still in high school makes my thirty-plus years suddenly feel ancient. For me, high school feels like a different life.

"Thanks for asking," Evie adds, almost like she's surprised I remembered.

I nod and tilt my head toward the music books. "I assume you eventually got...good?"

She laughs. "I did. Good enough, anyway. I graduated with a degree in music and everything."

"That's why you're down here. Something to do with your violin?"

"Sort of?" she answers. "Less *my* violin, and more just stringed instruments in general. I'll be learning how to build them, repair them, refurbish them."

38

"Megan said you'll be a luthier? I honestly didn't even know that was a thing."

"Most people don't. At least, not people who aren't musicians."

"Why'd you pick it?" I ask, mostly because I really like listening to her talk.

She shrugs. "I don't know. My degree is in violin performance, and I'm sure I'll get back to that eventually, but since I'm raising Juno on my own, I needed something with more flexible hours. As long as there are people who *play* stringed instruments, there will always be a need for luthiers, so I figured...good job security? Plus, this is a really great opportunity. Victoria is one of the best in the business, so I'm lucky I get to learn from her."

I step to the side while Camden and Nathan bring in Evie's mattress and lean it against the wall.

"There are a few pillows in the back if you can't handle anything heavier," Nathan says, eyeing the crate of books with a grin.

The last few weeks, I've been spending a lot of time with the trainers after practice, icing my knee, babying it like I have to if I have any hope of staying in the game. But then yesterday on the ice, Coach Davis made a comment about my age. *"You aren't as young as you used to be, Sheridan. This season, you have to play with your brain as much as your body."*

Since then, the guys have been ribbing me with merciless consistency. My level of play hasn't been impacted—at least I don't think it has been—so the teasing has all been very good-natured. But I'm guessing if the guys knew the kind of pain I'm ignoring, they'd take the whole situation a little more seriously.

Still, I can't fault them for what they don't know, and I'm not sure I'm ready to talk about it yet.

"What was that about?" Evie asks as we watch Camden and Nathan walk back to the pod.

"What was what about?" I ask. "The teasing? They just like to make fun of me for being old."

She eyes me curiously. "Okay. But it seemed like your face did a thing."

"A thing?" I raise my eyebrows, but it's not lost on me that Evie just picked up on something being off when, so far, none of my friends have done the same.

Less than an hour later, we finish unloading, and Evie closes up the pod.

While she walks back to Ruth's to check on Juno, I head inside the house with Felix to take a look at the water damage. It's bad. Worse than I expected. There's no way she's moving in until this place has been completely gutted. It's going to need new floors, new baseboards, possibly even new drywall.

"What do you think?" I ask Felix.

He runs a hand through his hair. "The sooner you get someone over to start cleanup, the better. We could do a little with a push broom, get some of the standing water out, but it's really a job that should be tackled by professionals." He pulls out his phone. "I'm texting you the number of the guy I know. He did fast work at my place. He could probably have guys out here before nightfall."

"You think I should go ahead and call him? Even with the landlord not knowing what's up?"

"I would," Felix says. "The longer the water sits, the worse things will get and the longer Evie will be without a home."

I nod as my phone buzzes with Felix's text. "All right, cool. I'll call right now."

I follow Felix out to the porch, where he says goodbye

then heads down the driveway to where Camden is already climbing into Nathan's Bronco. The three of them wave before Nathan pulls away from the curb, probably anxious to get on with their evening.

There's still no sign of Evie, so I drop onto the porch steps and call the number Felix sent me. It only takes a few minutes to explain the situation, and the guy on the phone assures me he'll have someone over to assess the damage and begin water removal within the hour.

While I'm on the call, my phone buzzes several times. By the time I end the call and open my texts to see, I already know what I'm going to find.

Sure enough, my teammates have blown up the dream team text thread we keep going between us. A while back, a journalist referred to the Appies starting line as *The Dream Team*, so we renamed our text thread as a joke. There are eight of us all total, seven who still play for the Appies, plus Wyatt who was with us last season, then signed with the Bruins and moved to Boston. Most of the time, I'm happy to stay connected with my teammates.

Other times, the dream team texts make me want to throw my phone into the nearest lake.

NATHAN

A heads up for those of you who weren't present. When Alec saw Evie for the first time, he basically swallowed his own tongue.

CAMDEN

Can confirm.

FELIX

Honestly, it was hard to miss. Pretty sure he drooled.

VAN

I'm sorry I missed it.

NATHAN

It's also worth noting that her house flooded
from an exploding water heater, which
means our good captain is probably going to
invite her to stay at his place.

FELIX

He'd better invite her. Alec, you do know you
can't let her stay in a hotel, right?

ALEC

Of course I will. But this will not be a thing.
Evie is like a sister. There was no tongue-
swallowing.

Definitely no drooling.

FELIX

Good. Then it shouldn't be a big deal when
she moves in.

VAN

How much younger is she?

ALEC

Nine years.

VAN

Nice. She can care for you in your old age.

I pocket my phone, knowing that at this point,
responding will only motivate them more. But Felix is right.
It shouldn't be a big deal for Evie to stay with me. And if she
actually *was* my sister, I wouldn't hesitate to offer. Which
makes me wonder why I'm hesitating now.

I look up and see Evie walking down the sidewalk with
Ruth, a baby in her arms.

I stand and make my way toward her, meeting them at the

foot of the driveway. The baby is facing outward in Evie's arms. She has a head full of dark hair the same color as Evie's and big blue eyes. As far as babies go, she's pretty cute. I've never seen one with so much hair.

The baby kicks her legs the slightest bit, and Evie looks down and smiles. "Are you saying hi to Alec?" she says to her daughter. She lifts her gaze to meet mine. "Alec, this is Juno."

I reach out and let Juno take my finger, her chubby fist closing around it with surprising grip. "Hey there, Juno," I say, shaking her finger like it's an official greeting. This makes the baby smile and something small turns over inside my heart.

"I think she likes you," Evie says. "Want to hold her?"

"Oh, absolutely not," I say, and Evie laughs. "I don't know anything about babies."

"There's only one way to learn," Ruth says with a knowing grin.

"Did your friends leave?" Evie asks, looking toward the curb. "I didn't get to say thank you."

"They did, but they don't need any thanks. They were happy to help. And they already agreed to come back when the house is done and you can officially move in."

Evie smiles, but it's tight around the edges, and I can sense how much she hates needing this much help. I definitely shouldn't tell her I just gave my credit card number to the disaster repair guy to secure their services.

I'm pretty sure her landlord will pay me back.

But even if he doesn't, I'm not sure I care.

"Now, Alec, help me convince this young lady that she does not need to stay in a hotel," Ruth says, one hand propped on her hip. "I've got a spare guest room that she's welcome to use, and I'd be more than happy to have the company."

A knot forms in my stomach. I should feel relief. Evie would probably feel more comfortable at Ruth's, and I'm sure the elderly woman knows a lot more about babies than I do. But what I really feel is a strange sense of disappointment.

"It's so kind of you to offer," Evie says. "But you already told me your daughter is coming to visit next week. I can't take up the guest room when she'll need it, especially not with a baby who doesn't care if anyone else in the house gets any sleep."

"As I said, there's a pull-out sofa in the office that Desiree can use," Ruth chides, but I understand Evie's hesitance, especially with the open-ended nature of her current situation.

"Actually, I've got more than a few empty guest rooms at my house," I say before I can overthink it. "They're on the opposite side of the house from my room, so you'd have plenty of privacy and your own bathroom. Plus, I'm on the road with the Appies all next week, and the house is empty when I'm not there."

Evie's brows lift, eyes wide. "You'd let me stay with you?"

Something in her tone makes my cheeks warm the slightest bit. "I mean, if you want. Megan would want me to offer."

"Well," Ruth says. "That sounds like a perfect solution."

Evie bites her lip, and for a moment, I expect her to protest. To say she'd be more comfortable at Ruth's after all. But then her head bobs once in a distinctive nod. Like she's made up her mind and committed herself to it, maybe despite her better judgment. "Okay," she finally says. "That would be great."

Okay. So I guess I'm getting a new roommate.

Juno blows a few spit bubbles before kicking her feet,

squirming enough that Evie flips her around and lifts the baby to her shoulder.

Make that *two* new roommates.

My heart speeds the slightest bit, and I realize I'm excited.

Weirdly excited. And not just because I know it's what Megan would expect.

Maybe it's because my house really is too quiet. Or maybe it's because I can't stop noticing the way Evie keeps tugging her hair over her shoulder, revealing the curve of her neck, the ridge of her collarbone, the slope of her bare shoulder. She's wearing overalls over a white tank top, a look I didn't know I liked until I saw it on her.

"So I guess, since I still haven't heard from my landlord, I just need to call someone about the house," Evie says. She looks at me. "Felix mentioned he knows someone. Did he happen to give you the number?"

"It's already taken care of," I say. "They'll be here before the end of the day."

Evie holds my gaze, lips pressed together for a long moment before she turns and hands Juno to Ruth then steps closer and wraps herself around my waist in a tight hug.

At first, the surprise of the gesture keeps me from responding, but it only takes a moment for me to catch up and settle my arms around her shoulders. She smells amazing, like apples and cinnamon, which is something considering the day she's had, and it's all I can do not to lower my nose to her hair and breathe in a lungful of her scent.

I'm sure I've probably hugged Evie before, when she was offering congratulations after a game. Or maybe after her and Megan's high school graduation. But I've never hugged her like this, and I'm distracted by how good it feels to have her against me.

"Thank you, Alec," she whispers. She gives me one last squeeze, then lets me go, stepping back as she lifts her hands to wipe at her eyes.

My throat goes suddenly dry and my skin prickles with heat and awareness.

What was that?

A hug, but something else too.

Ruth clears her throat, and I lift my gaze to hers. She raises her eyebrows, then looks pointedly at Evie.

Right. Evie just said thank you, and I'm standing here like an idiot, cataloging every inch of my body that touched *any* inch of her.

"It's no problem," I stutter out. "It just took a phone call."

Evie shakes her head. "It's more than that. It's everything. The phone call. The house. You offering a place for us to stay. I had no idea I was going to need a hero today, but since I very clearly did, I'm really glad it was you."

"Come on," I say easily, like it's no big deal. "We're basically family. I've only done what any good brother would do."

I don't know why I say it.

Panic, probably.

After all, I told my sister she didn't have anything to worry about when it comes to Evie and me. That means I shouldn't be feeling this much attraction. Maybe my subconscious was trying to reestablish boundaries and remind me to behave?

Evie blinks once, twice, then she smiles. "Right. Right, of course. And I really appreciate it."

I could be wrong. But as Evie turns and reaches for Juno, pulling her daughter back into her arms, I think I see a flicker of disappointment flash through her eyes.

CHAPTER 5

EVIE

I REALLY DIDN'T SEE this coming. I knew Alec lived in North Carolina. That he would help me move, that if I ever wanted tickets to a hockey game, I could probably text him and he'd hook me up.

I did *not* expect to follow him through Harvest Hollow to his house, where I will be staying for the next few days, possibly even longer depending on how long it takes to dry out my rental.

Not that I'm surprised Alec offered. He's always been a good guy.

It was, admittedly, a tiny gut punch to hear him refer to me as a sister, especially right after the hug to rival all hugs. Wrapping my arms around Alec's waist, feeling him tug me even tighter against his chest...it basically lit my skin on fire.

Which is an enormous deal because I haven't felt any kind of *fire* in months. I wasn't even sure I was still capable.

47

But his words were the douse of cold water I needed, especially now that we'll be living together.

We've only been driving a few minutes when Megan calls.

"Hey," I say, once she's connected through my car's Bluetooth.

"Hey! I just got off the phone with Alec. Are you okay?"

"Thanks to him," I say. I'm relieved to hear that Megan's voice sounds mostly normal. I don't know why it wouldn't, but it does feel slightly weird to be talking to her when I'm minutes away from moving into her brother's house. I've only ever known Alec through the context of him being Megan's brother. And we've never been around each other without Megan there. If I were in Megan's shoes, this would probably feel weird to me.

"Yeah, Alec told me what happened. I'm so sorry about your house."

"It's okay. I'm sure it'll be fine eventually. Just a weird inconvenience." In front of me, Alec slows and turns into a gated community, pulling up to a gatehouse where a security guard steps out to greet him. "Um, have you ever seen Alec's neighborhood?"

"It's so freaking nice," Megan says.

"We just pulled up to the security gate. It feels very fancy."

"Wait until you see the house," she says. "He sent me a picture when he moved in. Totally ridiculous."

Alec pulls his truck forward, and the security guard waves me through, smiling as I drive by. Enormous houses line both sides of the wide, paved road, all with expansive yards and perfectly manicured landscaping.

"I knew the Appies were successful," I say, peering at the houses as I follow Alec deeper into the neighborhood. "I maybe didn't realize they were *this* successful."

"I definitely don't think his bank account is hurting. How did Juno handle the drive?"

I glance at my rearview mirror and catch Juno's reflection in the car seat mirror mounted in front of her. She's sound asleep, her head leaning to the side. "She was a total champ. I'm lucky she's such an easy baby."

"If anyone deserves a little luck, it's you," Megan says. "And I'm so glad Alec is there for you. If you were in some random city alone, I'd be on an airplane right now coming to help, and that would not help me pass my pharmacology exam."

I don't know what Megan is worried about. I don't think she's ever gotten anything but an A on *any* exam, even in her hardest nursing classes.

"You know you'll do great," I say.

"Meh. Maybe. I hope so. So how has it been with Alec? Is it weird to be around him without me there?"

I think about Alec breezing into Ruth's living room and calling me *nerd*. "I thought it might be, but it's totally fine. He's been really nice."

"Good. I warned him he'd better be on his best behavior."

Juno whines a little from the backseat, so when we stop at the next stop sign, I shift the car into park and turn around long enough to give her a pacifier. "What does that mean?" I ask Megan. "Why does he need to behave?"

"Come on," she says. "You know you used to have a crush on him when we were kids."

"Please tell me you didn't tell *him* that."

"Pretty sure he could tell," Megan says. "But no, I didn't mention it. I just told him he'd better not try to woo you now that you're all grown up and a smoking hot bombshell."

I scoff. "Woo? Who still says woo? Besides, I promise he won't try. He literally *just* told me he sees me like a sister."

"I mean, probably not *exactly* like a sister," Megan says. "But that does give me some comfort."

In front of me, Alec slows and pulls onto a wide concrete driveway. When he reaches the house, he opens the garage door and pulls his truck inside, leaving plenty of room for me.

I park and turn off the car, then climb out, phone pressed to my ear.

"It brings you *comfort*? Is the idea of me and Alec together that horrible for you?"

It's a stupid conversation. Megan knows better than anyone what I've been through in the past year. She's the one who held my hand through the divorce. Who helped me through Juno's delivery when my idiot ex-husband didn't want to be there. I shouldn't be insulted because she doesn't think a purely hypothetical relationship with her brother is a good idea.

"Are you kidding?" Megan says. "There's nothing I would love more than having you as an actual sister. At least, I would if I thought Alec was ever going to settle down. But he's been married to his hockey team for years. And you just went through so much, Evie. I don't want you to get hurt, and I definitely don't want my brother to be the one who hurts you."

"That's fair," I say, somewhat mollified. I open Juno's door and put Megan on speaker, tucking the phone into the front pocket of my overalls, speaker end sticking out the top. I reach into the car and pull out Juno's carrier, then set her down on the driveway. She's awake now but still a little dazed and sleep drunk, blinking like she doesn't know which end is up.

You and me both, baby girl.

Alec appears beside me and holds his hand out for Juno's carrier. "Can I take her inside?"

"Yeah, thanks," I say. "I'm just talking to Megan."

"Hi, Alec!" Megan yells through the phone. "Have I told you you're the best brother ever?"

Alec grins as his eyes drop to my phone. "Is there anything else I can carry?"

I retrieve the portable crib from the trunk, then hand it over, along with the diaper bag and a second bag full of extra diapers and wipes. Both shoulders are laden with bags by the time he makes his way inside, the crib in one hand and Juno's carrier in the other.

I spend an extra long moment admiring the way his back and shoulders flex with the effort, then slam my trunk closed with a sigh. "I should get inside," I say to Megan. "But trust me. You don't have anything to worry about."

"Stop it," Megan says. "Don't make it sound like that. I'm not worried about *you and Alec*. I'm just worried about *you*, in general. Your scars are still fresh, Evie."

"It's been almost a year," I say. "Which, I'm not saying that because I want to date your brother. I'm just saying, maybe you don't need to worry so much. I'm doing okay."

Megan's quiet for a beat before she asks, "You really think so?"

"I mean, my bank account balance is abysmal, I still can't fit into my favorite jeans, and I'm hormonal enough to cry at every single dog rescue video that comes across my feed. But otherwise, yeah. I really think so."

I circle the car and open the back door to get my duffel bag.

"In that case," Megan says, "I think I should probably tell you something."

"Okay," I say through a grunt. This bag is *really* heavy.

"I have some news about Devon."

I freeze, dropping the bag and letting it fall back onto the seat. "What about him?"

"I don't know the details. Just that he's no longer a part of *The Great Gatsby* cast."

"What? Who told you that?"

"I ran into Gina on campus the other day. She says hey, by the way."

"What did she say about Devon?"

"Not much, honestly," Megan says. "But if I'm reading between the lines, I kinda got the sense he screwed up pretty big and was fired."

I breathe out a sigh. It isn't that surprising that I haven't heard anything about Devon. I make a pretty conscious effort to stay *out* of the loop when it comes to my ex-husband. But losing a coveted Broadway role when he worked so hard to get one in the first place doesn't really track with what I know about him.

"Did Gina want you to tell me?" I ask. "Is that why she brought it up?"

Gina was definitely more Devon's friend than mine, though she was more sympathetic during the divorce drama than a lot of our other friends.

"I don't know," Megan says. "She didn't really say one way or the other. I'm sorry for mentioning it. I just thought you might want to know."

"Yeah, I'm glad you did. Thanks."

"Call me tomorrow?" Megan says.

"Yep. Love you, Meg."

I end the call and pocket my phone before hoisting the duffel onto my shoulder and knocking the car door closed with my hip.

Whatever Gina's intention in telling Megan about Devon,

he made it clear when we divorced that he wouldn't worry about me. Which means I'm not going to worry about *him* either.

Alec meets me when I'm halfway up the sidewalk, lifting the bag from my shoulder and carrying it the rest of the way. I frown as I watch him walk. I could be wrong, but he looks like he's favoring his right knee. I don't remember noticing anything when we were unloading all my furniture which makes me suddenly worry he somehow injured himself. Especially after the way his teammates teased him.

I'm deep in a narrative in which Alec's hockey career is over and it's all my fault and he'll never forgive me much less speak to me again when I realize Alec has said something and is waiting for me to respond.

I scour my brain for the words I know I heard but clearly didn't process, but I come up empty. "Sorry, what was that?" I ask. "I spaced there for a second."

Alec lifts an eyebrow. "I just asked about your conversation with Megan."

"Oh! It was good. Great. She's worried about her pharmacology exam." It's a true response, even if we only talked about pharmacology for the first two minutes, then spent the rest of our conversation talking about him.

He nods knowingly. "Sounds about right. I don't know why she worries so much. She always does great."

"That's what I tell her!" I say, making a mental note to circle back to Alec's leg. Even if it's something minor, I'll feel terrible if he hurt himself on my account. "Still, I'm glad you were around today because otherwise, Megan would have flown down here herself, and then I'd never hear the end of her stressing over the school she'd miss as a result."

Alec pauses in his open front doorway and looks back, shooting me a warm grin. "You know my sister well."

I think of the expression on Megan's face as she gripped my hand through the last hour of Juno's delivery. "I honestly don't know how I would have gotten through the last few months without her."

Alec holds my gaze for a long moment, his brown eyes flashing with something I can't quite read. "Megan is great," he says, "but I watched you today. Something tells me you'd be okay no matter what."

We move into the entryway, where Juno is still sitting in her carrier, awake now, her little feet kicking as she happily sucks on her pacifier.

I huff out a laugh. "I'm sorry, were we at the same house today? Pretty sure if not for you and Ruth, I'd still be sitting on my front steps crying over the missing porch swing."

He moves and closes the front door, stepping close enough that I feel the warmth of him as he reaches past me. "Your house is supposed to have a porch swing?"

I shrug. "It did in the pictures. But it feels dumb to worry about that now."

He pushes his hands into his pockets and looks down at me. He's standing close enough for me to see the specks of gold in his brown eyes. He smells good, manly and woodsy and a little musky. "It's not dumb," he says softly.

He holds my gaze for another second before giving his head a little shake and stepping away. He reaches for the duffel he discarded when we first stepped inside, then adds the crib and diaper bag to his shoulders. He clears his throat. "Let me show you where you'll be staying."

I grab Juno's carrier, then let Alec lead me through the entryway, past some sort of a music room with a grand piano right in the center and a dining room with a table that looks big enough to seat Alec's entire hockey team. There's an enormous staircase in the center of the house, but Alec doesn't stop until we reach a living room right off the kitchen. It's warm and welcoming and actually looks lived in, at least compared to the rest of the house. It's still nice, but it doesn't feel *fancy*. I'm guessing this is where Alec spends most of his time.

The L-shaped couch looks soft and comfortable, covered in throw pillows in dusty shades of blue, and there's a fluffy blanket draped over the back. The opposite wall has bookshelves on either end, flanking a massive TV, making the whole space perfect for a movie night. Give me a bowl of popcorn and that fluffy blanket, and I could be happy in this room forever.

"There are three bedrooms upstairs," Alec says, motioning to a second stairway in the corner of the room. "All with the beds made up and ready, so you can have your pick and use as many as you want."

"You keep all three guest rooms ready?" I set Juno's carrier down on the floor, then crouch down to unstrap her and lift her out. She's been an absolute dream today considering how much time she's spent in the car. But I can tell her patience is about to run out. She needs a bath and a meal and a little bit of uninterrupted mama time.

Alec shrugs easily as he glances around the room. "I bought the house fully furnished, so they were like that when I moved in."

I look around the room one more time. "That explains the grand piano."

"How do you know I haven't started playing?"

"Have you?"

He grins. "Well, *no*, but I might now that I have a piano." He pushes his hands into his pockets. "The people who sold me the house moved to Europe and didn't want to ship over all their furniture. Most of my stuff is still in boxes out in the

55

garage, but I haven't had a lot of time or reason to unpack everything."

I get the convenience of moving into a house like this. But I have to wonder. If Megan is right about Alec not wanting to settle down, why did he buy a four-bedroom house in a quiet, family-friendly neighborhood?

Alec looks down at Juno, then reaches forward, his hand curling around her foot. It's a gentle gesture, almost a thoughtless one, but it makes me happy to see him acknowledge her, despite his earlier claim that he knows nothing about babies.

Juno looks up at him, and he smiles. "She looks like you."

"You think?"

"Yeah. She definitely has your eyes." He lifts my bags a little higher on his shoulder. "Come on. I'll carry these upstairs for you."

Ten minutes later, he leaves me in the largest of the upstairs bedrooms, one with a sitting area off the main room that will be perfect for Juno's portable crib, and an ensuite bathroom with a huge soaking tub and a gorgeous tile shower.

I spend the next hour with Juno, going through her nightly routine, crossing my fingers that despite being in a strange house, she'll go down without too much trouble. She usually falls asleep around seven or eight; if I'm lucky, she won't wake up again until midnight.

Once she's settled in her crib, I take a shower and put on a pair of leggings and my Cornell hoodie. Megan's parents bought it for me at one of Alec's college games, and it's been one of my favorites ever since. I almost pick something else —I don't want Alec to think I picked it because of him— but it really is the softest and the warmest, so I leave it and push my worries from my mind. For all I know, Alec has gone to bed and won't even see my hoodie.

I'm tempted to climb into bed and crash myself, but Ruth's chicken pot pie is the only thing I've eaten today, and that was hours ago. I'll head to the grocery store tomorrow, but for now, I hope Alec has a stocked pantry.

I'm halfway down the back stairwell when my nose picks up the smell of something cooking, and my stomach lets out a low rumble.

I find Alec in the kitchen in front of the stove, sliding a sandwich onto a plate. After everything he's done for me already, it feels selfish to hope he's making it for me, but my mouth is watering before I've even reached the counter. When Alec smiles and nudges the plate toward me, it's all I can do not to whimper out loud.

"I'm not much of a cook," he says. "But I thought you might be hungry."

"Starving," I say. "Whatever it is, it smells amazing."

"Fried egg, cheddar, and bacon," he says. "Breakfast food is pretty much all that's in my wheelhouse."

I pick up the sandwich and take an enormous bite, not even caring that Alec is watching me so intently. I close my eyes as a low groan sounds in the back of my throat. "Oh my gosh, that tastes amazing," I say through a mouthful of food.

The yolk on the egg is runny, just the way I like it, and my second bite gets messy, egg dripping down the side of my hand.

Alec reaches for the paper towels, tearing one off before sliding it across the bar.

"Sorry," I say in between bites. "Breastfeeding makes me ravenous." I look at the paper towel, then look at my sandwich. If I put it down, I'm only going to get messy again when I pick it back up. "You know what? I'm committed. I'm just going to finish, then clean up after."

Alec chuckles. "Okay, but maybe..." He moves around the counter and picks up the paper towel, then lifts it to my face. I sit stone still as he slides it across my cheek, wiping away a smear of egg I hadn't even realized was there. "So it doesn't get in your hair," he says. He uses his free hand to slide the rest of my hair off my shoulder and away from my face. His fingers lightly brush across my neck before he moves his hand away, and goosebumps erupt across my skin.

My gaze reflexively lifts to his, like I might be able to tell from his expression whether he realizes that him standing so close makes me feel like my heart is beating on the outside of my chest.

Alec's eyes are warm, but there's nothing in his expression outside of genuine concern and kindness. Nothing to make me think he noticed my reaction or that touching me impacted him the same way it did me.

Which honestly, it's a completely ridiculous thought. First, I talked about breastfeeding, then I smeared food all over my face, and now I'm wondering if Alec is feeling attraction? I don't think I could be less sexy if I tried.

"Nice sweatshirt," he finally says, and heat warms my cheeks.

"Thanks. Your parents bought it for me back when I was going to all your games with Megan."

He nods. "I remember. You guys were an excellent cheering section."

"We were, weren't we? I still have a Cornell jersey with your name on the back."

Something happens to Alec's expression then, his eyes narrowing the slightest bit, his mouth falling open like he's lost in thought, but then he gives his head a little shake and steps away, moving back around the counter. He keeps his eyes down while he fixes two glasses of water, giving one to me, then returns to the bar with a second sandwich for himself.

I have no idea what happened. If I made him uncomfortable by mentioning his jersey, or if it triggered an entirely different thought and his momentary weirdness didn't have anything to do with me. Either way, he seems okay now, so I dig back into my sandwich.

We eat in easy silence until I finish and slide my plate forward, then use my napkin to wipe my face and hands. "That was amazing," I say. "Thanks for feeding me. And for everything today, really. Unloading the pod. Giving us a place to stay. All of it."

"It's no problem," he says in between bites. "I've got plenty of space."

"Yeah, why *do* you have all this space? This house is huge."

"It was more about the neighborhood and less about the house," Alec says. "I like the security. And it's quiet. Mostly families. My last place was in a busier part of town, people always coming and going, and my neighbor was always having crazy parties." He pauses and offers me a sheepish grin. "I sound really old, don't I?"

"*So old*," I repeat, but then I smile. "I get it, though." I slide off the barstool and carry my plate to the sink. "So talk to me about your knee."

He frowns. "Why would I want to talk about my knee?"

"Because I saw you limping when we came inside. Are you injured? Please tell me you didn't hurt yourself today."

"I didn't hurt it today," he says, and I can tell he's telling the truth.

"So it's a hockey injury?"

59

He breathes out a sigh. "You're asking a lot of questions."

"Oh come on." I return to the stool beside him. "You said I was like a sister, so talk to me like one."

He lifts an eyebrow at this, but then he finally shifts on his stool and turns to fully face me. "It's an old hockey injury," he says. "Do you remember when I had surgery on my ACL during my senior year at Cornell?"

"Oh, that's right! You didn't play in any games until after Christmas."

"Exactly. Then I blew it out again my first year with the Appies, and it hasn't been the same since. I've had three surgeries total, and the past few years it's been pretty solid. But here lately, it's been acting up again."

"What does 'acting up' mean?"

He shrugs. "It gets stiff, especially later in the day. And it swells up if I'm not icing it regularly."

I look down at his knee, though it's not like there's anything to see through the dark joggers he's wearing. "Does it impact your playing?"

"Not so far, but..." He hesitates and runs a hand through his hair. "But my trainers seem to think it's only going to get worse if I keep playing on it."

If he keeps playing.

Does that mean he's thinking about *not* playing? He isn't saying so much in words, but I can read a lot in his body language. In the tightness across his shoulders, in the way he's avoiding eye contact. Hockey has defined Alec's entire adult life. It isn't hard to imagine how gutting it might feel to think about all of it ending.

I nudge his knee with mine. "Hey. You know you're more than a hockey player, right?"

He looks up sharply, like my words have surprised him.

"You're a brother, a son, a friend, a human. You'll still be all those things when you stop playing hockey."

He shakes his head and lets out a little disbelieving laugh. "I don't think it's going to come to that," he says, but the tension in his body makes me think he's worried it might be.

"What do your teammates say?" I ask.

He props his foot up on the bottom of my barstool, bringing his knee into direct contact with mine. I will myself not to move away even though the heat of him feels like a brand through the thin fabric of my leggings.

"My teammates don't say anything because they don't know." He rolls his shoulders, and I get the sense he's admitting things, saying things out loud that he hasn't said before. "I've played through the pain before, and I've had surgery before. I'll have another one if I have to. It's the job, right?"

He's making it sound so simple, like it's no big deal. But what if it *is* a big deal? "Will you...would you ever stop? Decide it's not worth it?"

He hesitates. "I mean, at some point, I'll have to. My trainers like to talk about future mobility. Making sure I can go on hikes or play outside with my kids—assuming I ever *have* kids—just do regular life stuff. But it's hard to prioritize that if it means I have to stop playing now."

Beside me, the sound of Juno stirring comes through the baby monitor I brought downstairs with me, and I will her to settle back into sleep. A conversation like this feels like a lot for two people who only just reconnected, but it also feels incredibly easy. Like we could talk about anything and it wouldn't give either of us pause. I have no idea why—why Alec decided I was the person he'd finally say all of this to, but I don't want the conversation to end just because Juno wakes up.

I hold my breath, bottom lip grasped between my teeth

until Juno quiets, her breathing falling back into a steady, reassuring rhythm.

"Have you given any thought to what you'll do when you *do* stop playing? Whenever it *does* finally happen?"

Alec shakes his head, his jaw tensing the slightest bit. "There's nothing else I *could* do." He stands and moves into the kitchen, keeping his back to me for several long moments.

"There's no denying you're great at hockey," I say slowly, "but you're also smart and funny and personable and charming. You could probably do a dozen different things without even leaving the sport. Coaching or broadcasting. You'd be great on television."

He lets out a dismissive grunt. "Nah. Analysts come from the NHL. Not the minor leagues."

"Most of the time, sure," I say. "But you're an Appie. You guys freaking beat an NHL team last season. Half the players on the team could be playing in the NHL if they wanted to be —you included. The same rules don't apply to the Appies."

Alec's eyebrows lift, and I'm suddenly embarrassed to have said so much. To have revealed just how closely I've followed his career.

But then he grins, and my regret fizzles and floats away. "So you weren't just reading textbooks at all of my games," he says.

I roll my eyes. "I already told you. That happened *one* time."

"Once a nerd, always a nerd," he says.

Juno's monitor lights up again, and this time, it doesn't sound like she'll settle back down.

I pick up my water glass, draining the last of it before putting it in the sink next to my plate. "She probably won't go back to sleep without me," I say, reaching for the monitor. "Thanks again for the sandwich."

"Of course," Alec says. "If you get hungry later, just make yourself at home. I don't have much, but whatever you find in the fridge or the pantry, you're welcome to it."

I'm halfway across the living room when Alec stops me.

"Hey, Evie?"

I turn back to face him. It's the first time he's called me by name, and the sound sends a delicious shiver racing up my spine. "Yeah?"

Alec pushes his hands into the pockets of his joggers. "Thanks for listening. You're pretty easy to talk to."

I smile. "Anytime."

He runs a hand through his hair and takes a step toward me. "Listen. I have no idea if it's even practical with Juno, but I'm happy to get you a ticket to Sunday's game if you want to come. Or any game, really. It doesn't have to be this one. I'm just saying generally. If you want to go to an Appies game. All you have to do is ask."

My heart squeezes at the kindness behind Alec's words. I haven't been to a hockey game in years. Not since high school. Once I started at Juilliard and met Devon, it wasn't as easy to get away, even though Megan frequently traveled to see whatever games he played in the northeast.

But Devon was a theater major, and he didn't understand my love for hockey at all. I tried to explain it was simply a part of my childhood, but I might as well have been speaking a different language.

So I let it go.

Devon had that effect on people. He drew people into his orbit and kept them close, and we all stayed there because it felt like such a privilege to have been chosen by someone so talented, so magnetic. We liked what he liked, listened to what he listened to, ate whatever he was in the mood for.

It was even easier for me because I was his favorite. The one he fell in love with and married on a warm summer day exactly one month after my twentieth birthday.

A part of me wants to go to Alec's hockey game just to spite Devon. But a bigger part wants to go just because of how much I miss it.

But Juno makes everything more complicated. Navigating the crowds and the cold and the often rowdy fans at a hockey game can be challenging when you *don't* have a baby along. Not to mention the noise.

"I'm just now comfortable taking Juno to Target," I say. "I don't think I'm ready for a hockey game yet. But thank you for offering."

Alec nods. "Another time then."

Later, when Juno has nursed and fallen asleep again, I lay in my bed for a long time thinking about the conversation with Alec. How easy and natural it was to talk to him. How good it felt to have him invite me to a hockey game, even if I couldn't take him up on the offer.

I am still absolutely positive that a relationship is the last thing I need right now.

But I can't seem to stop smiling anyway.

CHAPTER 6

ALEC

I DON'T SEE much of Evie over the next few days.

This early in the season, our practice schedule is still pretty intense, so I'm not home much, and it seems like she's lying pretty low, which makes sense. She and Juno are both probably exhausted after all their traveling. But I still find myself looking for her car whenever I pull into the driveway or spending a little more time than usual in the common areas of the house.

Not that I need to see her.

I don't. I have zero reason to keep track of where she is, and she has zero reason to give me a play-by-play of her plans. I texted her the code to the front door the first night she was here, and I added her to the security guard's list so she's free to come and go as she pleases.

On Saturday morning, I spend an extra long time making breakfast, but she never comes downstairs. I must have missed her altogether because when I leave for practice a few minutes later, her car isn't even in the driveway.

Where could she be at nine-thirty on a Saturday?

Better question. Why am I thinking about this so much? And why am I disappointed?

As I pull into the parking lot at the Summit, I try to muster up some enthusiasm for the day ahead. We aren't actually practicing today, though I will be on the ice. Today is social media day, so the team will be filming videos and taking photos with Parker, the Appies' social media manager.

She always has a long list of stuff for us to do at the beginning of the season, and since our social media presence is such a huge part of the Appies' success, we all know better than to protest.

I usually don't mind most of it. It's part of the job. But I'm not much in the mood today. Partly because I'm still feeling off about all things Appies. Partly because I can't stop thinking about Evie.

When we were talking at the counter the other night, her knees tucked in between mine, she didn't feel like a sister at all. I was much too aware of the warmth emanating from her skin and the freckles dotting the bridge of her nose. But she didn't feel like a date either. There was no pressure, no expectations, which made it easy to be honest, to say things I haven't said to anyone else.

Maybe that's why I can't stop thinking about her.

It was nice having someone to talk to who *isn't* connected to my team.

After three hours and two different viral dance trend videos, we're almost done.

On the other end of the rink, a professional photographer is set up with lights and an Appies backdrop and has been taking solo shots of each of us, but Parker has been filming too, catching what she calls B-roll footage that she'll use in the many videos she puts out every season.

She has one last thing she wants to film though. And from the way the other guys are looking at me, it has something to do with me.

"Okay, I need Alec and Nathan," Parker says, confirming my suspicions as she skates across the ice, camera in hand. "And where did Felix go? Wasn't he just here?"

"I'm here," Felix says, stepping back onto the ice, his goalie gloves in hand. "I had to grab a new glove."

Parker lines us up, Felix standing in front of the goal, with Nathan and I flanking him on either side. "Alec, turn to the left a little so I can see your captain's C," she says. I reposition myself on the ice, and she nods as she skates around us. "Perfect." She films for a few seconds before dropping her camera and looking back across the ice. "So here's what's going to happen," she says. "It's everyone else against the three of you. A dozen pucks on the ice, and your goal is to stop as many of them as you can. There's been a lot of talk about this particular defensive pairing, so let's show everyone you're as good as they say you are."

Parker skates to the center of the rink where Eli, Logan, Camden, and the rest of the team are waiting. Three against twelve is hardly a fair matchup, but that's the point with stuff like this. Parker knows what gets clicks, and usually, the stupider we look, the better.

She skates back our way, pulling to a stop right in front of me. "Also, one more thing," she says. "I just told the twins they can crash at your place for a little while. They're young and homesick and they aren't doing great living on their own and you have that big old house that's basically empty, so it makes the most sense. Good? Great. I knew you'd agree."

She pats me on the shoulder, then spins on her skate and hurries away before I can protest.

"Uh, what just happened?" I ask, looking over at Nathan.

He shrugs. "I think you just got two new roommates?"

I already *have* two new roommates, but I don't have time to protest because Parker blows her whistle, and a wall of offense advances toward us at full speed.

I grip my stick a little tighter, ignoring the tightness in my knee as I prepare for what's coming. I'm not necessarily opposed to having the twins stay with me. It's the way things generally operate with the Appies. The older players are expected to look out for the younger, newer recruits. And I *do* have a big empty house. But it's a lot less empty with Evie and Juno around, and the last thing I want to do is make Evie feel uncomfortable.

I fend off a shot from Van, then circle the goal and steal a puck from Camden, sending it sliding in the opposite direction before Logan plows into me, pinning me against the boards, while Eli flies by and makes a shot over Felix's shoulder.

This is when I know there's more to this exercise than I thought because Logan doesn't let me go. Instead, he pulls my stick out of my hands, tosses it to the ice, then spins me toward Theo, who's twirling a lasso over his head in perfect circles. An actual lasso. The kind you'd see at a rodeo, not in a hockey rink. I have no idea where he got the rope, but he clearly knows how to use it because when he sends the lasso soaring, it falls perfectly over my head, then tightens around my shoulders, pinning my arms to my sides. Fifteen feet away, Nathan is getting the same treatment from Carter.

In a matter of seconds, they've hauled us both to right in front of the goal where they tie us together, back to back, before throwing their arms over their heads in victory.

Parker's still filming, and she zooms in on the twins.

"That's how they do it in Texas," Theo says, his smile wide.

Right. I'd forgotten the twins were from Texas.

Behind me, Nathan sighs. "We probably should have seen this coming."

"We definitely should have."

The twins are skating circles around us now, cheering loudly while the rest of the guys look on. They're a defensive pairing just like Nathan and me, so it makes sense Parker would think up something like this. The rookies are solid players. I've been watching them play in our preseason games, and I can see them both having lucrative careers. But I'm not worried about them taking playing time away from me and Nathan, even though it honestly might be good if they did. For my knee, anyway, if not for my stats. Either way, it's easy to take this as the good-natured prank Parker meant it to be.

It also helps that the twins, for all their youthful cockiness, aren't jerks. Carter especially seems eager to learn and grow and figure out what it truly means to be an Appie.

I breathe out my own sigh.

Had Parker asked me—told me?—a few days ago that the twins were coming to live at my house, I might have protested. But after my conversation with Evie last night, I find myself more inclined to say yes.

Maybe because she said I was a good leader, and I want to live up to her assessment. Maybe because she reminded me that there are things I can do besides just *play* hockey. Or maybe it has to do with the fact that I'm supposed to view Evie as a sister, and having two more people around might make it easier to keep any *not-so-sisterly* thoughts out of my mind for good.

I'll put the twins in the bonus room over the garage—there are a couple of futons up there, plus an enormous television they'll love to use—so they won't be in Evie's space at all. And I *do* think it'll be good for them. Maybe good for me too. The pessimism that's clouded my judgment the past few weeks seems to have cleared a little bit, though that could just as easily be Evie's influence.

"Listen," Logan says later in the locker room after I've showered. "Parker didn't know you already have people staying at your house. If the twins need to crash with me until Evie leaves, I don't mind. I've got enough room for them."

"It's fine," I say. "We'll mostly be on the road next week anyway. By the time we're back, Evie's house should be almost ready, and then she'll move out. It shouldn't be a big deal."

Before I leave the Summit, I give the twins my address, then call the security guard to add them to my list of approved guests.

The twins have been staying in an Airbnb near the Summit, so they're coming over tonight, just as soon as they pack up, which only gives me an hour or so to let Evie know.

I don't expect her to care. But I still feel nervous about mentioning it. Or maybe I'm just nervous about seeing her generally?

I have no idea what it means, but I'm choosing not to overthink it when my heart jumps at the sight of her car in my driveway.

Before I get out of the car, I notice a new text message from Riley. I haven't heard from her in weeks, so it takes me by surprise. But I'm more surprised by my lack of interest in reading the message. It's a stark contrast to how anxious I am to get inside and see Evie.

70

I pocket my phone without reading the message and head inside.

I find Evie in the kitchen, her hair piled on top of her head and Juno strapped to her chest in some kind of colorful fabric sling looking thing. Music is playing from a portable speaker on the counter, and Evie is dancing around the kitchen.

She spins one more time, her hands cupped around Juno's feet, and finally sees me. She yelps and jumps back, her arms wrapping around the baby like I'm some kind of predator.

I grimace. "Sorry," I say over the music.

She smiles and shakes her head as she retrieves her phone from the counter and turns off the music.

"I didn't mean to scare you."

"It's fine. I was just..." She looks down at Juno who is awake and wide-eyed. "She likes the music. Plus, I get some exercise, so it's a win-win." She looks over at the stove. "Are you hungry? I cooked. And by cooked, I mean I warmed up a pizza and there's some left over. But I did make these!" She pulls a kitchen towel off the top of a baking dish full of cinnamon rolls. "It's actually your mom's recipe," she says. "She gave it to me as a baby gift when Juno was born."

Evie is buzzing with energy, her cheeks pink from exertion, her eyes bright. With Juno in her arms, she looks like *life*. Like happiness.

I lift my eyebrows. "Mom guards that recipe with her life. She hasn't even given it to *me* yet."

"It took years of wearing her down," Evie says. "And maybe a tiny bit of guilt-tripping after the divorce? I'm still not sure I've perfected her process, but this is the best batch I've made so far." She cuts a corner off one of the rolls and pops it into her mouth, closing her eyes as she chews. She

71

lets out a little groan, then licks a dollop of icing from her finger.

I watch, transfixed, as her tongue slides over the ridge of her knuckle.

"Dark brown sugar," she says. "That's what makes them taste like caramel."

I clear my throat and force my eyes to the ceiling. I have got to stop staring at this woman's mouth, but she isn't making it easy.

"They *do* taste like caramel," I say. "I remember."

She cuts off a second corner from the same cinnamon roll and walks it over to me. "Spoil your dinner with me?" She holds the cinnamon roll just in front of my mouth.

She could be offering me a chocolate-covered cricket and I'd probably still say yes.

I lean forward and take the bite, my lips brushing over her fingertips.

The contact is brief, but it's enough to send an unexpected reaction sparking across my skin.

Fortunately, the cinnamon roll provides at least a temporary distraction. It tastes like my childhood, and a wave of nostalgia washes over me as I chew. I can't count the number of times we crowded into the kitchen waiting for Mom to pull these out of the oven. She'd barely get them frosted before we were begging to have one.

As often as she wasn't, Evie was beside Megan, begging right along with us, but it's still a surprise that Mom shared the recipe with Evie. She always talks about how it's her mother's recipe, and it will, as far as she's concerned, always stay in the family.

It's a *good* surprise though. Somehow, it seems right that Evie has it. Though that could just be because she's in my kitchen, and I'm the one benefiting from her knowledge.

"Tastes pretty perfect to me," I say, and Evie beams.

"Really? I didn't bake them too long?"

I shake my head and move closer to the pan, where I cut myself another bite. "They taste just like Mom's."

She looks down at Juno. "Did you hear that, Juno? They taste just like Mama Sheridan's. She'll be so proud of us!"

Something catches in my heart as I think about Mom encouraging Evie and loving on Juno, and an ache of homesickness makes my gut tighten. It's been less than a month since I saw my parents, but we were so busy getting them moved out of their house and into their retirement community, it didn't really feel like we got to spend much time together. It was all about logistics, time management, making sure they were fully settled before Megan's last semester of nursing clinicals started. We definitely didn't have time for cinnamon rolls.

"So how was your day?" Evie asks. "What did you do?"

"It was press and social media day at the Summit," I say.

"What does that mean? Photos? Interviews?"

I nod. "And an ambush involving a lasso and a pair of eighteen-year-old twins from Texas."

She lifts her eyebrows. "Do I want to know the details?"

"Just make sure you're following the Appies on social media. I'm sure you'll *see* the details eventually."

She grins. "You guys really do a lot of funny stuff."

"I can't take credit for any of it." I move toward the stove. "Is there really pizza left over? I should probably have some real food before I eat an entire pan of cinnamon rolls."

"Yes!" She moves in beside me and opens the oven, pulling out a cookie sheet holding half a pizza. "It's the good kind from Trader Joe's and everything. Juno and I did a grocery run this morning."

"Yeah, you guys were up early," I say. "I was surprised to see you already gone by the time I woke up."

"That's Juno for you," Evie says. "She never sleeps past seven. Plus, shopping early is easier since there aren't any crowds, then I can get home in time to put her down for a morning nap."

Juno gurgles, blowing little tiny spit bubbles between her lips.

"So basically you're saying Juno is in charge," I say in between bites of pizza.

Evie laughs. "You have no idea."

We fall into easy conversation after that. About the dance I had to do with Eli and Van. About her violin and how she hasn't played it a single time since Juno was born. About her conversation with her landlord, who finally called her back today and confirmed that he's talked to the disaster repair people we called yesterday, so everything is good on that front, and he'll be back in town at the end of the week. He promised to have her home repaired and livable within a week of his return and agreed to prorate her rent for next month to compensate for the delay.

Evie stays on her feet the whole time we're talking, swaying back and forth to keep Juno happy, and I lift myself onto the counter, sitting next to the leftover pizza, which I finish.

There's something very *domestic* about the whole situation. And not because Evie is in the kitchen and made food. It's more that she's just...*here*. That we're talking about our days and she's interested in how I am and what I have to say.

There's no pretense with Evie and realizing as much helps me identify what I don't love about Riley. Riley *always* has an agenda. Something to prove.

I realize Evie has reasons for being in Harvest Hollow that

don't have anything to do with me. But it's still triggering a *want* I didn't know I had.

I'm so preoccupied with our conversation, so distracted by how much I like talking to Evie, that I completely forget to mention the twins coming over until the doorbell rings.

Evie lifts her eyebrows. "Are you expecting someone?"

I wince as I jump off the counter. "Yes, and I meant to explain before they showed up. You know the twins I mentioned earlier? They need a place to crash. They're brand new to the team, and they're having a hard time living on their own."

"The twins who lassoed you?"

"Yes, but what made you think they lassoed *me*?"

She grins. "Intuition? Or possibly the look on your face when you mentioned it. Should I be concerned? Will they try to lasso me too?"

I breathe out a chuckle. They *might* try to lasso her once they see her like this, looking alive and happy, a little bit of powdered sugar dust on her cheek. "I promise to make them leave their lassos outside." I pause before leaving the kitchen and look at her over my shoulder. "Hey, I don't want you to think they're going to be in your space. I'm going to have them stay in the bonus room over the garage, so you won't be passing them in the hallway or hearing them when you're trying to get Juno to sleep."

"You have a bonus room over the garage?"

I nod. "It's got a couple of futons in it."

She chuckles and rolls her eyes. "Alec, this house is stupid huge. I appreciate you being concerned, but this is your place, not mine. If you trust them, I trust them. Juno and I will be fine if they stay in the other bedrooms upstairs."

"I do trust them, but it's important to me that you feel

comfortable here. And I don't want them to mess with Juno's sleep."

"It's probably more likely that she'll mess with *their* sleep."

"Either way, the bonus room is on the opposite side of the house, so they shouldn't hear you, and you shouldn't hear them."

She nods as the doorbell rings one more time. "Go let them in then. They can have a cinnamon roll."

I grin. "Nope. Those are all for me."

When I open the front door, Theo and Carter barrel into the house, their shoulders laden with enormous matching duffel bags.

"Dude, this house is insane," Theo says as he looks around the entryway. He spins in place and his bag knocks into a lamp sitting on a hall table. I reach out and steady it before it crashes to the floor, and Carter meets my gaze over Theo's shoulder, rolling his eyes.

"Sorry," Carter mutters. "He doesn't get out much."

Theo's hair is cut shorter than Carter's, which makes it easy to tell them apart. But even if the hair didn't give him away, Theo is much louder and rowdier than his more reserved brother. He'd only have to open his mouth for me to immediately know which twin he is.

"Come on," I say, leading them into the house. "I'll show you where you're staying."

Evie appears in the doorway of the kitchen as we approach, still wearing Juno, hands setting loosely on her daughter's back. The baby turns her head, eyes wide as she looks at the new arrivals. She bounces a little, almost like she's excited, her little hands flailing up and down.

"Are you saying hi?" Evie says, looking down at her

76

daughter, smiling like she thinks Juno's reaction to the twins is just as entertaining as I do.

"Whoa, you're married?" Carter asks. "With a kid? How did we not know that?"

"This is Evie and her daughter, Juno," I say, shooting Evie an apologetic look. "She's a friend. She just moved to Harvest Hollow, and she and her daughter are staying here for a few weeks until her place is ready."

"So you're single?" Theo says, taking a step toward Evie. "Because...*Hey. My name's Theo.*"

"Dude, she just had a baby," Carter says, punching his brother in the shoulder.

"So? I always wanted to be a dad." Theo looks at his brother. "I'd be a good dad."

"Okay, that's enough," I say, steering Theo down the hallway and away from Evie. "There will be no more hitting on Evie for the duration of your stay." I ignore the tightness in my chest as we go. It's stupid to feel jealous of someone as young as Theo, but it's not lost on me that he's closer to her age than I am.

As soon as I dismiss that very stupid thought, another replaces it.

Would *I* be a good dad?

Not that it matters, but I'm more than a little envious of how easily Theo claimed he would be.

Behind us, Evie laughs. "It was nice to meet you both," she calls.

Carter looks over his shoulder. "Nice to meet you too, ma'am. Please forgive my brother."

Once we're in the bonus room, it takes the twins less than five minutes to drop their bags and connect their PlayStation to the enormous television mounted on the far wall. They stopped for burgers on their way over, so they don't

77

need food, and they seem happy to spend the rest of their evening playing *NHL 25*. They invite me to play, but I'd rather go see if Evie is still in the kitchen.

I don't find her there, but I do have a text message waiting for me.

EVIE

Sorry to disappear on you. Juno decided she's done for the night. Thanks for hanging out with me. I won't tell anyone if you really do eat all the cinnamon rolls yourself.

I tap my phone against my palm, processing my disappointment. Because I *am* disappointed.

I like hanging out with Evie. After her first night here, I was hoping for the chance to do it more. She's easy to talk to and fun to be around, and I like that we have so much shared history.

She's also beautiful. Which, I can't pretend like that isn't part of this.

It never occurred to me to notice or even look when she was younger. She was *so much younger* that it would have been weird if it had. But now...is nine years too much of an age gap? She has Juno, and that makes her seem older, but she really *isn't* older.

Plus, she's only been divorced a little over a year.

There are a million reasons why I shouldn't be so disappointed that the twins showed up and interrupted our time together. Reasons why I shouldn't be looking at my little sister's best friend with anything but brotherly affection.

I run a hand through my hair, then type out a quick response to her message.

ALEC

No worries. Enjoy the rest of your night.

There. Simple. To the point. Not even a little bit suggestive.

Once I finish, I finally open the message Riley sent earlier.

RILEY

Hey. It's been a while. I've got a work thing happening in Charlotte at the beginning of next month. Think you could make it over? I'd love to see you.

I stare at her text, knowing how I'm going to respond without even having to think about it.

ALEC

Thanks for the invite, but I don't think that's a good idea.

RILEY

Hmm. You didn't just say you're busy, which means...you've met someone, haven't you?

It's entirely too early to be thinking like that.

But the first thought that comes to mind is *yes*.

CHAPTER 7

ALEC

WE'RE PLAYING an afternoon game on Sunday, so even though it's only ten AM, I'm already dressed and ready to head to the arena. With how we've been missing each other, I'm surprised to find Evie in the kitchen, drinking a mug of tea while she scrolls on her phone. Juno is in some kind of baby seat thing in the living room. It's rocking back and forth, the colorful toys hanging over her head swaying from the motion of the seat.

When I step into the kitchen, Evie looks up, and her mouth falls open.

I've always appreciated the tradition of game-day suits—I like having a reason to dress up—but Evie's expression makes it even more worth it.

"Wow," Evie says. "You look really nice."

"Yeah?" I slide a hand down my tie, then hook my thumbs on the edge of my pants pockets.

Evie is wearing her overalls again, and she's barefoot,

looking perfectly relaxed and comfortable. She has glasses on, and I don't think she's wearing any makeup. I like the glasses, and I like how at home she looks in my space. It's a nice change from the big empty house I'm used to.

She stands and shifts around the counter, moving toward me. When she reaches me, she lifts her hands to my collar. "You really know how to wear a suit. You just need to tuck your tie in right here."

I catch the scent of her as she adjusts my tie—apples and cinnamon—and I feel a sudden impulse to lift a hand and wrap it around the curve of her waist, tug her against me.

The desire startles me with its potency. I haven't felt anything like it in a long time, which makes it easy to ignore the reasons I thought I had for staying away. I debated long and hard after Riley asked me if I'd met someone. So what if Evie is my sister's best friend and a little bit younger than I am? Now that I've spent a little time with Evie, those reasons feel pretty thin. But she *is* still vulnerable. And she's trusting me and living in my space, and I don't want her to think I'm allowing her to live here because I'm hoping for something more.

I also don't know how to stop my heart from pounding whenever she's close.

"Thanks," I say, forcing myself to stay still, to resist the allure of touching her.

"You're welcome." She slides her hand down my lapel then gives my chest a quick pat. "Now you're perfect." She holds my gaze, and my blood heats several degrees.

She's perfect.

I clear my throat and take a step backward. "Right. I should head out."

She nods and shoves her hands into her back pockets. "Good luck. I hope you guys win."

I'm halfway to the Summit before I realize I didn't check in with the twins before leaving. They have their own transportation—they can definitely drive themselves to the game. But it seems dumb to have left without waiting for them— without asking if they wanted a ride since we're headed to the same place.

But I lost all sense of reason when I made eye contact with Evie, when I felt the heat of her gaze. I didn't even remember the twins were in the house, much less members of my hockey team.

Clearly, I haven't gotten my good sense back because before I head to the locker room, I find myself in the gift shop at the Summit, braving the crowds to look at infant-sized Appies merch.

It's a ridiculous thing to do on so many levels.

One. I have no idea whether Evie would ever put her baby in Appies gear.

Two. I have no idea if our relationship—friendship?— justifies this kind of a gift.

Three. Even though it's still hours before puck drop, already fans are hanging around, and I'm getting more than a few excited looks.

"Um, this is brave of you."

I look up to see Summer, Nathan's girlfriend, eyeing me, her expression curious. As part of the Appies' in-house legal team, Summer is at the Summit all the time. But today, she's swapped her business attire for an Appies jersey, one which I'm sure has Nathan's name across the back.

"Yeah, I'm just…" My gaze lands on a pair of kids standing behind Summer, their eyes fixed on me. They're both wearing Appies jerseys, and the size of their eyes tell me they know exactly who I am. I give them a brief nod, then look back at the baby clothes. I lift a hand to my jaw. "Do you know if any of this would work for a baby girl?"

Summer presses her lips together like she's fighting a smile. "I think it's all meant to be pretty gender neutral. Are you thinking of Evie's baby?"

I look up to meet her eye. I haven't had a conversation with Summer about Evie, but I shouldn't be surprised that Nathan told her. He probably tells her everything.

"Nathan mentioned she was staying with you," Summer says, confirming my suspicion. "How old is the baby?"

"I'm not exactly sure. Four-ish months, I think?"

Around us, several other groups have gathered, all of them looking like they're waiting for an opportunity to approach. Summer looks around, clearly noticing the same thing I am.

"Are you in the mood to sign some autographs?" she asks quietly.

I push my hands into my pockets. "Yeah, probably not. But I'm not sure I can avoid it at this point."

She nods and moves her hand to my arm, gently nudging me toward the door, placing herself between me and the waiting fans. "We can at least get you out of the baby aisle," she says. "What if you let me pick up something for Evie's baby? I'll make sure it's in the locker room for you by the end of the game."

"Are you sure?"

"Are you kidding? You've just given me an excuse to shop for baby clothes." She pauses and frowns. "Maybe don't tell Nathan how excited that just made me."

I grin. "Your secret's safe with me."

We make it out of the gift shop, and I stop in the concourse outside the arena, where I spend a few minutes talking to the fans who followed me out and signing jerseys and hats and team posters. The longer I stand here, the more people will gather, so I need to go before things get out of hand, but it's hard to turn away from fans, especially the kids.

Finally, Summer holds up her palm like she's my handler. "Thanks, everyone. Alec needs to get down to the ice for warmups." She steers me out of the crowd and stays beside me as I head toward the stairs that will take me below.

"You're good at that," I say as we hurry past watching fans.

"Nathan's given me a lot of practice," she says. "I can't take that man anywhere without a crowd gathering." We reach a locked door into a stairwell, and Summer swipes her ID badge, allowing us to pass through. "I don't know that Nathan would ever just wander up to the concourse right before a home game though," Summer says, eyeing me as we start down the stairs.

"Yeah, I don't know what I was thinking."

She smirks. "I'm pretty sure I know exactly what you were thinking."

"I wasn't—it's not like that," I say a little too quickly.

Summer only shrugs. "Okay. But if it *is* like that, you wouldn't have to justify yourself to me."

"She has a baby," I say as we reach the rink level of the Summit and step into the hall outside the stairwell.

"Fine," Summer says, her voice still totally neutral.

"And she's my little sister's best friend."

"Sounds perfect."

"Which means she's...young," I add.

"Okay," Summer repeats, her tone telling me she *still* thinks this is no big deal.

"Okay?" I ask. "That's all you have to say?"

"Age is just a number," she says. "If you like her, you like her."

Down the hall, Felix and Logan push into the locker room, followed by Coach Davis, which means I need to get myself in there sooner than later. Especially if I want to heat wrap my knee before the game.

I look back at Summer. "You'll get the...?" I lift my head in an upward motion, gesturing in what I think is the general direction of the upstairs gift shop.

Summer nods. "I've got you. Now get in there with your team and have a good game."

We *do* have a good game. We dominate the first two periods and start the third with a two-point lead. Halfway through the third, Coach adjusts our defensive rotation and pulls Nathan and me, adding the twins, who are eager for as much ice time as possible. I'd normally hate to sacrifice the minutes played, but this time, I'm happy to let them have it.

My knee keeps locking up, and a locked-up knee on the ice could mean jacking up my hips or messing up my *good* knee.

I pull off my helmet as soon as I'm on the bench and reach for a water bottle. Nathan drops down beside me. "You're off, man," he says. On the ice, Camden flies past us, then hits the puck to Logan who scores, increasing our lead to three.

"We're winning, aren't we?"

"Not because of anything you've done," Nathan says. I know better than to be insulted by Nathan's assessment. He won't mince words to spare my feelings, something I usually appreciate. He knocks his stick against my skate. "Is it your knee?"

86

"I'm fine," I say, eyes on the game. The other team is in possession now, and Carter and Theo move toward each other, crossing in front of Felix as the opposing offense moves closer.

"You aren't fine," Nathan says. "And when you aren't fine, I'm the one who has to pick up the slack. You know I'll do it." He whacks my skate one more time, and I finally lift my eyes to meet his. "You know I'll do it," he repeats. "But you gotta tell me what's going on so I know what we're dealing with."

My jaw clenches, pride making my anger flare, but Nathan's right. He's my other half when we're out there. If I can't play the game like I usually do, he's the one impacted the most. "It keeps locking up," I say. "But I'm on it. I'm taking care of it. It'll be fine by next game."

"Alec. You can't—"

"Just leave it," I say, and Nathan clamps his mouth shut. "I'm fine," I repeat.

It's a lie, and I'm pretty sure Nathan knows it's a lie. When we're back on the ice, I fight through more pain than I have in a very long time.

We take the win, but for me, it's tainted by a nagging realization that at this rate, I may not have the luxury of playing out a full season. My knee may force me to quit long before we get there.

Felix tells the team he's got a pot of chili big enough to feed anyone who wants to stop by his place, but I stay back at the Summit and treat myself to an extra-long ice bath instead. Theo and Carter are planning to go, and I'm glad about that. They need to spend time with the rest of the guys, but right now, I'm happy to let the others take charge of the teambuilding.

Nathan gives me a knowing look on his way out, but I ignore him. At some point, I'll have to have a longer conversation with him about what's happening with my knee and how it might impact my play. But I'm not ready to do that yet.

Talking about my knee means talking about what comes *after* hockey. And save the one conversation I've had with Evie, I haven't really worked my way through that yet.

I sink deeper into the ice bath and duck my shoulders so the water is over my head. The cold is bracing, but it feels good on my sore muscles. When I emerge, Eric, the Appies head trainer, is standing at the foot of the tub.

"Hey," I say, rubbing the water from my face.

"Dr. Samuelson's here," he says, his voice calm.

I breathe out a sigh. I should have expected as much. If Nathan noticed me favoring my knee during the game, Eric definitely did. I can hide the pain I'm feeling from my teammates, but I can't hide it from Eric. Or from the sports medicine doctor who takes care of the team.

"Go ahead and shower," Eric says. "Take your time. He'll be in the med suite waiting for you."

I'm the only player still around when I leave the shower, which is better because when I make it back to my stall in a towel, I find an Appies merch bag sitting on the bench. I peek into the bag enough to see something that looks small and soft and Appies turquoise, but I don't pull it out. I trust Summer, and I don't know enough about baby clothes one way or another to have an opinion. I'm sure whatever she picked out is great.

As soon as I'm dressed, I leave the locker room and head down the hall to the Summit's medical suite. I pass a room on the right where players typically meet their families after games. It's empty now, except for Dominic, one of the younger guys on the team, who is sitting with his girlfriend in the corner. He played a good game and seems to be celebrating by swallowing her face.

A beat of restlessness pushes through me.

I don't fault the guy. Or *any* of the guys who have wives or serious girlfriends. But I'm getting tired of the reminders that everyone seems to have found someone but me. When Evie straightened my tie this morning, my brain jumped all the way to imagining her here, waiting in *this* room, wearing an Appies jersey with my name on it. The woman has been in North Carolina less than a week, and I'm already imagining her as my girlfriend. I can't decide if that makes me really confident or just really pathetic.

I think of the merch bag Summer left for me in my stall and wonder if I should take whatever she bought back upstairs to return it. But I'm at the med suite now, so I ignore my waffling thoughts and push my way inside.

"Hey, Doc."

Dr. Samuelson is leaning against an exam table, studying an iPad. He looks up and offers me a friendly smile. "I wish I could say I'm happy to see you."

I run a hand across my face as I drop into an empty chair in the corner of the exam room. "Yeah. Same."

"Talk to me about your pain, Alec," the doctor says. "What are we dealing with?"

Fifteen minutes later, I've been scolded and humbled and gotten both a cortisone injection and an injection of hyaluronic acid—a combination we've never tried before.

"I can't make any promises," Dr. Samuelson says. "But this might buy us a little time. Just keep me in the loop, all right? And listen to your body. You try to play the hero on that knee, you're liable to wind up in the OR again."

I nod. "You think I'll make it to the end of the season?"

He frowns. "You want me to be honest here?"

"Always."

"Your inflammation is the worst I've seen it. Which makes me think you'll be lucky if you do," he says. "Alec, it's time to start thinking about what happens next."

CHAPTER 8

EVIE

I SINK BACK into the couch in Alec's living room and shift Juno from nursing on one side to the other, quickly burping her in between. She yawns before she latches back on, and I notice the perfect bow of her upper lip, shaped just like Devon's.

Stupid, *stupid* Devon.

Months without a message from my ex-husband.

Months.

Months of living in the same city, of ultrasound visits and prenatal classes and doctors' appointments. Then, after Juno was born, four more months of living with my parents in White Plains, learning how to be a mom, exhausted and emotional and barely keeping myself together.

And through it all, Devon never showed. I was a short train ride away from where he lived in Manhattan, and he never visited. Never laid eyes on his daughter.

And now he's texting me.

Now, when I'm living in a different state, trying to start over and move on with my life, he's texted and said he wants to talk.

The message came in an hour ago, and I've basically done nothing since. I managed to order dinner delivery, and the TV is on, but the volume is muted, and I haven't glanced at the screen in ages.

I just keep staring at my phone.

Reading Devon's message over and over.

DEVON

Can we talk?

Only three words, but they could mean anything. My gut says they probably have something to do with him losing his job. But what does that have to do with me? The thought of finding out for sure makes me feel ill.

I don't want to know because I don't want him in my life.

Juno lifts a hand up and brushes it along my chest, her fist curling around the hem of my shirt and making my heart squeeze. She's still Devon's daughter, and he technically has visitation rights, at least according to the state of New York. If he's come to his senses and wants to meet Juno, will I stand in his way? Will I keep him from having a relationship with her?

There's no question that he'll never have a relationship with me. Not after what he put me through.

But Juno? She'll want to know her father. Logically, I know I should want the same thing. I just don't want her to know disappointment from him like I have. And I don't know how to protect her from that.

I screenshot the text and send it to Megan, followed by an all-caps *HELP* and a string of question marks. When she doesn't respond right away, I toss my phone across the couch, letting it slip in between the couch cushions.

I don't go after it, because I'd rather it stay there anyway. I'm not going to respond to Devon until I've consulted with Megan, and if I don't see her response right away, I can stop thinking about it for a while.

I reach for the remote to turn up the volume on the TV, but I pause when I hear the front door open. I streamed Alec's game earlier, but I didn't expect him to show up anytime soon. I assumed he'd be out with his team, celebrating their win.

He strolls into the living room carrying a bag from a local burger place and an enormous diet soda. "Dinner delivery," he says as he sets the bag on the coffee table, then drops his duffel bag onto the floor.

"What? Really?"

"You ordered it, didn't you?" he asks. "I met the delivery guy in the driveway."

"Yeah. I just didn't expect it so soon."

"Betty's always delivers pretty fast." He smiles at me. "Hi."

Heat warms my cheeks because *good grief*, the man has an incredible smile, and my heart does a little shimmy. But *no*. Nope. No shimmying should happen—not based on the Instagram posts I stumbled across earlier.

It was purely accidental. I was scrolling through the Appies official account, looking at posts other people had tagged them in, and a woman named Riley popped up. Her post was relatively benign. Just a photo of her with the Appies game visible on the television over her shoulder. But the caption caught my eye, because she named Alec specifically. *Watching Alec kill it on the ice today!* Followed by way too many heart emojis.

At first, I thought she might be a really enthusiastic fan, but curiosity made me click through to her profile, and that's when my stomach dropped into my fuzzy socks.

There were two posts pinned to the top, and both were of her and Alec looking extremely cuddly. In one photo, she's kissing him on the cheek while he smiles wide into the camera.

She's beautiful—because *of course* she is—something made perfectly clear by the dozen or so posts I scrolled through before Juno woke up from her nap and saved me from myself.

It is not in my best interest to compare myself to a fashion designer and influencer with more than twenty thousand followers. Not when my wardrobe is mostly stretchy pants and overalls because that's all that currently fits. But the discovery did give me a much-needed wake-up call.

No matter how easy it is to talk to him, no matter how nice Alec is being by letting me stay here, he's not for me.

"Hi," I say, reaching for Juno's blanket. I drape it over my shoulder, making sure I'm at least partly covered. Juno tends to get hot when she nurses, so I won't cover her completely, but the way she feels about Alec's voice, if he starts talking, I can't guarantee she won't pop off just to look around and see what's going on. I'd rather avoid an accidental nipple flash if I can, so I feel better at least having the blanket close.

"Are you hungry?" I say, lifting Juno the slightest bit so I can reach for the bag without breaking her latch. "I had a hard time deciding what I wanted, so I actually ordered *two* burgers."

Alec lifts an eyebrow as he drops onto the couch beside me. He traded his gameday suit for a pair of joggers and a pullover in Appies gray and turquoise, but he almost looks just as good in these. "You ordered two burgers?"

"Don't judge," I say, trying and failing to get my straw

open using only one hand. "Nursing makes me feel like I'm starving. I couldn't decide between the barbecue burger because it has an onion ring on it and hello, that sounds delicious, and the one with a fried egg and smoked gouda."

"You should eat that one," Alec says, reaching over and helping me with my straw. "It's my favorite."

"You like Betty's Burgers?"

"Of course I do. They're the best in Harvest Hollow."

"You have to eat that one, then," I say, reaching into the bag and pulling out the paper-wrapped burger marked with a scribble of magic marker that simply says *egg*.

"But then you won't get to try it," he argues.

"But it's your favorite. I'm sure the other one is amazing too."

"I'll do you one better." He stands and takes both burgers into the kitchen. A minute later, he returns with two plates, each holding half of two different kinds of burgers. "Now you can try them both." He looks from me, to Juno, then back again. "Are you going to be able to eat this with one hand?"

Right after Juno was born, when she first started nursing, it was hard for me to feel comfortable feeding her in front of *anyone*. But it's definitely gotten easier over the last few months, or maybe I've just gotten used to it? Either way, it's notable that Alec doesn't seem to be bothered by it. Unless he has a secret life I've never heard about, I doubt he's been around a lot of breastfeeding women, but he doesn't seem thrown at all.

"Just put it on the coffee table," I say. "She'll be done in a second, and then she'll hopefully sit in her seat long enough for me to eat. But don't wait for me. You go ahead."

"You sure?" He reaches for the fries and dumps them all on my plate.

"No fries for you?"

"It's your dinner," he says, but something in his tone makes me think that's not his entire reason.

"And you'd rather not eat greasy salty fries?" I lean over and grab one and pop it into my mouth. It's hot and delicious and perfectly crispy.

"I cheat every once in a while," he says. "But eating healthy is part of the job."

I grab another fry. "I think I'd have to get a different job."

He chuckles. "Says someone with the metabolism of a twenty-three-year-old."

"Whatever. You probably burn a billion calories a day. Your metabolism is just fine."

He grins and takes a huge bite of the barbecue burger. He lets out a little groan that makes a tiny ribbon of heat unspool in my belly. "Oh man. Okay, that one is really good too."

"Where are Theo and Carter?" I ask.

"At a team dinner," he says before taking another bite. "At Felix's."

I frown. "You didn't go?"

"Nah. I stayed back at the Summit to ice my knee, then just came home instead."

There's definitely something Alec *isn't* saying. While it would be nice to think he came home just so he could hang out with me, I don't think that's it.

Juno finally finishes and leans back, craning her neck the slightest bit like she wants to look at Alec.

I shove my boob back into my bra and tug my t-shirt down.

Alec glances my way as I lift Juno to my shoulder to burp her, and his cheeks turn the lightest shade of pink, a contrast to several days' worth of stubble growing along his jawline. I glance down and realize my t-shirt is still hiked up, the bottom half of my bra only half concealed by Juno's body. "Oh gosh. Sorry. Didn't mean to flash you there." I shift Juno to the side and adjust my shirt.

Nothing like exposing Alec to the more glamorous sides of motherhood right out of the gate.

"It's fine. You didn't," he says quickly. He clears his throat, and I suddenly wonder if my earlier assessment was wrong, and Alec really *isn't* comfortable with me breast-feeding in front of him.

I'm not going to be happy if he isn't, but this is his house, and beggars can't be choosers, so I feel like I have to at least ask. "Does it bother you that I'm feeding her out here?"

His eyes widen. "No! Absolutely not," he says quickly. "Feed her wherever you're comfortable. I was just wondering if..." His words trail off, and he clears his throat. "Actually, never mind. I'm not going to ask you that."

"Wondering what?" I repeat back. "Just ask me."

He looks at Juno, then takes another bite of burger, chewing and swallowing before he finally asks, "I was just going to ask if it hurts."

I lift my eyebrows as Juno lets out an enormous burp. "Good girl," I say, patting her on the back. "What? Breast-feeding?"

He nods.

I stand and buckle Juno into her bouncy seat, then reach for my plate, balancing it on my knees. I'm surprised that Alec is asking, but I'm also *glad*. A lot of the friends who came to see me after Juno was born mostly just seemed uncomfortable with all the ways my body has changed. "It did at first," I say as I reach for another fry. "The first few weeks or so. She made me bleed."

I don't realize how shocking my words sound until I look up and see Alec's horrified expression.

97

Maybe *this* is why my friends were uncomfortable.

But I don't want to diminish the things my body has endured. There is a grittiness to motherhood, a vulnerability that has left me bold and bare and honest in new ways. This is my reality now. There's no reason to sugarcoat it.

"Are you serious?" Alec asks. "That's horrible."

I shrug and let out a little laugh. "Honestly, after everything else I went through to get her here, bleeding nipples didn't feel all that bad."

Alec coughs, his eyes widening like he's starting to choke. He's clearly moving air through his lungs, so I don't think he needs the Heimlich, but his distress is still pretty obvious.

I scoot closer and thwack him on the back a few times. "You okay?"

He finally recovers, a fist lifted to his mouth as the coughing subsides. He wipes tears from his eyes. "I'm good. Sorry. Just went down the wrong pipe."

"I'm the one who's sorry. I probably should have given you more of a warning before mentioning my nipples." I wince. "Oh geez. I keep doing it!"

Alec laughs. "It's okay. I *did* ask."

"I think something happens when you're having a baby. I thought I would be so private, that I wouldn't want anyone in the room with me. But then when you're in labor, it becomes about so much more. Your body is doing this incredible thing, and...I don't know. With so many people coming in, poking, prodding, I guess I stopped caring as much. It was more about function, about allowing them to take care of me."

I stand up and reposition Juno in her bouncy seat. She's kicking her feet, sliding herself closer to the bottom edge, so I tighten the buckles to keep her in place. "What are you so excited about, huh?" I squeeze her little toes. "Are you in a

98

good mood?" She smiles and gurgles, kicking a few more times and making the seat bounce up and down.

Alec is quiet for a beat, his expression reflective, before he says, "Honestly, I think your body is pretty amazing."

I lift my eyebrows, fighting a grin. "Do you, now?"

"Wait. That's not what—I mean, *yes*. I do in that way too. But I meant that it's amazing what your body can *do*. What it *did*."

If Alec weren't being so incredibly adorable right now, I might get hung up on the fact that he just admitted he thinks my body is *amazing*. If he saw me naked, he might not think so, because everything from my collarbone down to my hip bones is a roadmap of stretch marks. But there's a sincerity in Alec's eyes that forces that shallow thought away and holds me in the moment.

He really means it.

I know my body is amazing. Bringing Juno into the world was practically a sacred experience. And of course, it was incredible to have Megan and Mom there with me, cheering me on, wiping away my tears and celebrating with me when Juno took her first breath.

But it still feels good to hear Alec acknowledge it. Maybe because he's a man, and I'm not sure men always get it. At least not until they see a woman do it. Maybe because Devon wasn't there. Now, Alec is validating some part of me I didn't know needed validation.

"You grew a whole person," Alec continues. "That's big."

I shrug. "I did, but...honestly, that's not what changed me the most."

"No?"

I tilt my head toward Juno. "She did. There are lots of ways to become a parent, and not all of them include pregnancy. I think your heart changes through the process no matter how it looks."

Alec holds my gaze. "That's pretty deep, nerd."

I grin. "Shut up."

"No, I mean it. I really do," he says. "I like what you said. My mom is no less my mom because she wasn't my birth mom. I get what you're saying."

I lean my elbow on the back of the couch. "Sometimes I forget your parents are actually your grandparents. I never think of them that way."

"We really don't either."

"Do you see your birth mom any more frequently than Megan does?"

He shakes his head. "Nah. She isn't interested in seeing us. She's got a different life. Other kids. But it's fine. I'm glad she's happy."

"That's very mature of you," I say, because it honestly *is*. Though knowing what I know of their parents, Alec and Megan probably had a lot of support processing and understanding their circumstances. Megan had a therapist when we were in middle and high school, and her parents were loving and supportive, fully engaged in her life. It stands to reason Alec would have had the same. If he and Megan's birth mom left a hole when she left, I have no doubt their parents filled it.

Somewhere across the couch, a vibration sounds deep in the cushions, and Alec's eyebrows lift. His phone is sitting on the coffee table next to my soda, so the buzzing has to be coming from mine. He sticks his hand in between the cushion and the arm of the couch and rummages around before pulling the phone up in a triumphant gesture. "Got it." He glances at the screen, his expression shifting just slightly before holding it out to me. "Yours?"

I take the phone, wincing when I see another text from Devon on my notification screen. This one is only two words long.

DEVON

Evie, please.

"Thanks," I say to Alec, but then I shut off the screen and lean forward, dropping the phone face down on the table.

I shouldn't be comparing the two men, but I can't help it. Devon and I talked a lot, but most of the time, we were talking about him. His life. His auditions. His friends.

As soon as I found out I was pregnant, everything changed because Devon couldn't be the center of the universe anymore. He hated the idea of sharing me, hated that I was prioritizing someone else's needs over his. Even when those needs were my own.

Alec is the complete opposite. Even with his fame, his following, his role as the captain of a very popular hockey franchise, he has prioritized me and my comfort over and over again, and we aren't even in a relationship. He's just a genuinely nice guy.

My phone buzzes one more time, and a question flashes in Alec's eyes. But he must sense I don't want to talk about it because he doesn't ask or push for information.

It's the right move because I don't want to think about Devon right now.

Instead, I smile and shift my focus back to Alec. "So tell me about the game."

CHAPTER 9

ALEC

THE COMPULSION TO ask Evie about her ex-husband is stronger than I expect. Even more surprising: the impulse to find the man and pummel him for causing the grief that just flickered across her face from a simple text. It was gone as quickly as it appeared, hiding behind a mask of determined indifference, but I saw it before Evie schooled it away, and I'm not sure I can forget it.

Does she miss him? Do they still talk? Is he involved in Juno's life at all?

I'm not sure it's my place to ask, which means it's definitely not my place to punch the guy on her behalf. But I still wish I could.

Bare minimum, I want to make her feel better, distract her from whatever she's feeling, which has me reaching for my duffel, rummaging through it to find the baby things Summer picked up for me.

Just as Summer promised it would be, the white plastic

merch bag was in my stall after the game. It stayed there until I finished with Dr. Samuelson and returned to retrieve it. My teammates were all long gone by then, but I still pushed the gift to the bottom of my bag before leaving the Summit. Not sure who I was hiding it from. Maybe myself.

Now that I have it in my hands and I'm really paying attention, the bag feels slightly more full than it should, and I wonder if Summer included a few extra things.

"You okay?" Evie asks.

The time it took me to find the shiny white plastic was just long enough for me to realize how this might look, and I start to doubt. "I'm fine," I say, but my voice is a little too breathy, almost squeaky.

I clear my throat and try again. "I'm fine," I say, my voice normal this time, but based on Evie's expression, I'm not doing myself any favors here.

Will this give her the wrong idea? Seem presumptuous? Is seconds after her ex-husband texted really the time to make a gesture like this?

I stand up and tuck the bag behind my back. Maybe I can get it into the kitchen and stash it in a cabinet without Evie realizing I'm holding something. I turn my body and back toward the kitchen without turning around, but she stops me by asking, "What's in the bag?"

I spin so my back is to her and shove the bag under my shirt. It's bulky and obvious and I'm being ridiculous, but suddenly, the idea of giving her a gift like this feels way too personal.

"Nothing," I say over my shoulder, using my arms to hide the bulge under my clothes.

Evie grins, her tone light as she asks, "If it's nothing, why are you hiding it from me?"

"I'm not hiding anything," I lie.

Evie stands and reaches down to give Juno her pacifier before rounding the couch and approaching me. She walks slowly, a smile playing on her lips, until she's less than a foot away. "I think you're lying to me," she says. Then, quick as lightning, she snakes one hand under my shirt.

My hands fly to my midsection, trapping and holding the bag in place, but I end up trapping Evie too, flattening her palm against my stomach.

I relax my grip, expecting her to tug her hand away, but instead she does the opposite. She slides her hand upward, grazing it over my skin until her fingers brush the bottom of my right pectoral muscle. I flex, my breath catching in my throat, and Evie grins, her expression sly as she drops her hand and yanks the bag free.

"That was way too easy," she says with a smirk.

I can't do anything but smile. Partly because my skin is still tingling from her touch. But more because the light in Evie's eyes that disappeared when Devon texted is back now, and seeing it sends warmth across my chest.

I like making her happy.

The next realization is a little more potent.

I just like *her*. And no amount of mental gymnastics will talk me out of it.

I grip the back of my neck, feeling sheepish as Evie peers inside the bag. She looks for one second, then two before her gaze jumps back to mine, a question in her eyes. "Is this...?"

"For Juno," I say.

Slowly, she pulls out two different footie pajama-looking things. One is turquoise and white striped with an Appies logo on the butt, and the other is solid turquoise with the words "Littlest Appies Fan" stitched on the front.

"I figured if you're living in Harvest Hollow," I say, "she needs to look like a true Appies fan."

105

"Alec," Evie says softly as she looks them over. "These are perfect."

"If they aren't the right size, I can exchange them," I say, but she shakes her head as she looks at the tag. "No need. They'll fit her right now." She moves around the couch, dropping the Appies bag onto the coffee table before she kneels down next to Juno, holding up the pajamas like she wants her daughter's approval. "Do you see what Alec brought home for you? You get to be an Appie just like him!"

An odd sensation washes over me, something I've never really felt before. It isn't just attraction, though I *do* feel attracted to Evie. It feels more protective. Like I have extra reason to check the door locks. Or go upstairs and make sure all the windows are securely fastened in her bedroom.

I'm still puzzling out what this means when the front door clicks open. It has to be the twins, and as much as I hate that they're interrupting my time with Evie—*again*—I'm a little glad for the distraction. Otherwise, I might start remembering the sensation of Evie's palm sliding over my skin or imagining how it would feel if she touched me like that for real.

"What's up, what's uppppp?" Theo steps into the room with Carter quick on his heels. "How's everybody doing?" Theo's cheeks are flushed, his words a little too soft around the edges, and I immediately know he's been drinking.

I exchange a quick glance with Evie. She's still on the floor next to Juno, and she wordlessly unbuckles her daughter and pulls her into her arms. Theo doesn't look the least bit dangerous, but I don't blame her for wanting Juno close.

I glance over at Carter. "Please tell me you weren't also drinking."

106

"No, sir," Carter says. "I was driving, so I didn't have anything."

"Where were you?" I ask. "You didn't just go to Felix's?" It's a stupid question because they obviously went somewhere else. Felix would never have let them drink at his place.

Carter at least has the decency to look chagrined. "We started there, but then we stopped by a party at the end of Maple Street."

"A *boring* party," Theo says. "The girls were lame." He moves around the couch and picks up the Appies bag, his gaze landing on the baby clothes Evie already pulled out. "Dude? Is this Appies stuff for the baby?"

He reaches into the bag, surprising me when he pulls out an adult-sized Appies jersey. He holds it up, and I catch a glimpse of my last name stitched in turquoise letters across the back. *Sheridan.*

Theo frowns. "I think this is probably too big for her."

I shift my eyes to Evie, heat climbing the back of my neck as her eyebrows lift.

"Is that for me?" she asks.

I clear my throat. "Yeah. Yes. Of course it's for you."

Theo chuckles. "Way to make a move, Captain. Giving her your jersey. *Classic.*"

I can't read Evie's expression, and for a moment, I have no idea what to say. If I protest Theo's comment, will it make Evie think I'm *not* making a move? That I would never make one?

I'm still mulling over an acceptable response when Evie stands, Juno tucked against her, and moves around the coffee table toward Theo. "I've been wearing his jerseys since I was nine," she says. "His sister and I both did. We wore them to all of Alec's high school games."

107

Theo snorts. "Is that how old you were when he was in high school?" He looks at me. "You're like...a grandpa."

Evie plucks the jersey out of Theo's hands. "He's *not* a grandpa. And you're turning this into something it isn't."

I study Evie's expression, wondering if that's what she truly thinks. It wasn't my idea to give Evie a jersey, but there's definitely been a vibe between us tonight. She can claim this is no different than her wearing my jersey when we were kids, but it isn't going to feel the same for me.

As if to illustrate that point, Evie lifts Juno into my arms. "Hold her a sec?" She quickly yanks the tag off the jersey, then tugs it over her head and pushes her arms through the sleeves.

A strange possessiveness pushes through me at the sight, but it's quickly eclipsed by my present reality.

I'm holding a baby.

Or...sort of holding a baby? I might as well be holding a basketball. Juno is dangling from my hands, little legs kicking, eyes wide as she looks up at me.

"Want me to hold her?" Carter asks, stepping toward us. "I've got a niece, so I know how."

A part of me wants to agree, but a bigger part doesn't want to give the baby up. Suddenly, Juno makes a cute babbling noise before her mouth lifts into an enormous grin. We're making eye contact, she's looking right at me, and she *smiles*. I pull her closer. "No, I want to hold her." I look down at Evie. "I just don't know how."

"Just tuck her against your chest." Evie reaches up and positions my arm just below Juno's butt, then moves the other so it's supporting her back.

Juno shifts her weight forward, one hand clamping onto my shirt, and Evie grins. "See? Just like that."

I bounce Juno lightly in my arms. "Hi, Juno," I say, feeling a strange sense of wonder. I look over at Evie, completely forgetting the awkwardness that punctuated the last few minutes. "This is pretty awesome."

"I love hanging out with my baby niece," Carter says, warmth in his expression. "But my sister says I only feel that way because I only hold her when she's happy."

Behind him, Theo drops onto the couch and leans his head back, lifting his feet to prop them on the coffee table.

"True, but this is a good place to start," Evie says. She smooths her hands down the front of the jersey, holding my gaze. "I love this," she says, her tone warm. "And the things for Juno. Thank you for thinking of us."

The Appies turquoise across the shoulder and down the sleeve brings out the blue in Evie's eyes. But more than that, the genuine gratitude in her expression keeps me from feeling any regret about giving her the jersey. Even if it wasn't my idea to do it.

"Can we watch something?" Theo says, reaching for the remote.

"Nah, man. Let's leave them alone," Carter says. "You're annoying when you're drunk."

"I'm not drunk," Theo says.

I don't love that Theo and Carter left the team dinner for another party. Had I been with them, I would have encouraged them to stay, to get to know their teammates. Avoid partying when our season's just starting. I can't fix the way things went down, but I can hopefully do a little bit of damage control now. "Actually, why don't you pick out a movie, Carter?" I say. "I'll make some coffee for Theo, then we can all watch."

"I can make coffee," Evie says, moving toward the kitchen. "And pop some popcorn. As long as you're happy holding the baby."

She moves around the island while I pace behind the couch, a soft bounce in my step as I rub my hand up and down Juno's back. Eventually, her head drops onto my shoulder, one hand lifting to her face as she rubs it against her eyes.

"Is it okay if she goes to sleep?"

Evie turns and looks at me across the island, her expression tender. "She's fine if you're fine," she says. "If she does, we can take her upstairs and put her to bed." Evie winces the slightest bit before quickly correcting herself. "Not we. I don't know why I said we. I just mean I. *I* can put her to bed."

I nod, growing more and more comfortable with having Juno in my arms. Honestly, I didn't really mind that Evie said *we*. I thought I meant it when I told Megan I didn't do babies, but that was before I met Juno. Before I realized how fun this is.

As I continue my pacing, I leave the living area and move into the hallway that leads toward the front door. There's a mirror on the wall halfway there, and I stop, turning to the side so I can see Juno's face. Her head is fully on my shoulder, her eyes heavy, but she's clearly fighting, trying to stay awake. I sway back and forth a few times until finally she takes a deep breath and her eyes fall closed, her weight sinking into me as she fully relaxes.

I haven't felt a stronger sense of victory since we took the Calder Cup last season. Juno is asleep—*in my arms*. I did this. And it feels amazing.

I snuggle her a little closer, my cheek dropping onto her baby-soft head.

When I look up again, Evie is watching me from the end of the hall.

I offer her a tentative smile. "I don't know what I did," I whisper.

She slowly walks toward me, her hand lifting to Juno's back. "You must have a magic touch."

"I don't know about that," I say, but Evie only shakes her head.

"Trust me. She doesn't go to sleep for just anyone."

"I'm happy to help anytime," I say. "I mean, as long as I'm here."

"That's right. You're leaving soon, aren't you? I remember you saying I'd have the house all to myself."

"Tomorrow morning," I say. "Bright and early."

Something like disappointment flickers across her expression, but then she smiles, her hand lifting to Juno's face where she brushes a stray curl off her forehead. "We'll have all the dance parties we want, Junebug," Evie whispers.

She leaves her hand on Juno's back for a moment, her body swaying toward me the slightest bit. There's an easy comfort to how we're standing, linked by Juno, our voices pitched low, and I find myself wishing we could stay like this a while longer.

"I know I said I'd take her," Evie says, "but do you mind coming with me and carrying her upstairs? I'm afraid we'll wake her otherwise."

"Not at all," I quickly say. "Lead the way."

I toe off my shoes at the foot of the stairs and follow Evie up to her bedroom. She leaves the room dark but flips the switch in the bathroom so there's enough light to see by as I walk Juno over to the portable crib.

"Over here first," Evie whispers. She lays out a blanket looking thing on the bed and motions for me to lay Juno on top. My knee pinches the slightest bit as I lower Juno to the bed, but I ignore it, watching as Evie maneuvers Juno's arms through the sleeves and zips up the blanket.

"Uh, that thing is really cool," I say, and Evie grins.

"It's a sleep sack. Easier than blankets because she can't get tangled up in them."

Once Juno is safely bundled, Evie lifts her and carries her over to her crib where she lowers her in. She grabs the baby monitor, then together, we walk into the hall and close the door behind us.

"It's crazy that she didn't wake up through all of that," I say.

"She's usually pretty good about staying asleep," Evie says through a yawn. "Sheesh. I'm tired. I hope the twins picked something exciting."

As much as I'd love to have Evie watch a movie with us, she has to be exhausted. She'd probably enjoy going to bed herself now that Juno is asleep.

"Listen, you don't have to watch a movie with me and the twins," I whisper. "I need to spend some time with them, but I don't want you to feel like you have to."

She waves away my comment. "I want to. I can already smell the popcorn, and now I want some." She leans against the wall, arms crossed. "What's going on with the twins?"

I shrug. "I'm not sure, actually. They're doing okay on the ice, but I don't love that they're leaving team dinners to party right in the middle of the season. I don't know. The transition can be tough when you start so young."

"How old are they?"

"Barely eighteen," I say, and her eyes widen the slightest bit.

"Wow. Yeah. That's young."

I let out a little huff. "You're one to talk. Did you have to tell them you were *nine* when I was in high school?"

She grins. "Sorry, old man. The truth hurts, but it's still the truth." She cocks her head to the side. "Hey, how's your knee?"

"So we go from calling me an old man to bringing up my knee problems? Hit me where it hurts, nerd."

"I'm sorry! That's not why I asked..." She purses her lips to the side. "Okay, actually, that's exactly why I asked. But I promise I really do want to know."

"It's doing okay. I saw the team doc before leaving the Summit," I say, recognizing how much easier it is to say this to Evie than it would be to my teammates. "He came up with a new plan to manage the inflammation. I just have to hope it works."

"You don't have any other options?" she asks.

I lean against the wall and fold my arms over my chest. "Surgery. But I've already had three. Another would probably take me out for the season."

"Are you in a lot of pain?"

"Nah. It's not too bad," I whisper. "Probably not as bad as bleeding nipples."

She lifts her hands to her face and covers her cheeks. "Please don't remind me I actually said that out loud."

"I'm glad you did. It keeps the playing field even because you're still the only person outside of the Appies staff who knows how bad things are with my knee."

Her expression warms, and for a split second, I imagine what it would be like to kiss her.

"Come on," she says, tilting her head toward the stairs. "Let's go watch a movie."

"Are you sure?"

Evie nods. "Yeah. I'm sleepy, but the idea of spending time with grown-ups sounds pretty nice."

"We're calling the twins grown-ups?"

She chuckles. "Practice grown-ups?"

"Better." Halfway down the stairs, I add, "So just putting this out there. I'll happily put Juno to sleep any time you need it."

She looks at me over her shoulder and grins. "Already so smitten."

Completely, I think, as I follow her into the living room.

And not just with Juno.

CHAPTER 10

EVIE

ALEC HAS ONLY BEEN GONE from Harvest Hollow for a couple of days, and I already feel a tiny bit unmoored.

Which is silly. I've been on my own for months, and I've been doing just fine. There's no reason to suddenly be clingy and needy now. But for the last few days, in a new state, in a new town, there's been something stabilizing about Alec's presence. Knowing he was coming home went a long way to keeping me in a good mood.

I lift my hand to adjust my rearview mirror to check on Juno. She's been fussy and cranky this morning and probably needs a nap, but I'm supposed to meet my soon-to-be boss for lunch, so I'm crossing my fingers Juno falls asleep in the car and stays asleep when I take her carrier into the restaurant.

"It's just you and me, Junebug," I say to her reflection. "Let's make it a good day, yeah?"

Except the other night, it wasn't just Juno and me. It was Juno and me and *Alec*.

I plug the name of the restaurant into my phone's GPS, then slowly back out of Alec's driveway.

It's hard to fully quantify what it did to my heart to see him holding Juno. To see my daughter relax into his arms and fall asleep.

Not that I can blame her. And honestly, considering how many times I've used videos of Alec's deep voice to soothe her, it's not a wonder.

But still. He was so gentle with her. So genuinely enamored.

It was a new side of him and did not help my efforts to *not* have a crush.

Which, speaking of...

I stop at the exit to Alec's neighborhood and call Megan. I bet she'll have the answers I want.

"What do you know about a woman named Riley?" I ask as soon as she answers the phone.

"Well, hello to you too," she says back.

"Sorry. Hi. How are you? How was your pharmacology test?"

"I got an A, and I'm fabulous," she says. "Thank you for asking. Riley who?"

"I have no idea," I say as I make a left turn out of the neighborhood. "That's why I'm asking you."

"With zero context?" Megan asks. "You're just randomly throwing out a woman's name and expecting me to know something? I think there was a Riley in my third-grade class. Is she who we're talking about?"

"Oh, oops," I say. "Sorry. I'm talking about Alec. The internet tells me he's dating a woman named Riley."

"What? Really?"

"According to her Instagram." I give Megan Riley's Instagram handle, which I not-so-weirdly remember considering how much time I spent stalking her profile, then wait while she pulls up the account.

"Ohhh, I love Flex clothes," she says after a few seconds. "Alec brought me all kinds of free stuff after he signed his branding deal with them."

So *that's* how Alec knows her. I guess it makes sense.

I make another turn, my GPS telling me I'm less than ten minutes away from the restaurant.

"But you don't know about Riley?" I ask. "He hasn't said anything about her?"

"Not that I've heard," Megan says. "Can we talk about why you're asking about a woman Alec might be dating?"

The question takes me by surprise, even though it absolutely shouldn't. Did I really expect to call Megan, of all people, asking questions about her brother, without her getting suspicious?

"No reason," I say after too many seconds of silence. "I was just curious."

Megan must not believe me, because she answers with a longsuffering sigh. "Evie," she says.

"Don't Evie me," I shoot back. "It was just a question. It doesn't mean anything."

"You're sure? Your crush hasn't returned even a little?"

I think about the baby clothes Alec brought home from the Summit.

I could keep lying. Dismiss Megan's concern. But she knows me too well. And honestly, now that we're having the conversation, it might be nice to have her input.

"Okay fine, maybe a little," I say. "But he's not playing fair. He's making me food and holding Juno until she falls asleep, and the other day he folded an entire load of Juno's laundry while we watched a movie. Plus, he brought home an Appies jersey for me from his game, and he's talking to me like I'm a real person and not just a frumpy, exhausted dairy cow. He's being so nice, Megan. Thoughtful in ways that are literally the exact opposite of Devon."

I turn into the restaurant parking lot and pull into an empty spot under an enormous oak tree, its leaves a rich, fall red. I shift into park, then turn to check on Juno. Right now, she looks peacefully, *gratefully* asleep. Still, I leave the car running, hoping the steady hum of the engine will help keep her that way.

Megan lets out a little laugh. "Alec actually *held* Juno? He told me he doesn't do babies."

"He told me the same thing," I say. "But he did great. Carried her upstairs to put her to bed and everything. The whole thing was pretty adorable."

"That *does* sound adorable," Megan says. "Okay, so...I'm scrolling through her profile, and I don't think Alec *is* dating this woman. I mean, maybe? But she's not on his profile at all, and all these pictures that she's posted look like they were taken on the same day."

"Not all of them," I say, because I noticed (and studied) the same thing.

"Okay, but *most* of them," she amends. "Also, the trees in the one pinned at the top of her profile look super green, like they were taken in the middle of summer. If they're still dating, wouldn't she have more recent photos?"

"Is this how far we've fallen? That we're studying the color of the leaves in her photos?"

"You started it," Megan says. "It's only creepy stalking if we start searching for her Mom's Facebook account so we can see pictures of her as a kid."

"Please tell me you've never actually done that," I say.

"We aren't talking about *me*, Evie," Megan says cheekily. "Why don't you just ask Alec? He'd probably tell you. And just because Alec hasn't settled down doesn't mean he's a player. He wouldn't flirt and lead you on if he were dating someone else."

"You really think?" I'm not sure if what Alec is doing *is* flirting. Nothing has been so bold that I couldn't just be reading into things. But it does make me feel better to hear Megan's opinion.

"I totally think," she says. "Do you want me to talk to him for you?"

"For real? You, who initially warned him he'd better not try to *woo* me, are now volunteering to speed things along?"

"He's the one who folded your laundry for you. My hands are tied! Besides, I said from the beginning I loved the idea of you guys together. But only if it's going to last forever and no one will ever get hurt. Because so help me, Evie, I am not choosing between the two of you."

"I could be making something out of nothing, so I don't want you to talk to him. But thank you for letting me talk *about* him."

"Anytime. Until you want to talk about sex, and then I'm out."

I laugh. "Noted."

"How's the garbage ex-husband?"

"Ugh. Still texting," I say. "He wants me to call him."

"Boo. Are you going to?"

"I have no idea. What would I even say?"

"I mean, he did just go through something," Megan says. "I don't know why he lost his job, but that role was supposed to be his big break. If he blew it, maybe it was enough to wake him up? Help him see what really matters?"

"Seriously? Have you forgotten who we're talking about?"

I'm not about to believe Devon has suddenly changed. The man was very good at being concerned and loving, but only when being so also served *him*. Did he need me to help him run lines? Then *of course* he'd make dinner. Did he want me to be his arm candy at a big premiere where he was hoping to impress a fancy producer and his casting director wife? Then he would *love* to buy me a new dress.

Right before I got pregnant with Juno, we went through a particularly rough patch where we weren't getting along at all. But my birthday was coming up, so Devon planned this big trip to Martha's Vineyard. A weekend away, just the two of us. A time to really celebrate *me*.

Except there was also a party happening that weekend... just two doors down from the cottage Devon had rented for us. Hosted by a soon-to-be famous playwright Devon absolutely had to meet that very weekend if he had any hopes of securing the lead role in a groundbreaking play that wasn't even finished yet.

When I refused to go to the party with him—it was my birthday, after all—he went by himself, promising to meet me for dinner after. I waited at the restaurant for two hours before walking back to the cottage alone. Devon didn't get home until after midnight, drunk and not even a little apologetic because he was *sure* he'd just made the connection that would launch his stage career once and for all.

Newsflash: The playwright *still* isn't famous, and that groundbreaking play he was working on? Still not finished.

"Okay, fine. That doesn't sound very much like Devon," Megan says. "But you never know." She's quiet for a beat before she adds, "He's still Juno's dad, Evie. Like it or not."

I breathe out a sigh. "If he wants to be her dad, he can come down here and tell me in person."

"Then tell him that," she says. "Make him work if he wants things to be different."

I like that idea because I doubt very seriously Devon would ever make the trip.

On my car's dashboard, the clock flips from 11:59 to noon. "Okay, I've got to go. I'm having lunch with Victoria right this second."

Despite the downer Devon conversation, a burst of nervous energy still bubbles up at the thought of meeting Victoria in person. It's possible I've started to idolize her over the past few months. Partly because she has one of the best reputations in the industry. I played with musicians in New York who traveled all the way to North Carolina just to see her. But mostly I really admire her work. She recently posted a ten-part video of a cello restoration on her YouTube channel, and I've already watched the entire series at least five times.

The biggest parts of lutherie involve the construction of new instruments and the repair of existing ones. But Victoria's restoration work—that's the piece that excites me the most. The idea of taking something everyone else thinks is too old or too broken and bringing it back to its full potential? That's magic I want to be a part of.

And I will be.

Assuming this lunch meeting goes well, and Victoria doesn't rescind the apprenticeship to work with someone whose life isn't one tiny spark away from a dumpster fire.

"Oh! Amazing! Let me know how it goes," Megan says. "I'm sure Victoria will love you. You've got this, Mama."

I say goodbye to Megan, then turn in my seat. The fact that Juno is still asleep loosens some of the tension coiled inside me.

This is going to be fine.

Easy.

Victoria and I have chatted over the phone a few times already, and those conversations have been amazing. We have good chemistry, and she knows about Juno, so there's really no way this can go wrong. Juno's a good baby. An easy baby.

An easy baby who was a complete terror for most of the morning, but we're past that! She's sleeping now! Everything is great!

By the time I make it inside the restaurant, I almost have myself convinced.

I find Victoria in a back booth, her white hair swept up into a twist and stylish glasses perched on her nose. She stands as I approach the table and opens her arms for a hug.

"Are you a hugger?" she asks as she wraps her arms around me. "I'm a hugger."

"I love a good hug," I say. "It's so lovely to meet you."

"Likewise, dear. And this must be Juno?" She looks into the baby carrier and smiles. "I didn't realize she'd be joining us."

My chest tightens. "I hope it's not a problem. I just got into town and didn't figure out childcare for today. But she'll probably sleep the whole time."

"Oh no, no," Victoria says. "It's not a problem at all. Even if she wakes up, that just means I'll get to meet her."

I'm encouraged by Victoria's kindness, but the feeling is short-lived. We're still eating our salads when Juno wakes up and she has fully reverted right back to the cranky mood that made our morning so memorable. There doesn't seem to be anything specifically wrong with her. She doesn't want to eat or burp or sleep. Her diaper is dry, her body temperature is normal. She's just grumpy. And she keeps spitting her pacifier out like it's the most disgusting thing I've ever offered her.

I try to eat one-handed while I bounce her in my free arm, but she's squirmy enough that she keeps knocking her fist against the edge of the table. When I bounce her a little more, shooting Victoria an apologetic glance, Juno flails in response, body stiffening as she arches her back, this time hitting her *head* against the table.

The cry she lets out in response is sharp and ear-piercing, and I want to sink into the floor.

What am I doing here?

I'm supposed to be talking about my symphony experience, my training at Juilliard, my reasons for wanting to be a luthier. Instead, I'm disrupting lunch for an entire restaurant and probably making a terrible first impression.

As if I needed more icing on this very terrible cake, Juno's cries make my milk let down, and it soaks right through my shirt.

Victoria looks at me with what can only be pity. "Perhaps you should take her out, dear," she says over Juno's wails. "I'll have your food boxed up, and I'll bring it to your car. It's really okay. We can do this another time."

Tears fill my eyes, but I don't have any choice but to nod, gather up my things, and head for the door. Juno's cries have slowed to hiccups by the time I reach my car, and I look down at her.

"Now you're happy, huh?"

She has the audacity to smile at me, and I catch sight of a tiny white line on her gum.

"Oh my gosh! Juno! Are you getting a tooth?" I drop her carrier onto the pavement next to my car and lift her a little higher to get a closer look. "You are!" I say. "No wonder you've been so grumpy."

There's still no sign of Victoria coming out of the restaurant, but there's a green space right next to the parking lot with several benches scattered under the trees. I carry Juno to the closest one and sit down to nurse.

Now that we're out of the restaurant and she has my full focus, Juno is totally chill and settles in to eat with her usual enthusiasm.

"That was bad form, girlie," I say as I stroke her wispy brown waves away from her face. "It really is good I noticed that tooth or I'd still be mad at you."

She kicks her little feet, smiling without breaking her latch, and what's left of my frustration completely melts away.

I am embarrassed and discouraged and extra exhausted, but I can't be mad at Juno for any of that.

I close my eyes and tilt my face up to the afternoon sun filtering through the leaves overhead. The weather down here isn't all that different from New York, at least for right now. But I wonder if the winter will be milder.

I pull out my phone, wondering if that would be a weird thing to ask Alec, but when I glance at the screen, there's already a message from him waiting for me.

It must have come in while Juno was having her melt-down, otherwise there's no way I would have missed it popping up on my watch.

My heart jumps the slightest bit as I pull up the thread and read his message.

ALEC

> Hey. Just wanted to thank you again for hanging out with the twins before we left. You're good for them, which feels like a weird thing to say. But I can tell they had a good time.

I smile as I type out a reply.

124

EVIE

You can just say it, Alec. I have a mom vibe.

ALEC

Apparently, I have a grandpa vibe, so…

EVIE

We make quite the pair.

ALEC

How are you?

EVIE

Been better? I just tried to have lunch with my new boss, and Juno had a total meltdown. She cried, then I cried, then I left the restaurant without my food, and my new boss probably thinks I'm a hot mess.

Instead of texting back, Alec calls.

"Is this a pity call?" I say as I answer. "It's fine if the answer is yes."

"Can we call it a cheer-you-up call instead?"

"Yes, definitely," I say. "Cheer me. I want to be cheered."

"Hmm. Let me think. Okay, right now, Nathan is asleep on the bus, and his girlfriend Summer is standing behind him putting dozens of tiny braids in his hair."

"He's sleeping through that?"

"He can sleep through anything," Alec says. "This is nothing. Hang on. I'll send you a picture."

My phone buzzes when the photo arrives, and I pull it away from my ear long enough to quickly look. "Oh wow," I say through a smile. "That's going to take him forever to undo. Does Summer work for the team?" She must, if she's on the bus, so I'm not surprised when Alec confirms.

"She's legal counsel. She doesn't always travel with us. Just sometimes."

"Lucky for Nathan."

"He gets all kinds of crap for it. Logan, too. His girlfriend also works for the team. So what's up with Juno? Why is she having such a rough day?"

I breathe out a sigh. "She's teething, apparently. I didn't notice until we came outside, but her front tooth just poked through her gum."

"That's big, right?" Alec asks. "First tooth? You should send me a picture."

"You want a picture of my daughter's first tooth?"

"Do I need to remind you what happened the night before I left? I'm hooked on your kid."

I close my eyes for a brief second. He has no idea what he's doing to me. What it means to have him interested in Juno's life. It's taking monumental effort not to turn this into something it isn't, but when he's saying and doing everything that my heart wants, how can I not?

Across the parking lot, Victoria emerges with two to-go boxes in her hands.

"Hey, I've got to go," I say. "My boss is coming. But thanks for calling. I'll text you a picture in a bit."

"Let me know if you need more distractions," he says. "I've got six more hours on the bus before we get where we're going."

"Are you sure *you're* not the one who needs a distraction?"

There's a smile in his voice when he says, "Maybe."

"Thanks, Alec."

"Later, nerd."

I set my phone down on the bench beside me and close my eyes, heart pounding in my chest.

I used to roll my eyes when Alec used the nickname he gave me as a kid, but now, I don't think I mind it so much.

EVIE

Good news. My new boss doesn't hate me.

ALEC

You're very likable, Evie. This doesn't
surprise me.

EVIE

You didn't hear Juno crying inside the
restaurant. It was pretty impressive,
honestly.

ALEC

But you talked to her? Everything's okay?

EVIE

Yeah. She was pretty understanding. And
she also asked me to go with her to a
symphony concert this Thursday. So that's
nice.

ALEC

That's cool. You'll see Felix's wife, Gracie.

EVIE

She's in the symphony?

ALEC

Plays the cello, I think? Is that the biggest
one? The one you have to sit down to play?

EVIE

You do have to sit down to play the cello,
but it isn't the biggest stringed instrument.

ALEC

Oh right. The biggest one is the bass, right?

EVIE

Very good. You pass.

ALEC

Thank you very much. Please don't check
my browser search history.

EVIE

Haha.

ALEC

Gracie definitely plays the cello.

EVIE

I'll have to look for her. Assuming I can figure
out childcare.

ALEC

Didn't Ruth offer?

EVIE

She did. But I still feel weird about asking
her. I'm basically a stranger.

ALEC

You aren't. You know me, and I know Malik,
and Malik is Ruth's family. AND you'll be
neighbors.

EVIE

A compelling argument. And I really like
Ruth. I just don't want to make her feel
obligated.

ALEC

Evie.

EVIE

Alec.

ALEC

Just ask her. Hang on...

I just asked Malik how he thinks Ruth would
feel about watching Juno for you. This is
how he responded:

She'd probably do it full time. She's been
looking for something to do. Tell her to ask
her. If I had kids, I'd trust Ruth to raise them
from day one.

EVIE

I hadn't thought about asking her to do it full
time. He really thinks she would?

ALEC

It can't hurt to ask. But definitely ask her
about the concert.

EVIE

Yeah. I should. Thanks for your help.

And thanks for calling me earlier. You really
DID cheer me up.

ALEC

As payback, can you text me for…three
more hours?

EVIE

I have a life to live, Alec. A baby to care for.

ALEC

What if I say please? The twins are singing
through George Strait's entire catalog, Evie.
I'm desperate here.

EVIE

Really? Are they any good?

ALEC

They are…very dedicated to the cause.

EVIE

Do you have headphones? And Spotify?

ALEC

Yes to both.

EVIE

K. Let's swap playlists. Then you'll have something to listen to and something to text me about.

ALEC

You want my playlist? Are you sure our friendship is ready for this?

EVIE

COME ON. I'll show you mine if you show me yours.

ALEC

Fine. Sent. But no judging.

EVIE

Guess who I just met?

ALEC

Flint Hawthorne.

Barack Obama.

Santa Claus.

Freddie Ridgefield.

This is a fun game. Should I keep going?

EVIE

I'm just sitting here trying to dissect your celebrity choices.

ALEC

Don't overthink it. I typed the first names that popped into my head.

EVIE

See, that's why I SHOULD overthink it.

But the correct answer is Gracie Mitchell. I found her after the symphony concert, and she was so nice.

ALEC

That's awesome. Gracie is great.

EVIE

I really like her.

ALEC

How was the concert?

EVIE

So amazing. Last time I heard classical music live I was IN the symphony, so it was nice to be there.

ALEC

And stuff with your boss was good?

EVIE

I want to be her when I grow up. She's amazing. I just hope she loves me as much as I love her.

ALEC

I'm sure she does. How could she not?

Did Juno do okay while you were gone?

EVIE

I missed her, but she was a total champ.

And Ruth is all set to keep her when I go to work on Monday.

ALEC

That's awesome. Are you nervous?

EVIE

Terrified. But I'm excited about the job, so that's helping.

ALEC

It's a very good second reason for moving to North Carolina.

EVIE

Second reason? What's my first reason?

ALEC

I'm wounded you have to ask.

EVIE

Because my first reason is...you?

ALEC

I mean, I was thinking of my stellar breakfast sandwich, but if you wanna say it's me, I won't complain.

EVIE

I don't know what I was thinking! OF COURSE I came all the way to North Carolina to eat your sandwiches. Not your Grape Nuts, though. Your cereal choices are very boring, Alec.

ALEC

Don't knock them until you try them.

EVIE

I DID try them. I was desperate. It was very disappointing.

ALEC

But have you seen their fiber content?

EVIE

Mmm. Please tell me more.

ALEC

You're mocking me.

YES. I would rather get fiber from sucking on tree bark. But I love that you love them.

We're talking about this again as soon as you turn thirty. You might feel differently.

Deal. It's on my calendar. I will happily enjoy my Frosted Flakes until then.

CHAPTER 11

ALEC

TEXTING Evie definitely makes time on the road easier to bear.

The conversation we started at the beginning of the week has been going on for days, mostly just through text, but we've had a few phone calls too, and we're talking about everything.

A lot about what she's been up to in my absence. Hiring Ruth to provide daily childcare for Juno. Getting a North Carolina driver's license. Meeting her landlord at her house to go over the list of repairs and improvements he plans to make before she moves in.

I don't like thinking about that part—about the fact that if everything happens as planned, Evie will move out of my house within just a few days of my return. It feels selfish to grumble about it when I know she's excited to set up her house and get settled, but hanging out with the twins without Evie around doesn't sound nearly as much fun.

We've talked about our families. My teammates. All our favorites. Music. Movies. Books. Food.

She told me the story of her water breaking on a train car halfway between Manhattan and White Plains, and how Megan was the only reason she didn't completely lose her mind while they waited for whatever malfunction had stalled them to be repaired. She made it to the hospital in time, but barely.

I told her about the time I fell asleep in the top bunk of a sleeper bus and didn't wake up until I was locked inside a bus lot in Chicago, five miles from the arena with less than an hour before puck drop.

For once, I don't mind so much that my closest friends on the team spend so much of their time texting their girlfriends or calling their wives. Because now, I have someone to talk to as well.

In all my past relationships, it's never been this easy. It definitely wasn't with Riley.

Not that I'm in a relationship with Evie. This is just friendship. I *think* it's just friendship?

We're outside of Philadelphia, an hour from our destination when a new message pops up.

> **EVIE**
>
> ALEC. There is a lot of Midnight Rush on your playlist.

I chuckle as I type out my response.

> **ALEC**
>
> It's two songs. That's not a lot. And they're good songs.

> **EVIE**
>
> It's FOUR songs.

ALEC

Real men aren't afraid of boybands.

EVIE

Can I put that on a t-shirt for you?

ALEC

I'd wear it.

EVIE

Consider it done. Your Instagram fans will love it.

ALEC

Evie, do you follow me on Instagram? Is that what you're admitting here?

EVIE

Don't let it go to your head. I find the comments very entertaining.

ALEC

AND you read the comments?

EVIE

Mostly so I can laugh at the lack of hockey knowledge people have. I swear, a lot of your fans don't even watch the games.

ALEC

Do YOU watch?

EVIE

Of course I watch! I mean, it's hard to watch the Appies because of how few games are televised. But I watch all the highlights on Instagram.

There's an upgrade I can add to my streaming package that will let you watch the Appies games. If you want. Not that you have to watch. I'm just saying if you do, I don't mind adding it.

EVIE

I would love that. If it's not too much trouble.

I like the idea of Evie watching me play. Though there's an undercurrent of uncertainty attached to the feeling.

Last night, I spent a few minutes studying my stats compared to last season. My minutes played are a lot lower than they should be. Nathan and I have always played so well together, we're usually on and off the ice at the same time, but lately, Coach has been shuffling defensive pairings. Last game, Nathan played quite a bit with Carter and Dumbo while I played with Theo and Tucker—something I didn't love because it required me to play offside since we're both left-handed. Overall, I still played with Nathan more. But I have to wonder what Coach is trying to do. Or what he's trying to *say*.

Dr. Samuelson has repeatedly made it clear the injections are a short-term solution. If Coach thinks I can't pull my weight, where does that leave me?

My phone buzzes in my hand, and I look to see another message from Evie.

EVIE

Alec! Oh my gosh! Juno just rolled over!

ALEC

Is that a big deal?

EVIE

It's a HUGE deal. She's never done it before!

A minute later, she sends a video. I pull it up and smile through a twelve-second clip of Juno flopping over from her belly onto her back, then start it over and watch again. At the end of the video, Evie turns the camera and smiles into the frame, eyes sparkling. Her face is perfectly centered on my phone when a hand drops onto my shoulder.

"Okay, time to talk," Felix says, his brown eyes serious as he sits down beside me.

Camden, Eli, and Van file into the row in front of us, standing so they can face me, and Nathan pops up behind me so I'm fully surrounded by my teammates.

I look at Felix, then shift my gaze from one guy to the next. They're all looking at me with matching expectant looks. Like this was some kind of planned ambush. "About what?"

"We think you know what," Van says.

I look over at Nathan, my jaw ticking. "Dude, I swear, if you said something about my knee..."

"What's going on with your knee?" Felix asks, and I frown. *Oops.*

Nathan rolls his eyes. "Evie," he says, like it should have been obvious. "We've all noticed. You're texting her all the freaking time."

"I'm not," I lie. "And it's not like any of you have room to talk. Van calls Amelia at least twelve times a day."

"And she answers every single time," Van says with a smirk.

"You *are* texting her all the time. Evie's face was on your phone not five seconds ago," Felix says to me.

"We're not saying it's a bad thing," Camden adds. "We're just curious where your head is."

I consider the question. Technically, I could dismiss their concerns, claim Evie and I are just friends, and leave it at

139

that. All we're doing is talking. Texting. But I *am* thinking about her all the time. And a part of me is curious to know what the guys think.

I run a hand through my hair. "Nothing is going on—not officially. But I do think I like her."

"*Are* you worried about the age thing?" Nathan asks. "Summer said you mentioned it."

"Nah," I say without even having to think about it. "If I think about it too much, it starts to feel weird, but when we're talking, I don't really notice it. She doesn't *seem* all that much younger."

"Does anyone else think it's weird that we're asking about the age thing but not the baby thing?" Eli asks. "A baby is a big deal."

"Does it have to be?" I ask, because honestly, so far, hanging out with Juno has been awesome.

"It's a *kid*," Van says. "I'm not saying you shouldn't date her. But we aren't talking about one of Eli's puppies. If you go down this road and you're serious about it, you have to be okay with that kid eventually being *your* kid. You'd be a dad, man. Like, *instantly*."

My gut tightens at the thought. So far, I haven't really thought of myself in that context, and it sends a wave of uncertainty washing over me. "I think we're getting ahead of ourselves."

"Are we?" Felix says. "If you're starting something, you have to think about Juno because Evie definitely will."

"I've never even held a baby," Eli says, shaking his head, but there's a glimmer in his eye that makes me think he's excited about the prospect. "Have you?"

"I held Juno before we left," I say, happy I can at least claim that much. "For like an hour. Long enough to get her to go to sleep."

"Wow. A whole hour," Van says dryly. "You're a pro."

"I like my sister's kids," Nathan says, ignoring Van's sarcasm. "This could be good for you. But Felix is right. You can't approach this like any other relationship. Juno will take priority over everything else."

I sink back into my seat, feeling the weight of the new reality my teammates are presenting. So far, texting, hanging out with Evie while she's living in my house has been easy and fun. Very in the moment. But if we were to date for real, how would that even work? Once she moves out, I won't see her near as frequently. She'll be working, juggling childcare for Juno. Would she even *want* to go out at night when she's been away from her daughter all day long?

My travel schedule already makes stuff complicated enough.

"Dude. What's with the face? We aren't saying you shouldn't do it," Felix says.

"No, I know," I say. "I'm just...recognizing a lot of the potential complications."

"I know a thing or two about complications," Van says. He *would* know since he's the one who married the coach's daughter. "If it's right, it's right, and you'll figure everything out."

"I hate to be the wet blanket here," Eli says, "but aren't we forgetting something?"

When no one responds, he rolls his eyes and pulls out his phone. He scrolls for a second, then holds it up.

"Aren't we forgetting *her*?"

A picture of Riley fills his screen.

Van lets out a low *ohhhhh*, but there's no reason for him to.

"She's not an issue," I say. "We were never exclusive, but either way, it's over. We aren't talking anymore."

"Does she know that?" Camden says, looking over Eli's shoulder at his phone. "Because you're all over her feed."

"Am I?" I reach for the phone. Sure enough, I find at least a dozen photos of me and Riley on her profile, including the top three posts pinned to the top.

"She knows," I say. "I had no idea she was posting like this."

"How?" Eli asks, looking over my shoulder. "You're tagged in all of them. This one was only posted a week ago."

"I don't spend any time on Instagram," I say. "And I haven't seen her in person in two months."

"Could she just be using you?" Felix asks. "Not in the relationship sense, I just mean with her posting. She's got a pretty big following, but not as big as yours."

I run a hand over my face. "Yeah, maybe."

"If you want to start something with Evie, you need to talk to her," Felix says. "Get her to stop posting. Because this reads like you're still together."

"You want to start something with Evie?"

I spin around to see Carter standing in the aisle of the bus.

I would cringe if not for the hopeful expression on his face. Despite his brother's questionable attitude, Carter is a hard kid not to like.

"If he does, you won't say anything about it," Nathan says, and Carter quickly nods.

"No, definitely not." He hovers for a moment, indecision crossing his expression like he can't quite decide if he should stay or go. A few seats ahead, his twin is dead asleep, which makes it easier for me to motion him over with a slight tilt of my head. I trust Carter, at least, if not his brother. And it might be nice to have an ally in the house.

Eli clears his throat. "You should probably consider the possibility that Evie has seen Riley's posts too."

My stomach sinks at the thought. Evie was just talking about following me on Instagram. It wouldn't be a stretch to assume she's come across Riley's profile, since Riley is still actively tagging me in her posts.

If Evie *has* seen the photos and it hasn't stopped her from texting me, maybe to her, the dynamic between us really is just friendly and I'm the one reading into things.

I swear under my breath. "What if Evie has seen them and she doesn't care? What if this is all just friendship to her?"

"I know I don't have the relationship experience you guys do," Carter says, "but I don't think Evie looks at you like she only wants to be your friend."

I breathe out a sigh and drop back into my seat. "Why does this suddenly feel so complicated?"

"It doesn't have to," Camden says, his quiet voice cutting through my spiraling thoughts. "You just have to ask yourself some important questions before jumping in. When a kid is involved, you have to count the cost up front and make sure you're willing to go the distance." He frowns and runs a hand across his face. "If you make it that far."

I really think about his question, wanting to be circumspect. But the answer clicks easily into place with little hesitation. "I don't think Juno is a reason for me to walk," I say.

Van reaches over and claps me on the back. "Then go for it, man."

"Just maybe go slowly," Nathan says. "She's been through some stuff. You might need to play the long game."

"Yeah, that's probably true."

"Evie plays violin, right?" Felix asks.

I nod. "She actually met Gracie the other night at a symphony concert."

"Gracie told me," he says. "So once we're back home, bring her over for dinner at my place. I'll cook and invite everyone. Low stakes. Lots of people around. But you'll still get to spend time with her."

"Yeah, that could be good," I say.

"Do I get an invitation to dinner?" Carter asks. He looks around at each of us. "Don't think we haven't noticed there are team dinners and then there are *Dream Team* dinners."

The guys joke and tease Carter about one day earning his spot on the invite list, but I zone out, falling into my own thoughts.

It feels good to own how I've been feeling about Evie. Saying it out loud makes it feel a little more real. But there's one part of the equation my teammates haven't mentioned, and it might throw a wrench into everything.

The only thing Evie and I haven't talked about this week is Devon.

I know he's still texting her. What I don't know is how Evie feels about it or if she's texting him back.

He's Juno's father, so he has every right to reach out. But he's also Evie's *ex*. And where her heart is relative to him has to be something I consider.

CHAPTER 12

ALEC

WE FINALLY MAKE it back to Harvest Hollow just after dinner on Sunday night. I'm anxious to see Evie, tired of my teammates and even more tired of being on a bus, so I don't linger at the Summit.

I'm halfway across the parking lot to my truck when my phone buzzes with a text.

> **EVIE**
>
> I have no idea if you'll be hungry when you get home, but I made soup and there's plenty left over.

My pace quickens but then a second text pops up, and my enthusiasm wanes the slightest bit.

> **EVIE**
>
> There's enough for Theo and Carter too, if you want to let them know.

I look over my shoulder at the twins, who are only a few paces behind me. We all rode to the Summit together when we left town, so they're riding home with me too. I turn and look over my shoulder. "Evie says there's food at the house. She made soup."

They both grin, their expressions identical in a way that still gives me pause. "Home cooking from the missus," Carter says. "Sign me up."

Theo only grunts, but after the bracing conversation I had with him before our last game, when I pinned him against the boards during warmups and made it clear it was time for him to check his attitude, I don't expect much more.

I didn't like getting in his face like I did, but he kept trying to pick a fight with Dominic, who, for all the trouble he gave us his first season on the team, has really stepped up this year. He made a perfectly reasonable suggestion to Theo about how to improve his passing accuracy, and Theo practically lost it.

Carter clearly got a double share of impulse control, leaving his twin with barely any at all.

Except, I'm not entirely sure that's what's happening.

Theo talks a big game. He's got enough swagger for the whole team, and he frequently pushes around his teammates, like he's just *trying* to make them respond. That's what he was doing with Dominic. But it seems less like a lack of impulse control and more like intentional antagonizing. Carter is a good bouncer, and he's talked more than a few guys down after Theo has annoyed them.

But how long will he be able to keep that up?

Eventually, people will tire of Carter protecting Theo as much as they tire of Theo's antics in the first place.

I just wish I could figure out what Theo was thinking. Why he seems so determined to sabotage the start of what

146

could be a very impressive career. I've always felt some sense of responsibility as captain to make sure everyone is doing okay, but lately, with these younger players coming in—and now, living with me—it feels like the stakes are higher somehow, and I really don't want to let them down.

If I can't be a hundred percent on the ice, I can at least get this part right. But how?

As soon as we pull into my garage, I force myself to move slowly, intentionally, as I pull my bag out of the back of my truck and wait for the twins to do the same. I don't want to look overeager, even though I absolutely feel that way.

But then we step inside and hear music, and I can't keep myself from hurrying.

It's nothing like the Taylor Swift Evie blasted in the kitchen while she was making cinnamon rolls. It sounds like a violin, and it's crisp and bright enough that I know it isn't a recording. It has to be Evie.

I drop my bag by the garage door and follow the sound of her playing.

I find her standing beside the piano, her violin lifted to her chin, fingers flying over the strings as she plays a melody that feels familiar even though I can't quite place the song. Juno is sitting in her bouncy seat beside her mom, eyes wide, feet kicking. She looks enamored with her mother, and I completely understand the feeling.

Evie is incredible.

She sounds amazing, confident and sure, but more than that, she *looks* amazing. Like she's doing something she was born to do. Her face is relaxed, her eyes filled with a peace I've never seen in her expression before.

Evie smiles when she sees me come in, but she doesn't stop playing, her eyes closing as she moves with the music.

"Dude, is that Maroon 5?" Carter says from behind me. "'Memories?' I love that song."

The second Carter names it, I recognize it as well.

Theo leans forward the slightest bit as he listens. "I think I'm falling in love with your woman," he says under his breath.

I shoot him a warning look because one, as far as he knows, Evie and I are only friends. And two, I have no clue if Evie can hear him, and my goal is to take things *slow* with Evie. I don't need his idiot mouth messing that up.

Theo lifts his hands. "Sorry, sorry. I meant that as a compliment. She's just..." He nods toward Evie. "She sounds really good."

"She went to Juilliard," I whisper back. "She should."

Evie plays out the last few notes, then finally lowers her instrument.

"I thought people only played classical music on the violin," Theo says before I can even say hello.

"You can play whatever you want on the violin," Evie says. "Technically, 'Memories' was influenced by Pachelbel Canon, which is absolutely classical. It's one of the reasons I have so much fun playing it." She lifts her instrument again. "See? Listen."

She plays another song, and I immediately pick up on the similarities. I don't know a lot about classical music or the violin, but suddenly, it's my new favorite instrument.

She stops after a few more seconds. "You hear it?"

"Totally," Carter says. "That's really cool."

She looks at me, eyes warm. "Welcome back," she says without breaking eye contact. "Are you hungry?"

"Starved," the twins say in unison.

"Go ahead and help yourselves," Evie says. "There's soup and a loaf of bread you're welcome to slice and eat."

"Thank you, ma'am," Carter says before dragging his brother toward the kitchen.

"Please just call me Evie," she says. "Ma'am makes me feel old."

"Yes, ma'am—I mean Evie," Carter says. He stops before he disappears completely and says, "I'm sure we'll be fine on our own while we eat so don't feel like you have to check on us."

I have to appreciate Carter's effort, even if it is a little pointed.

Once they're gone, I look back at Evie, holding her gaze for a long moment. "Hi," I finally say, wondering if she can tell how quickly my heart is beating. It hasn't slowed since I first pulled into the garage, knowing I was on my way in to see her.

"Hi," she says back. "You're home." She turns and sets her violin on the back of the piano, then takes a small step forward, her bottom lip tucked between her teeth. "In my head, I thought I would hug you once I saw you again." Her tone comes out a little sheepish, and her cheeks flush a light shade of pink. "But now I feel a little...I don't know."

I cross my arms and lean against the door jamb, offering what I hope is an encouraging smile. I'd love to pull Evie into a hug. In fact, as soon as she mentioned it, my muscles practically vibrated with the ache of wanting her in my arms. "It's not too late."

She quickly shakes her head. "It would be weird now. I imagined greeting you at the door, jumping into your arms." She grimaces and drops her gaze to the floor. "That sounds so stupid now that I've said it out loud."

She wasn't the only one who imagined what it would be like to see her again. With all the texting and talking we've done over the last week, it definitely feels like we're closer.

But closer in text messages is different than closer in person, and there's a slight awkwardness hovering between us.

I step forward and offer her my hand. When she slips her fingers into mine, I tug her toward me and wrap my arms around her shoulders. "It's not stupid at all," I say into her hair.

She leans into my chest, her arms looping around my waist, and breathes out a sigh as she relaxes against me. "This feels really good. I've been...weirdly lonely the last few days."

In an instant, the awkwardness is gone. There's a rightness to holding her like this that doesn't leave room for any other emotion.

I shift my hands to Evie's shoulders as she steps back, giving them a quick squeeze before I drop my hands. "You finally got good at that thing," I say, motioning to her violin.

She rolls her eyes. "The last time you heard me play, I was what, eleven? Twelve? I'm feeling pretty rusty, honestly. This is the first time I've played since she was born." She tips her head toward Juno, who kicks her feet like she can tell her mom is talking about her.

"You sounded amazing," I say, and Evie smiles.

"Thanks. It felt good."

"Are you ready for tomorrow?"

"Gah," she says, lifting her hands to the top of her head. "I don't know. I'm so scared. I came all this way, you know? And now it's finally here and I'm starting, and I just don't want to screw up."

"You're going to do great," I say. "You've got this."

Her hands drop to her hips as she takes a deep breath. "You think?"

The vulnerability in her expression tugs at me, and I feel a sudden need to lift her up, to ease her worries in some way.

"I don't just think," I say gently. "I know. You're going to be amazing."

She bites her lip and breathes out a long sigh. "Remind me again tomorrow? And probably the next day too?"

"As many times as you need it," I say. I push my hands into my pockets. "So I was thinking, since you met Gracie already, maybe we could all get together for dinner at Felix's. Just like a group thing," I add, emphasis on the word *group*.

Evie's eyes narrow the slightest bit—that was possibly a little too pointed—but then she smiles. "I would love that. Would they mind if I bring Juno?"

"They won't mind at all. I'm sure they'd love to meet her."

"Count me in, then. That sounds like fun."

"Cool," I say, doing my best to minimize the excitement in my voice and find that perfect balance between *I'm looking forward to this* and *I'm so eager you should probably be concerned.* "I'll talk to Felix and figure out a night that works."

She crouches down and picks up Juno, tucking her against her before heading toward the kitchen. "Perfect. Now come eat before the twins devour all the soup."

I follow after her, keenly aware that for the first time, this too-big house full of furniture I didn't buy feels a lot like home.

CHAPTER 13

EVIE

YOU KNOW those scenes in movies where a woman finally gets her big break and is starting her dream job, only on her first day of work, her car won't start and her shoe gets caught in the drainage grate and she spills coffee on her shirt and she meets her boss for the first time when she's crying in the elevator?

I'm living one of those scenes. Except, plot twist, the only obstacle ruining my first day is an almost-five-month-old baby girl. Sometime in between her very smiley evening flirting with Alec and the twins while they ate their soup and talked about their time on the road and right now, Juno was clearly possessed by demon spawn that robbed her of the ability to sleep.

Maybe it's the full moon? A new tooth coming in?

All I know is it's nearly two AM, she will *not* fall asleep, and I'm supposed to be at Victoria's tomorrow at ten AM sharp.

I guess it could be worse. I could have to work at seven. Even eight would feel tough.

But I still can't stop doing the math. If Juno falls asleep right this second, I'm still only getting four hours of sleep before I have to wake up, feed her, get her ready to spend the day with Ruth, then make it to work. And I really wanted to get to Ruth's early, with plenty of time to spare just in case Juno had a hard time settling in.

Which she probably will now that she's also getting *zero* sleep.

Juno lets out a whimper, and I reposition her on my shoulder as we pace back and forth across our bedroom. The fact that I'm so keyed up, worrying about work tomorrow can't be helping things because Juno has to be feeding off my energy.

But we've tried everything. She doesn't want to eat or burp. She's clean and dry and there are no tags or loose threads on her pajamas that might be bothering her. She's just grumpy.

I reach the bathroom door on the far side of my bedroom, then turn and pace back toward the window. As long as I'm moving, Juno seems to do okay, but I'm not sure how much longer I can keep this up. I'm tempted to just put her in her crib and let her cry while I take a shower long enough to calm myself down, but this isn't my house, and I have no idea if the sound will carry across to Alec's room.

He just got home, and he looked exhausted. There's no way I want to ruin his sleep with a wailing Juno.

When I pass the bedroom door one more time, I change course and head out into the hallway. Maybe a change of scenery will help?

I head downstairs without really thinking, but I hesitate at the bottom, glancing down at the very skimpy tank top sleep dress I'm wearing. It's my favorite because the fabric is thick without being too heavy, and it makes nursing really easy. But it's not exactly something I'd choose to wear in front of people. Especially not men, and there are three of those somewhere in the house.

Still, it's well after midnight and the house is quiet, all the lights off save the tiny one over the stove in the kitchen, and I'm the only one in the house with a baby. It's not likely I'll run into anyone else, and honestly at this point, I'm too tired to care. Definitely too tired to go back upstairs to change clothes *just in case*.

Juno squirms in my arms and lets out another whimper, lifting her tiny fists to her face. It's a gesture I recognize, and it means she's exhausted, so why won't she just sleep already?

I pass by the television in the living room and get an idea. I haven't used Alec's video since moving to Harvest Hollow, though I can't pinpoint why. Maybe because it seems silly when we're living in his house? But it was tried and true a month ago, so maybe I'll get lucky and it will work on Juno now.

I usually watch it on Instagram, and I left my phone upstairs, but I bet I can find it on YouTube, and I can do that from Alec's TV. It takes a couple minutes of searching to find the right video, but I eventually do and push play, breathing out a weary sigh as I do.

"This better work, Junebug." I keep the volume low, then pace back and forth in front of the TV, bouncing Juno in the glow of Alec's face. I guess this might run the risk of waking someone up too, but it has to be better than wailing baby cries.

Juno stills in my arms, her eyes transfixed on the screen. On Alec.

155

"I can't blame you there, baby girl," I say softly, running a hand up and down her back.

Alec smiles as the interviewer asks him a question—something about his responsibilities as captain and how he interacts with his team. Even though I've seen this video a million times—thank you, Juno—watching it on Alec's enormous television hits a little differently. He really is so unbelievably handsome. Confident and charming, but somehow still self-deprecating and humble. And that glint in his eye... *gah*, it's just so sexy.

And he invited *me* to have dinner with him and his friends.

Logically, I know it's not really a big deal. A big group thing. That's what he called it. Just a casual gathering of friends.

But it doesn't feel casual to me.

During the symphony concert with Victoria last week, I easily spotted Gracie. Both because she's principal cello and because she was by far the most beautiful woman on stage.

At the reception after the concert, Victoria introduced me to several musicians, including Gracie, and I had a few moments to explain my connection to Alec. She smiled wide and gave me a big hug, saying she couldn't wait to get to know me better. She was so kind, and I immediately liked her, but once I was home, I looked her up on Instagram. Her profile is full of pictures of her and Felix and her best friend, Summer, who I already know is dating Nathan. Summer's profile led me to several others, all people who seem connected to the Appies. I couldn't quite piece together exactly how, but I'd be willing to bet a lot of the people I found will be included in the group dinner. Which is only problematic in the sense that every single one of them is young and vibrant and happy and beautiful and very much part of a couple.

Then there's me.

With my postpartum body and my milk-filled boobs and a tagalong baby.

I'm not one who usually struggles with confidence. I don't think I'm the most beautiful woman in the world, but I have great hair and decent skin, and when I wear makeup, I really know how to make my blue eyes pop. But even when it's being kind, childbearing is *tough* on a body. I'm a little looser, a little more jiggly than I ever was before. My boobs are different, my hips are different. *Everything* is different.

Which is fine, honestly. The expectations society heaps onto women are ridiculous anyway. But I'm only human, and this human is having a hard time not comparing myself to all the beautiful women I'll meet whenever this dinner happens, especially when I would really love to impress Alec.

Alec's video reaches the end, and I pick up the remote and restart it. That's when a truly horrifying thought pops into my brain.

What if Riley comes to dinner?

It's an irrational question because Riley's Instagram profile makes it very clear she lives in Chicago. But Chicago has airports. Even if Megan is convinced she isn't *really* dating Alec, I can't know for sure. Maybe she's perfectly willing, in all her Flex-clad glory, to hop on an airplane to attend a dinner party with her very sexy boyfriend.

Except, that doesn't sound right. Megan was right when she said Alec isn't a player. If only to respect his commitment to someone else, I think he would have different boundaries with me if there were another woman in the picture.

The long hug, all the texting, the baby gift. Those things don't necessarily mean Alec wants more than friendship. But they do feel like more than he'd be doing if he had a girlfriend.

If he and I really were dating, I'd be pissed to find out he was texting someone as much as he's been texting me. I just don't think he'd do that.

Juno and I are halfway through a second listen of Alec's video when the floor creaks behind me, and I spin to see the man himself standing at the edge of the living room. He's shirtless and barefoot, pajama pants slung low on his hips, looking sleepy and disheveled and entirely too sexy.

My eyes graze over the dips and curves of his bare chest, the sculpted muscles dusted with hair and marked with a small tattoo on the top of his left pectoral. From here, it looks like the Appies logo.

"Hey," I say. "I hope we didn't wake you."

"Nah, I got up for a drink," he says. "Then I heard myself talking and..." His words trail off like he can't quite figure out why his face is filling his television screen.

"Juno likes it," I say, heat climbing my cheeks. I'm at least grateful it's dark enough that he probably can't see. "Something about the register of your voice, or the tone. It usually calms her, puts her to sleep when nothing else will."

Juno's whimpers escalate into more of a cry, and I let out a frustrated whimper of my own.

Alec walks a little closer. "She's having a rough time?"

"We've been at this for hours. I can tell she's exhausted, but she just won't sleep. She's not exactly setting us up for a great first day tomorrow."

Alec studies me for a long moment, his bottom lip caught between his teeth. "Can I try?" he finally asks.

I lift my eyebrows. "Really?"

He nods. "You look like you could use a break. If she likes my voice, I'll just...talk to her. See if it helps."

158

He steps closer—close enough for me to feel the warmth of his big body—and lifts a hand to Juno's back.

Juno lifts her head, her cries trailing off as she looks at Alec.

"Are you sure?"

He chuckles. "It might not even work. But yeah. I'm willing to try."

I shift Juno into his arms. He looks awkward at first, but it only takes a moment for him to relax, Juno tucked firmly against his chest.

He tilts his head toward the tv. "Turn that off?"

I nod and reach for the remote, pausing the video but leaving it on, since it's the only light to see by. I watch as Alec makes his way around the perimeter of the room, a light bounce in his step as he rubs his hand up and down Juno's back. It's not quite a natural movement. He looks like he's trying really hard, thinking about his steps, thinking about the way he's holding her. But the longer he walks, the more he seems to relax, settling into a rhythm that seems to be working for them both.

And then my heart climbs into my throat because Alec starts to sing.

At first I can't quite make out what, exactly, he's singing, but then he turns so he's facing me again, and I pick up the chorus to Phil Collins', "You'll Be in My Heart." It's an old song. Stupid old. I only know it from the *Tarzan* movie that played on repeat in the waiting room of the children's hospital where my little brother got all his chemo treatments.

But how does Alec know it?

However he does, he sounds good. Completely on key, his tone rich and smooth.

Having spent two years married to a theater major with a

minor in vocal performance, I recognize a good voice when I hear one. And based on this little, tiny teaser, I'm betting Alec is as good as some of Devon's classmates.

I have no idea why Megan has never mentioned that her brother has such a beautiful voice or how I missed this growing up, but I am completely transfixed. Forget his Instagram reels. I just need to record this. Juno will never struggle to sleep again. It's only been a couple of minutes, and she already looks calmer, her body relaxed, her head resting on Alec's shoulder.

I, on the other hand, may never sleep again. I'll just keep replaying this moment over and over.

When he sings the line, "For one so small, you seem so strong," tears fill my eyes.

I don't know what's happening to me. On the one hand, the image of a shirtless Alec cradling my baby girl against his chest while he *sings to her* is a level of sexy I could not have dreamed up myself. But it's more than that. Seeing Alec hold Juno brings into stark clarity just how much she's missing by not having her dad around. Not that I can imagine Devon ever being this gentle, this patient with Juno.

I tug a blanket off the back of the chair and wrap it around my shoulders, then drop onto the end of the couch. Momentum with a dash of desperation has gotten me through the last few months. It propelled me all the way to North Carolina, even though I only feel like I barely know what I'm doing. With Juno, with life, with everything.

But right now, I feel exhaustion all the way down to my bones.

I don't know how I'm supposed to do this. How I'm supposed to raise a baby all by myself while also figuring out how to have a career and a life. Most of the time, Juno is a great baby. But babies are nothing if not unpredictable, and they're not exactly known for planning their tantrums and meltdowns around their parents' work schedules.

Or parent *singular*. One parent. Just me.

I lean back onto the couch and close my eyes. Alec has no idea the gift he's given me. It feels so good to just breathe for a second. To trust that at least for this small moment, Juno is safe in someone else's arms.

I wake up with my head resting against Alec's chest as he carries me up the stairs, one arm under my back and the other under my knees. My senses wake up slowly as I try to process where I am and how I got here.

Alec smells amazing, clean and woodsy and masculine, and his skin feels warm and smooth where my arms are draped around his neck.

Even though I'm rocking my post-baby curves like it's my full-time job, it doesn't seem like he's working to carry me *at all*. I mean, I know he's a professional athlete, but I'm not some tiny delicate flower of a woman. There's some heft to this body—to these boobs, which, *oh geez* I hope my boobs are covered.

Speaking of boobs and the infant they're responsible for feeding...did Alec leave my baby downstairs to carry *me* upstairs?

"Juno," I whisper.

"Already in her crib," Alec says, his voice low to match mine.

We reach the top of the stairs, and he carries me through my open bedroom doorway. The room is mostly dark, but the bathroom light is on, so there's just enough light spilling in for me to see Juno tucked into her portable crib, her chest rising and falling in peaceful sleep. She's even bundled up in her sleep sack—something Alec must have remembered from

161

when we put Juno to bed the night before he left for the road.

"You're a magic baby whisperer," I say as Alec lowers me onto my bed. He tucks my feet under the covers and pulls them up to my chest.

"I don't know how long it'll last," he says, "but I hope you can sleep while it does."

I close my eyes, suddenly overwhelmed by his kindness. Maybe it's because my emotions were already so close to the surface when I fell asleep, but tears fill my eyes for the second time tonight, one spilling over onto my cheek.

Alec sits down on the bed beside me, and I open my eyes. His face is heavily shadowed in the dim light, but I can see enough to recognize the concern in his expression. He lifts his hand and wipes the tear away with the pad of his thumb, his palm lingering near my face. "You okay?"

I nod and sniff. "Just tired." I take a slow breath, my eyes falling closed again. "Tired of doing this alone."

Alec's hand brushes down my cheek, and I can't keep myself from leaning into his touch.

"You aren't alone," he whispers. "Now try to sleep."

I'm already halfway there, my eyes closing as my awareness grows hazy. When I feel Alec shift and lean forward, pressing a soft kiss to my forehead, I'm not entirely sure it isn't part of the best dream I've had in a very long time.

CHAPTER 14

ALEC

I GO for a run the morning after I found Evie and Juno up in the middle of the night. Normally, I would just head to the Summit and run on one of the treadmills there rather than put my knee through the stress of running on concrete, but after last night, I'm keyed up, filled with a restless energy I can't define.

I want to *do something*. I just can't figure out what.

Hitting the pavement at six AM seems like as good an option as any.

It's cold when I step onto my front porch, cold enough that my breath fogs in front of me, and the grass is crunchy with a sparkling sheen of frost. I pull a beanie onto my head to keep my ears warm, then rub my hands together and set off down the sidewalk. The longer I run, the clearer my mind becomes, and slowly, I start to make sense of the energy pulsing through me.

Yesterday afternoon, when the bus finally pulled into the

Summit parking lot, I was comfortable admitting that I like Evie. That I want to get to know her. But last night, there was something else going on too. Feeling that baby fall asleep in my arms tapped into something in my brain that I've never experienced before. Something primal. I don't just want to date Evie, I want to protect her, take care of her. I'm talking fight her battles, kill the bad guys, rid the world of anything and anyone who might ever hurt her. And I want to do the same for Juno, which is the most foreign part of all.

I've always been the guy who will move my date to the inside of the sidewalk or keep a steadying hand on her whenever we pass by strangers on the street. I open doors, open jar lids, carry heavy suitcases. But all of that just feels like being a nice guy who's aware of his surroundings.

This feels different.

I hit three miles before my knee starts to hurt, but as soon as it does, I slow to a walk. I'm happy to push through the pain on the ice, but there's no reason to do it here. I round the bend on the cul de sac just south of my house, then walk up the hill, making a mental note of where the pain is the worst so I can mention it to Eric.

The house is still quiet when I make it back inside, but Evie should be up soon since I know today is her first day of work. I'm not sure what time, but I'm guessing whatever time it is, she could probably use some coffee sooner than later, considering her night. I take a quick shower and throw on some joggers and a t-shirt, then head to the kitchen.

While I wait for the coffee to brew, I send Megan a quick text, hoping her clinicals schedule will mean she's up early.

ALEC

How does Evie like her coffee?

MEGAN

SHUT UP YOU ARE TOO SWEET.

Which is exactly how she likes it. Cream and
the amount of sugar you think a normal
person would like, plus the same amount
one more time. Dessert coffee.

ALEC

Got it. Think she's already awake?

MEGAN

She's up! I already talked to her.

ALEC

Perfect. Thanks.

MEGAN

Just for the record. I know what's happening
here. And I just want you to know I LOVE IT.

ALEC

No more warnings or threats?

MEGAN

I only warned you because I didn't want her
to get hurt by your shameless flirting. It's
totally different if you're serious.

I think about the way it felt to hold Evie last night, how
good it felt to take care of her.

ALEC

I'm definitely serious.

MEGAN

YAY.

I make the coffee, then carefully carry it upstairs.
This could completely backfire, but I'm trusting my gut

and just going for it. I knock on Evie's door, then wait, heart hammering in my chest.

"Come in," she finally calls.

When I open the door, she's sitting cross-legged on her bed, a hoodie pulled over her pajamas. Juno is on the comforter in front of her.

"Hey," I say. "Thought you might like some coffee."

She smiles wide and lifts her hands out, wiggling her fingers in a "give me" motion.

I hand her the cup, then sit down on the foot of the bed, watching as she takes a sip. Her eyes widen. "It's perfect. How did you know how I like my coffee?"

"I asked Megan," I say. "She's also the reason I knew you were awake."

"Is that what she's going to do with us now?" Evie asks. "Call us in tandem? Maybe we should just call her together and put her on speakerphone, get all the conversations out of the way at once."

"We only texted, but don't give her any ideas," I say. "She'd probably love to have us on the phone together."

Evie takes another sip, then sets the coffee down on the nightstand beside her bed. "Thank you. That's delicious. Exactly what I needed."

"Did you sleep?"

"Yes! Thanks to you. Juno didn't wake up until six."

"That's amazing."

"She's in a much better mood this morning too," Evie says. "She's super smiley, if you want to see." She spins Juno around and scooches her toward me.

I lean down on my elbow, stretching out across the foot of the bed, and tug Juno a little bit closer so I can easily make eye contact. When I do, Juno kicks her feet and coos.

"Good morning, Juno," I say, lifting a hand and patting

her belly. I smile, and she immediately smiles in return. When I make a silly face, she *laughs*.

I look up at Evie, eyes wide. "Did she just laugh at me?"

She grins. "She totally did. Pretty amazing, right?"

I repeat the face and watch in wonder as Juno laughs again and again, feet kicking in excitement. An ache forms deep in my chest that I can't identify at first, but then it shifts and sharpens, and I recognize it for what it is.

I want this.

I want lazy mornings in bed with my wife, a kid tucked between us. I want to make coffee for someone as easily as I make it for myself. I want to talk about a baby laughing or rolling over for the first time. I want to be a *dad*.

I focus on Juno's smiling face and ask myself a surprisingly hard question. Does having them around make me want this generally? Like, now that I've gotten a taste of having a woman and a baby in my home, I know I want it for myself with a nondescript future someone? Or did Evie and Juno stir this awake in me because I want it specifically... with *them*?

It only takes a few moments of thought to decide it's the second one. When I try to picture that future life, it isn't with some random, faceless woman. It isn't Riley or anyone else I've ever dated. It's Evie's face I see.

Acknowledging as much only makes the feeling intensify, and I have to take a steadying breath to keep myself from saying something out loud.

Evie is studying me closely, a curious expression on her face. "I should probably get ready to go," she finally says, though something in her tone makes it sound like she doesn't want the moment to end any more than I do.

"Right. Absolutely." I sit up and look down at Juno. "Do you..." I hesitate, not wanting to impose but also knowing

I'd like to help. "Can I hang out with Juno while you do? Would that help?"

"Really?" Evie asks.

"Sure. I could take her downstairs. Watch some game tapes. See if she has any feedback for me."

Evie laughs. "If you don't mind, that would be amazing. I would love to shower without having to worry about her."

"I'd be happy to. I don't have to be at the Summit until ten."

Evie tosses off the covers and stands, and I do my best not to stare at the long stretch of her bare legs.

"Are you up for getting her dressed?" She crosses the room and rummages around in a drawer. "I already changed her diaper, so it'd be pretty easy. Onesie, stretchy pants, little socks."

"Sure," I say. "That sounds doable." I stand and pick Juno up, noticing how much easier it feels. How much more comfortable I am with her in my arms. Evie hands over the clothes and walks with me to the bedroom door.

"Thank you for this," she says. "Seriously. I shouldn't be longer than forty-five minutes or so."

"Take your time. I'm sure we'll be fine."

We *are* fine. More than fine. Juno is bendier than I expected her to be, and it's pretty easy to wiggle her into her clothes and get everything snapped and adjusted. She's still happy and smiling when her mom comes downstairs looking refreshed and more beautiful than ever.

Evie bustles around the kitchen, putting together a lunch and a few snacks to make it through her workday. She pulls several bags of milk out of the freezer, adding them to the diaper bag, then retrieves a few of Juno's bottles from the dishwasher.

Little pieces of her, traces of her life, are present all over the house. The baby gear, the bottles, the piles of tiny laundry. The house has never felt so lived in, and I really, *really* love it.

"You're going to do great today," I say once I've walked her to the front door.

She looks up at me, blue eyes wide and brimming with hope and excitement. "Thanks." She holds my gaze, then puts Juno's carrier and all her bags on the ground beside her before stepping toward me and wrapping her arms around my waist. "Thanks for your help this morning."

I hold her close, hands pressed to her back, and breathe her in.

She leans back and looks up at me, a vulnerability passing over her expression. "And last night too. I don't know what I would have done without you."

"I was happy to help," I say, because it's absolutely the truth.

As soon as I'm back inside, I pull out my phone and call Riley.

The faster she takes down the photos of us, the better. I want it clear to anyone who's curious. Right now, there's only one woman taking up space in my mind. And it's Evie.

CHAPTER 15

THE DREAM TEAM

ELI

Yo. Alec. Requesting an update on the Evie situation.

ALEC

What kind of update?

VAN

Have you kissed her?

ALEC

No.

VAN

You've thought about it though, right?

ALEC

No.

ELI

Don't lie. You know we know when you lie.

ALEC

Fine. Yes.

FELIX

Have you figured out the Riley thing?

ALEC

I called her. She was chill. Said she'd take the pictures down.

WYATT

Can someone summarize for the guy who doesn't live there anymore?

FELIX

Evie is Alec's little sister's best friend.

NATHAN

Also his current roommate.

WYATT

Right. Because her house flooded. I got that part. And something about Alec drooling when he saw her?

ALEC

There was no drool.

CAMDEN

But he IS into her.

LOGAN

But it's complicated because she has a kid.

FELIX

A baby who is only four or five months old.

WYATT

And Riley is the woman in Chicago? Who Alec dated?

ELI

Yep. But they aren't dating anymore even though her Instagram profile made it look like they still were.

ALEC

Which is why I called her.

WYATT

Got it.

ELI

And now we're back to Alec's next move.

ALEC

This does not need to be a group discussion. I've got this. We're doing a dream team dinner thing at Felix's. She already agreed to come.

WYATT

I miss dream team dinners at Felix's.

ALEC

We miss you too, man. How's Boston? How's the team?

WYATT

Boston is cold. Team is great.

CAMDEN

I miss dream team dinners that weren't couples dinners.

ALEC

Been there. Camden. Sorry, man.

FELIX

We'll do one with just the team soon.

Alec, you should invite Evie to the Halloween party at the Summit.

ALEC

Already thought of that.

LOGAN

Is she working? She started her new job,
right?

ALEC

Yeah.

LOGAN

Take her lunch.

NATHAN

That's a good idea. Surprise her.

ALEC

Okay. Hadn't thought of that.

ELI

See? You do need us. How's life with a baby
around?

ALEC

I don't hate it.

VAN

Are we supposed to read between the lines
here? Does that mean you also don't love it?

ALEC

I didn't say that.

ELI

So you DO love it.

CAMDEN

In other words...

VAN

Captain's got it bad...

CHAPTER 16

EVIE

VICTORIA'S WORKSHOP is everything I dreamed of and more.

First of all, it's adorable. A vine-covered cozy cottage at the edge of her property behind the spacious farmhouse where she lives with her recently retired husband. The setting alone is enough to make me love it. But it's also full of natural light and clean workspaces, and it has incredible views of the tree-covered mountains out the back windows. It smells of cedar and maple and wood glue and varnish, and there is always classical music playing in the background. The entire place has a calming, relaxed vibe that skyrocketed it to my top five favorite places ever in a matter of minutes.

I'm only three days in, and I already want to move here. Live here forever. Raise Juno right here on this property and let her bury me under the giant maple in the front yard.

Or, you know. Maybe I can just work here.

The point is, this place is magical, and I love it with my whole entire heart.

Which helps because if I were leaving Juno for something I hated, I would have already quit by now.

Juno is doing great with Ruth.

I, on the other hand, have cried myself to work three days in a row. I'm fine when I leave the house, mostly because Alec makes me coffee every morning and takes care of Juno while I get ready, so I'm buoyed by his attentiveness. But when I leave Ruth's all by myself, all that positivity seeps right out of my bones and into the floorboards.

I manage to pull myself together by the time I walk in, and after a while, I'm stable and ready to tackle the rest of the day. But for those first few minutes, I need every ounce of the patience Victoria seems to have in spades. She never had kids of her own, but she has this gentle nature that makes it seem like very little could rub her the wrong way.

As for the actual *work* happening in Victoria's workshop, it's a little more overwhelming than relaxing.

If only because there is still so much that I don't know.

The walls are covered in tools. Planes and saws and reamers and shapers and clamps and a hundred other hand tools I couldn't name. There is wood for repair and wood for original builds. Shelves full of glue and varnish and wax. Drawers full of bows and bridges and tailpieces. Boxes of strings and trays of hand carved tuning pegs and at least a dozen instruments in various states of deconstruction and repair.

I'm still nervous every time I touch something, though that's slowly getting better as time goes by. I just know how delicate instruments can be. How a weirdly cut bridge or a misplaced sound post can alter or even ruin the sound an instrument can achieve. But hearing something is off is different than knowing how to fix it, so there's definitely a learning curve.

"All right. Try it now," Victoria says. She holds out the viola she's been working on for the past twenty minutes.

When the viola first arrived, I was affronted that Victoria would be asked to repair such a cheaply made instrument. But Victoria only smiled when she took it from the frazzled mom and promised she'd see what she could do.

I reach for the bow resting in the instrument's case and tighten the hair, then take the viola from Victoria. It only takes a couple of notes for me to hear a difference.

All we did was replace the bridge and adjust the sound post, but it sounds like a different viola altogether.

I play a few more measures of a Mozart sonata before finally lowering the instrument from my chin. "That's incredible."

"The little things matter," she says as she takes the viola and puts it back in its case.

"Does it not bother you to have people bringing in instruments that are so poorly made? Why not tell them to return it and get something from a more reputable source?"

She shrugs easily. "People do the best they can with the knowledge they have. And they often buy what they can afford. I'm happy to help because I'd rather they play *something* than nothing at all." She closes the case and carries it to the front of the shop where she sets it with the completed repairs awaiting pick up. When she spins around to face me, her eyes are sparkling with new excitement. "Now that we've got *that* out of the way, I feel like doing something fun. Are you interested?"

"Always," I say without even a hint of hesitation. Three days in, I completely trust this woman. If her idea of something fun involved packing a bag and crawling into the Volkswagen van parked outside of her house for a spontaneous road trip, I'd probably do it. Well, as long as Juno could come too.

Victoria smiles. "I was hoping you'd say that." She walks to the corner of her shop and uses a key fob looped around her neck to unlock a heavy cabinet door.

I watch as she pulls out what looks like a very old violin case and sets it on the empty worktable behind her.

"Georg Winterling," Victoria says reverently. "Made in 1905 and purchased by a German man who emigrated to the United States in 1950. He brought the instrument with him, but he was the only one in his family who played, so after he died, it went into the attic, where it sat for the next sixty-five years. Until his family sold the house and had an estate sale and did not think to evaluate the worth of their grandfather's very old, very dusty violin."

"Shut up," I say, my voice reverent to match hers. "How much did you pay for it?"

She presses her lips together like she's fighting a grin. "Two hundred dollars," she says, and I gasp.

"You're kidding."

"I'm not. I'd feel bad about it, but honestly, Evie, they kept calling it a 'dusty old thing,' like they couldn't believe I had actual interest. I think they'd have thrown it away had I not bought it from them." She opens the case and pulls out the violin. "It's in terrible shape, but if we can restore it..."

Her words trail off as she slides a hand across the cracked body of the violin.

"It'll be worth thousands," I say, finishing her sentence.

She looks up, a gleam in her eye. "If I do it justice."

Something sparks in my heart, a sense of purpose and excitement that soothes the ache I've been carrying in my heart since I left Juilliard. I love to play my violin. I love to be in a symphony, to feel the music, to be a part of something that is so much greater than the sum of its parts.

When I lumbered across the stage at my graduation, seven months pregnant, completely heartbroken, I thought I would never find that purpose again. The music scene in New York is cutthroat. If you aren't all in, you are quickly ousted out. But I couldn't be all in as a brand-new single mom.

But hearing Victoria talk, that sense of purpose is sparking again. I love the history hiding in this violin. The stories it's heard, the music it's made. If I can be a part of bringing it back to life, maybe it'll be okay if I'm not playing as much as I used to.

"What do you say?" she asks. "Want to help me?"

"I would be honored," I say, matching Victoria's smile with my own.

Her gaze lifts over my shoulder, widening the slightest bit before shifting back to me. "Good. We'll start right after lunch."

"What? Why not right now? Who needs to eat?"

She chuckles and tilts her head toward the front door. "Why don't you peek outside and see if you still feel the same way?"

I spin around to find *Alec* standing on the cottage's front porch. He's turned to the side, eyes on his phone, but it's clearly him. He's dressed in joggers and an Appies hoodie, like he just came from practice, and he's carrying what looks like a to-go bag of food in his free hand.

My phone buzzes from my back pocket, and I pull it out to find a text he clearly just sent from the porch.

179

Hi. Are you busy? I'm here with food, but I'm
afraid to knock because I don't want to
interrupt.

I look back at Victoria. "How did you know he was here
for me?"

"I didn't," she says. "But based on the way he was looking
at you through the window, all sheepish and uncomfortable, I
guessed." She smiles. "A friend of yours?"

I nod and bite my lip, my heart climbing into my throat.

Alec is *here*.

I can't truly put into words what it's been like the past
few days. Ever since he got home on Sunday night, things
have been different. Charged with this current of anticipation. We're talking and texting as much as we did while he
was out of town, but now we're seeing each other too.

Eating dinner together. Watching TV with the twins.
Talking about the day while we do dishes.

I'm trying so hard not to read into things because I'm still
not sure about the whole Riley situation. But every day that
goes by, it's getting harder and harder. I just like him so
much.

"Evie, dear, are you going to let him inside, or shall I?"

My attention snaps back to Victoria. "What?"

She motions toward the door one more time. "He just
knocked."

"Right. Yes. I'll let him in." I hurry toward the door,
wiping my hands on my jeans as I go.

"Hey! What are you doing here?" I ask as I push open the
door.

"I brought lunch." He holds up the bag. "A burger from
Betty's. And sweet potato fries. Since you didn't have them

last time, I really thought you should try them because they're amazing."

"Did you seriously skip practice to eat burgers with me? I don't think your trainers would approve."

"I have a salad for me, and I'm not skipping anything. We finished early today."

I move out of the way and motion him inside. "Come on in, then. I'll introduce you to Victoria."

I make quick introductions before Victoria excuses herself, claiming she has a date with the leftover chili her husband made last night. But I don't miss the look she gives me over Alec's shoulder, eyes wide as she mouths the word *Wow*.

"She seems really great," Alec says as he follows me across the shop. There's a cozy living nook on the right side of the workshop with a couch, a coffee table, a small refrigerator, and a table just big enough for two people. It's tucked away and private, so it's been a perfect space for my twice-daily pumping sessions. I store the milk in the tiny fridge so I can take it home to Juno every day, but so far, that's all I've used it for. Even though I've packed a lunch, Victoria keeps insisting that I go up to the main house to eat lunch with her.

Alec sets the food down on the table while I grab a couple of water bottles from the fridge.

"She's amazing," I say as I steal a sweet potato fry from one of the open containers. "Oh my gosh. Those really are good."

"Right? I told you."

I sit down, and he slides my burger in front of me. It looks like the barbecue one—a solid choice—and my mouth immediately starts to water. "This was really nice of you, Alec."

"Don't worry about it. It was on my way home."

"It is *not* on your way home. This place is not on the way anywhere."

He grins. "I was hoping your limited knowledge of Harvest Hollow might work to my advantage."

"I'm bad with directions," I say, holding up a fry and pointing it at him. "But not that bad."

"Fine. You caught me. I'm here for the fries that I'm not allowed to buy for myself." He reaches over and steals a handful of sweet potato fries.

"Hmm. So they don't have any calories if you steal them from someone else's plate?"

"Exactly."

I take a bite of my burger, letting out a little groan as the tang of the barbecue sauce hits my tongue. "Oh gosh. That's so good."

"So I made the right choice?"

I nod through another bite. "You absolutely did. It's definitely my favorite of the two we tried. So, easy day today, huh? Must be nice after so much traveling."

"Yeah. I think we were all ready for a break."

"Next game is tomorrow?"

"Home game tomorrow, then another on Saturday."

"I don't know how you keep up with such a crazy schedule," I say as I lick a dollop of barbecue sauce off my finger. "I'd be exhausted all the time."

He shrugs, but not before a hint of something unreadable passes over his expression. "You get used to it."

I almost push. Ask him if he's getting tired of it all or if it's just the pain in his knee that has him worried. Is it harder this season? Are the injections in his knee still working? Has his playing time been impacted? But I've sensed a growing tension whenever we talk about hockey lately, and I don't want to push him when we only have a short time to be together, so when Alec changes the subject, I don't stop him.

"So, I was thinking," he says as he digs into his salad. "The team is doing a community thing next week for Halloween. All the junior hockey teams and their families come to the Summit and trick-or-treat around the arena, have a costume contest, that sort of thing. Would you want to bring Juno and go with me? It's usually pretty fun."

"I'm sorry, am I hearing you correctly? Alec Sheridan of *I hate Halloween* fame is actually inviting me to a Halloween event?"

His lips lift into a chagrined smile. "Sometimes I forget how much you know about my past."

"Alec. Everyone in all of White Plains knows how much you hate Halloween. You complained about that hotdog costume for months."

"It was a really terrible costume," he argues. "Layers and layers of polyester. And tights, Evie. Bright red tights."

To his credit, Alec still *wore* the terrible hotdog costume, because a ten-year-old Megan desperately wanted him to be a hotdog to her cheeseburger. But I still vividly remember how much he hated those tights. "You're a good brother."

"The scars run deep, because I still don't love Halloween. But the thing at the Summit isn't optional, so if I have to be there..." He gives me a pointed look.

"Misery loves company?"

His eyebrows lift playfully. "I was thinking more...maybe it won't be miserable if you're there with me?"

My face flushes with heat. He has no idea what he's doing to me. But also, he *shouldn't* be doing this if he has a freaking girlfriend who lives in Chicago. I put down my burger and force myself to swallow the bite suddenly lodged in my throat.

I have to ask him.

I have to ask him *right now* because if I don't, the question is going to eat at me and eat at me and then I might throw up which would be a colossal waste because this is a really delicious burger.

"Alec, are you still dating the woman in Chicago?" I blurt out. "The one with all the pictures of you on Instagram?"

Alec's hand stills over his salad, but his eyes are clear when he looks up to meet mine. "No," he says simply. "I'm not. Evie, I wouldn't be talking to you like this if I was."

I take a shaky breath, exhaling and letting the tension drain out of my body. In its place, a warm, buzzy glow fills my limbs, making my skin tingle and my blood heat.

I wouldn't be talking to you like this if I was. That means Alec really is flirting with me.

He clears his throat. "If we're talking about people we *aren't* dating," he says, "are you still talking to your ex-husband?" Alec's tone is even and steady, and the thrill of the previous moment whooshes out of me all at once. "I saw that he texted. I wasn't trying to snoop, but it did make me wonder if the two of you are still talking, or..."

"We aren't," I say, almost eagerly. Probably *too* eagerly. But my answer isn't entirely true. "I mean, not in the way you mean," I add. "He did text me recently. But only because of Juno. Not because there is anything between us." The warmth in Alec's expression immediately puts me at ease, making it easy to add, "I wouldn't be talking to *you* like this if there was."

His lip ticks up the slightest bit. "Good. I'm glad we're on the same page, then."

Oh my gosh.

Me.

And Alec Sheridan.

Megan's freaking older brother Alec Sheridan.

Are on. the same. page.

And not just *any* page. A page torn out of an actual romance novel.

"So...Halloween?" he asks, like we're still just having a normal, casual conversation.

I force my brain to focus. To not freak out. To be chill and calm like this is not one of my childhood fantasies coming true because it sounds like he's asking me on a date. "Juno does look pretty cute in her puppy dog costume," I manage to say.

"I'm sure she does. So you'll come?"

"I'd love to come."

"Perfect," Alec says, practically blinding me with his full megawatt smile. "And I was thinking dinner at Felix's on Friday night? It works for the rest of us if you're free."

"Dinner on Friday and Halloween next week? You don't think you'll get sick of me?"

He tosses me a flirty smile. "Not likely."

After I figure out how to breathe again, I spend the next twenty minutes talking about the repairs I've watched Victoria do and the restoration we're starting this afternoon. Once I get going, I completely forget that Alec basically just admitted he caught the same feelings I did. That's how much I'm enjoying this work. But Alec is also a really good listener. He keeps asking questions. *Real* questions. Questions that make it obvious he's paying attention and not just humoring me.

"And that's what's so exciting about it," I finally say. "A lot of older instruments are complete crap and shouldn't be restored because they never sounded great to begin with. But instruments that are well made will only sound better with age. And a Georg Winterling violin is definitely going to sound amazing."

He studies me for a long moment. "You're really happy here, aren't you?"

I lift my eyebrows, surprised by the question. "What, like, in Harvest Hollow?"

"Sure. But I really mean *here* here. Doing this. Working with Victoria."

I can't stop the easy smile that comes at his question because I really *do* love it here. Even though it's only been three days, I already feel like I've found a true friend in Victoria, and the work both inspires me and challenges me. I pick up my last french fry and stand up. "Come here. I want to show you something."

Alec follows me into the workshop. On the far wall, there's a wooden sign with the words *A Place for Healing* stamped over the outline of a violin. I motion toward the sign. "I know it's supposed to be about the instruments," I say. "But when I got here Monday morning and read that for the first time, it felt like a message just for me. A reminder that I'm going to be okay."

He pushes his hands into his pockets and studies the sign. "I'm really happy for you, Evie," he finally says.

His words are genuine, but there's a sadness behind them I can't quite define, enough that it shifts the happy mood of the past half-hour. "Hey." I look over at him and bump my shoulder into his arm. "You okay?"

He gives his head a quick shake. "Yeah. Absolutely. I *am* happy for you."

"I believe you," I say. "But there was something else to your look there. Something you didn't say out loud."

"It's nothing," he says.

"You sure?"

He breathes out a sigh. "I was just...thinking about you finding your purpose while I might be losing mine."

My heart clenches at his words. "Alec. Don't talk like that. You're going to be okay. There's more to life than hockey."

He winces at my words, and I immediately wish I could take them back. It hasn't been that long since I sat at Alec's counter and ate a breakfast sandwich, telling him he was more than a hockey player, but the words seem to hit him differently this time. Enough that I have to wonder what's happening on the team. No matter what it is, *there's more to life than hockey* is a stupid thing to say to someone in Alec's position.

"That was a dumb thing to say. I'm sorry. I didn't mean to make you feel—"

"It's okay," Alec says, cutting me off, his words a little too sharp around the edges. "You didn't."

It's my turn to wince, and Alec immediately frowns. "Evie, I'm sorry," he quickly says, reaching out to take my arm. His grip is gentle as he gives it a quick squeeze before sliding his fingers down to take my hand. "You didn't say anything wrong."

"No, I did. I didn't mean to diminish what you're going through with a stupid platitude."

"It's okay. Hockey is just hard for me to talk about right now."

I'm not sure it *is* okay, but that's a selfish thought. Just because Alec isn't talking to me doesn't mean he isn't talking to anyone. And what even am I to Alec right now? We only just admitted that we're interested in dating each other. That doesn't mean he's ready to reveal all his deepest, darkest thoughts.

But it does mean I'm worried about him.

His thumb brushes across my knuckles before he finally drops my hand. "I should probably go so you can get back to work."

I don't want him to go. I want to pull him into a hug and beg him to tell me everything he's feeling.

But that would be weird and entirely uncalled for, so I nod and smile instead. "Yeah. Probably. Victoria should be back any minute."

He looks over my shoulder toward the table where our empty food containers are still sitting. "Should I clean up, or…"

"I'll totally do it," I say. "Don't worry about it at all."

I walk with him to the porch, pausing at the top of the steps.

In the distance, Victoria is winding her way down the path that leads from the house to the workshop.

"Hey," I say as Alec starts down the steps. He pauses on the second one and turns, and for once, we're eye level. "Thank you. This was an amazing surprise." Before I can second guess and talk myself out of it, I lean forward and wrap my arms around his shoulders, pulling him into a hug.

His arms slip around my waist as I breathe him in, cataloging every element of his hug. The feel of him pressed against me, the slight musk of his skin, the way his grip tightens just before he lets me go.

"I'll see you tonight," he says, his voice low and gravelly.

He waves at Victoria as he climbs into his truck, then he looks back one more time and waves at me.

I'm still standing on the porch when Victoria reaches me, watching as Alec's truck disappears around the bend.

"Please tell me that man is someone special to you," she says as we head back into the shop.

"My best friend's older brother," I say. "Does that count?"

Her eyebrows lift. "It makes it more fun, but no. That's not enough."

I laugh as I move back to the table and pick up the trash from our lunch. "Well, give me a little bit of time. Hopefully we're moving in the right direction."

"Is he an athlete?" she asks, one hand pressed to her chest. "He looks like an athlete."

"A hockey player," I tell her. "He plays for the Appies."

"Oh. Oh! I've heard hockey players are *very* good with their hands."

"Victoria!" I say, laughing at her suggestive tone.

"What? They would have to be, wouldn't they? With all the...stick handling and...puck moving?"

"Why do I think you don't know anything about hockey?"

She huffs out a sigh. "Because I don't. But I have read a hockey romance or two, and let me tell you, that man could star in one of them."

I laugh. "I'll let him know you think so." I wipe down the table and throw away our trash from lunch, but after my conversation with Alec, a thought keeps niggling at the back of my brain.

I didn't lie to Alec when I said I wasn't talking to Devon. Not really. I have no desire to get back together with my ex-husband, no matter why he's calling.

But if something *is* going to happen with Alec, I need to figure out what's going on so Devon doesn't blindside me with a surprise visit or suddenly wanting to be involved in Juno's life. Unlikely, but it could be awkward with Alec. I need to know why Devon is calling. Why it's so important to him that we have a conversation when, as far as I'm concerned, everything we needed to say to each other has already been said.

"Hey, Victoria, do you mind if I make a quick phone call

189

before we jump back into work? It should only take a few minutes."

"Of course, dear. Take your time."

I take my phone onto the porch and drop onto the top step next to an assortment of bright orange pumpkins. Apparently, Victoria's husband is an avid gardener and has an enormous pumpkin patch every year. She already sent me home with a few to put on Alec's porch, one she said would be perfect for carving a jack-o-lantern.

I took them to humor her, knowing Juno is much too young for me to go through the effort, but Theo and Carter were excited enough for all of us when I showed up with pumpkins, and now Alec's front porch is adorned with two surprisingly well-carved jack-o-lanterns.

I pull up my text thread with Devon and read through the messages one more time.

DEVON

Can we talk?

EVIE

Texting is fine.

DEVON

Evie, please.

I really need you to call me.

I sigh and close my eyes, digging deep to find my courage —and my backbone. Then I open my eyes and make the call.

CHAPTER 17

ALEC

THE TWINS ARE in the kitchen eating cereal when I show up searching for coffee on Friday morning. Theo is staring at his spoon with bloodshot eyes, like even the idea of lifting it and dipping it into his cereal bowl is exhausting, so they must have been out late. We played and lost a messy game last night, so we were all in a low mood when we came home. When I got home and realized Evie had already gone to bed, I went straight to my room and crashed and assumed the twins did the same, but I was zoned out enough they could have gone back out without me realizing.

I swallow my judgments as I fill a travel mug with coffee. It's not like I never partied when I was their age, but partying was never more important than hockey, and that meant taking care of my body.

I shoot Carter a concerned look, and he shrugs as if to say there's nothing *he* can do about it. The trouble is, there's a lot Carter is already doing that he doesn't realize. I'd put money on him being the older twin because he looks out for his brother in ways that Theo never reciprocates. Carter is the one who makes sure they get to practices and games on time. Carter is the one who takes care of their meals, who does their laundry. He shouldn't have to do any of that, and I'm not sure why he does.

Except, Theo probably has the edge on the ice, and they're both better together than they are on their own. That might be enough motivation for Carter to cave and keep acting the adult. He knows he has a better shot of a big career with Theo beside him.

That will all go away if Theo doesn't stop messing around. He needs a lot more than raw talent to make it in this sport. He needs focus. Discipline. Work ethic. And leaning on his brother will only get him so far.

I lean against the counter to face them. "So about the dinner tonight," I say to Carter, hoping Felix will forgive me. "The dream team dinner. Why don't the two of you come?"

Carter lifts his eyebrows. "Really?"

I push my hands into the pockets of my joggers. Here lately, Carter has been a lot more amenable to hanging out with the team than Theo has, which means it almost never happens. Usually, Carter caves and does whatever Theo wants to do instead. I can't figure it out. The longer Theo is here, the more time he spends on the ice, the more miserable he seems to be. "Yeah. Really. I'd like you to be there."

Carter looks over at his brother, but Theo quickly shoots him down.

"Can't," he says through a mouthful of Raisin Bran. "We've got plans. Dates."

Dates at least feels safer than the two of them going out and partying on their own. Still, I'd rather they be somewhere I can keep an eye on them.

"Bring them," I say.

"We could—" Carter says, but Theo cuts him off.

"Sorry," he says, eying his brother. "There's this place on the other side of town I want to check out. I already told the girls about it."

"What place?"

"For real? Do you grill everyone on the team like this?" Theo asks, and my jaw tightens.

"Not trying to grill you, man. But I've been at this a lot longer than you have. I'm just trying to look out for you."

His shoulders drop the slightest bit. "It's called The Steam Engine. It's kinda like a club, but on Friday nights, they have college night with a theme and everything, and tonight it's line dancing." He motions to his brother. "That's one thing we know how to do, so we're going."

I look at Carter.

He nods enough to confirm Theo's story checks out, so I breathe out a sigh. "All right. But we have an early game on Saturday. That means we have to be at the Summit even earlier, so don't mess around. And no drinking."

Theo rolls his eyes. "Don't worry, Dad. As soon as we leave the club, we'll come back like good little children and do exactly what you say."

I look from one brother to the other, remembering so easily what it was like to be as young as they are. I had a little more structure than they do, playing four years at Cornell, which made it easier to transition into adulthood. But these guys were basically thrown into the deep end, and they're barely adults. It's a lot to ask.

But Theo is acting like he doesn't want to be on the team at all. I don't need him to do everything I say, but I am his captain, and that's a title that deserves at least some level of respect, especially from someone so new to the team.

I pull a barstool away from the counter and position it directly across from Theo. "Carter, can you give us a minute?"

He shoots a concerned glance at his brother, then slides off his barstool. He puts his plate in the sink, then leaves me in the kitchen with Theo.

"Hey," I say, waiting for him to make eye contact. When he finally does, I add, "Why don't you tell me what's really going on here?"

He shrugs dismissively. "Nothing's going on." He lifts his hand to his mouth and starts biting at his thumbnail, eyes averted.

"When did you start playing hockey?" I ask.

He clearly wasn't expecting the question, because he looks right at me, eyebrows raised.

"What does that have to do with anything?"

"It doesn't. I'm just making conversation."

He's quiet for a long moment, his gaze assessing, before he says, "We were little. Barely walking. My dad plays, or... played, I guess."

"Was he pro?" I ask, and Theo shakes his head.

"Just beer leagues. He maybe could have done more, but he was in a car accident in college that screwed up his back. He was never the same after." He slides his bowl forward, the spoon clattering against the ceramic. "He always hoped we would, though."

"And now you are," I say. "That must make him proud."

"I wouldn't know," Theo says, his voice distant. "He died last year. Another car accident. What are the odds, right?"

Suddenly, everything Theo is doing makes so much more sense, and my heart nearly breaks for the kid. He's not angry because he's a stupid punk kid. He's angry because he's grieving.

194

"I'm sorry about your dad, Theo. That really sucks."

He shoves back from the counter, his barstool scuffing against the floor. "Look, you don't have to do this," he says, waving his hand in my general direction. "Help, or whatever. I just want to play hockey. I don't need a heart-to-heart with the team captain to do that."

I push my palms against my thighs, debating how I should play this. Theo needs compassion—his dad only died a year ago—but he also might need some tough love.

"You do if your captain is worried you're screwing yourself over."

He rolls his eyes. "Whatever, man. How about I worry about my game, and you worry about yours? And you *should* worry. Word is there are a couple of rookies who are looking to take your spot."

My jaw clenches, but I don't move while Theo stalks out of the kitchen. He's trying to antagonize me, and I won't give him the satisfaction of thinking he has.

Last night, in a post-game locker room interview, a journalist got particularly pointed with her questions. "There's been talk from inside sources that your knee is giving you trouble. In light of the numerous surgeries you've already had, your physical limitations, and the strength of rookie defenders like the Williamson twins, are you giving any serious thought to retirement?"

It's one thing to have the team talking about my knee. To have the general public speculating about my future like it's no big deal is a new level of frustration. To them, it's just a question. A matter of who will be on the ice next season. For me, it's my life. My *livelihood*.

"Well, that was an intense conversation to have before coffee."

I turn to see Evie standing in between the living room and

the kitchen, Juno in her arms. She's dressed for work in jeans and a plaid shirt tied at her waist, Juno's diaper bag draped over her shoulder. Her hair is pulled back in a ponytail, and I'm struck for the millionth time by how beautiful she is. At the sight of her, some of the tension in my shoulders melts away.

"You heard that?" I ask.

"I stopped at the bottom of the stairs because I didn't want to interrupt." She takes a step closer and drops her bag onto the couch. "He shouldn't have said that, Alec. About you and your spot on the team."

"I'm not worried about that," I say, even though it isn't the full truth. This season hasn't gone at all like I wanted it to, and I hate thinking about what happens next. But that's on me. It doesn't have anything to do with Theo.

"I could be wrong," Evie says, "but it sounds like Theo might be doing a little bit of self-sabotage."

"What do you mean?"

"Maybe he feels guilty about playing? About enjoying his life when his dad isn't around to see him do it?"

I lean forward and prop my elbows on the counter. "Yeah, maybe. I just wish I could help him. I don't want to push, but none of the other guys know what he's been through. I don't want him to get himself in trouble, and if something doesn't change, he will."

"That might be what he wants," Evie says. "If he gets kicked off the team, he can't feel guilty about playing."

"But I think he really *wants* to play," I say.

"Does the team have a psychologist on staff?"

"Not on staff. But there's one the team refers us to if we need it. He's great. I've seen him a few times. Nathan, too. And he and Felix are basically best friends."

She tilts her head and smiles. "So you're saying real men aren't afraid of boybands *or* therapy."

I chuckle. "I'd also wear that t-shirt."

"It's a lot that he even told you about his dad," she says. "And you're showing him you're a safe space by not taking his attitude personally. Maybe just give him a little more time. He might still open up."

I stand and move toward her, crouching down so I'm eye level with Juno. "Yeah. I just hope he doesn't screw himself over in the meantime." I take Juno's hand and let her wrap her fist around my pointer finger. "Hey, Juno." I look up at Evie. "She looks bigger today. Is that possible?"

"I actually had the same thought," she says. "I have no idea how, but yeah. She totally does."

Juno drops my finger, and I lift a hand to her head, brushing it lightly over her wispy curls. When my gaze shifts back to Evie, there's a sadness to her expression that I can't quite define. It wasn't there moments before, but it's there now, and it makes my gut tighten with unease. Have I missed something going on with her because I've been caught up in my own problems? Caught up with the twins?

I lift a hand to her face, every other frustration and worry vaporizing in an instant. Right now, I only see her.

"Hey. What's wrong? Why are you frowning?"

She leans into the touch, and for a split second, I think about what it would be like to kiss her.

But then Evie gives her head a little shake, and her expression shifts. "Nothing," she says before licking her lips. "I'm good. Just...it's nothing."

I narrow my eyes. It's definitely *not* nothing. As far as I know, work has been going great for her this week. And Juno has done well with Ruth. Could it be Devon who's made her upset?

Down the hall, the twins' footsteps sound as they head toward the garage, and I glance at my watch. We've been riding to practice together, and it's just about time for us to go.

"Early practice?" Evie asks, and my hand falls away from her face. Every other morning this week, I've still been home when she's left for work. But I have to be at the Summit an hour earlier than normal to review game tapes before tomorrow's match-up.

"Yeah. But the twins can wait for me. Are you sure you're okay?"

She breathes out a sigh. "I'm okay. I just...seeing you like this, with Juno, it makes me think of her very absent father."

So it *is* Devon making her upset. The thought makes anger curl in my stomach. How is he not *here* right now? Watching Juno grow up? Supporting Evie like she deserves to be supported? Somehow, I simultaneously want the guy to step up because Evie and Juno both deserve so much better than what they're getting, and also stay far, far away. Because if he's out of the picture, there might be room for *me* to be the better they deserve.

I still have no idea what it would look like if I were to play a permanent role in Evie and Juno's lives. I just know that whenever I'm standing next to her, my desire to try is stronger than any fear suggesting I shouldn't.

"Does he not want to see her at all?" I ask, the words tasting sour.

"Apparently, he does now," she says, a bitter edge to her words. "That's the problem." She reaches up and rests a palm on my chest. "I want to have this conversation with you, but it will probably be easier if we have more time. Tonight, maybe?"

I nod. "Of course. Are you still good to go to dinner at Felix's place?"

Her lips lift into a smile, but it doesn't quite reach her eyes. "I definitely want to go to dinner. Maybe we can talk on the way?"

Reluctantly, I nod and move back into the kitchen to grab my keys and the coffee still waiting for me on the counter. But then I find myself crossing the room back to Evie, needing one more touch, one more connection before I go.

Without thinking, I lift my hand to Juno's back and lean down, pressing a quick kiss to the top of her head, then I shift over to Evie. I slide my fingers around the back of her neck, letting my fingers brush against her hair. She looks up at me, her expression warm and open, and I intuitively know she'd let me kiss her if I tried.

Right here. On an early Friday morning. I could lean down and kiss her goodbye just like couples do. I could, and it would feel like we're a family. Living together, spending mornings together. But that would be doing things backward. Evie is only staying here temporarily, and I can't let the forced proximity rush us through the moments that really ought to matter more.

I force my eyes away from her lips. I will not kiss Evie for the first time on my way out the door, while her daughter is in her arms.

Evie narrows her gaze. "Alec Sheridan, what are you thinking right now?"

Based on her flirty smile, I'm guessing she knows exactly what I'm thinking. But I won't admit it out loud.

I chuckle. "I'll never tell."

She cocks her head to the side, lips pursed like she's studying me. Then she shifts Juno a little higher on her hip, pushes up onto her toes and presses a lingering kiss to my

199

jaw, just below my ear. "I bet you will eventually," she whispers, her words brushing across my skin.

Fire slices through my veins. Maybe I don't actually need to go to practice today.

Maybe Carter needs to come in here and hold Juno—he did say he knows how—so I can kiss this woman properly.

"Hey, Captain, you coming?" Carter asks, sticking his head into the room from the hallway.

I breathe out a sigh. "I'll be right there," I say to Carter. Then I look back at Evie.

She smiles and pats my chest dismissively, like she knows exactly how hard she's making it to walk away.

"Time to go be a hockey captain," she says, and I drop my head, pressing my forehead to hers.

"I'm really looking forward to seeing you tonight," I say.

"Me too," she whispers.

The heat of her kiss is still lingering on my cheek when I reach the garage and find the twins waiting for me, leaning against my truck. It takes *all* my effort to force my mind off Evie's lips and back onto the twins, so the first few minutes of the drive pass in silence, though Carter does keep shooting me concerned looks from the front seat.

Rightly so, since he still has no idea how my conversation with Theo went.

Through the rearview mirror, I watch as Theo pulls a pair of headphones out of his bag and slips them over his ears. He folds his arms over his chest and closes his eyes.

"Sorry, man," Carter says under his breath. "He isn't usually such a jerk. He's just...going through some stuff."

I glance at Carter. "Yeah. He told me about your dad."

Carter's eyes widen. "He told you about him?"

"Just that he passed away," I say. "I'm sorry."

Carter nods. "Is that...all he told you? That he died?"

"There's more to it?" I ask, and Carter breathes out a sigh.

"Theo was driving," Carter says, his voice almost too soft for me to hear. "It wasn't his fault. They were t-boned. The other driver went straight through an intersection. But...I think he still blames himself."

"Carter, that's—I'm really sorry, man."

He nods. "Thanks. It...sucks. Theo hasn't really been the same since."

"Has he talked to someone about it?"

"What, like a shrink or whatever?" Carter says. "Mom tried but Theo wouldn't do it. I can't even get him to talk to *me,* and he talks to me about everything."

"How are *you* holding up?"

He looks over his shoulder at his brother. "I'm the oldest. Only by a few minutes, but I've *always* been the oldest. One of us has to keep it together, right?"

I drive in silence for a beat, considering Carter's words. He's a good kid, and I understand well what it feels like to look out for a younger sibling, to be strong so they don't have to be. But he has just as much right to grieve as his brother.

"I think he just misses Mom," Carter says more to himself than to me. "But he'll be all right. I'll make sure he is."

"Carter, do *you* need to talk to someone?" I ask. "There's no shame in it."

"Nah," he says, his Texas drawl a little more pronounced than it usually is. "I just need to skate. Stay busy. I miss my dad, but...I know what he'd want is for me to play, focus, make something of myself. So that's what I'm trying to do."

"I can respect that," I say. "But it doesn't have to be one or the other. If you need to talk to someone, there's a therapist the team uses. A lot of guys go. I've been a few times myself. Just say the word, and I'll make it happen. Or if you don't want something so official, you can always talk to me."

He nods. "Yeah. Thanks."

"Can I give you some advice about hockey?" I ask, and Carter nods. I'm going out on a limb here, guessing at the dynamic based on my observations, but I'm pretty sure I'm right. "I know you want to take care of your brother. And there's nothing wrong with that. But you have just as much potential to be a star as he does. Don't treat him like he's your only shot at making it to the NHL. I'm glad you told me what he's going through. And I respect your desire to take care of him. But at least when it comes to the team, don't fight his battles. It won't help you any more than it helps him."

Carter is quiet for a beat before he says, "I just don't want him to get himself in trouble."

"I get that," I say. "But he'll take you down with him, Carter."

"Then I'll go down with him," he says. "Because I won't play without him." He clenches his jaw as he shifts his gaze out the window, and I know our conversation is over.

When we pull into the parking lot at the Summit, I watch Theo with new eyes as he shoves his headphones into his bag and climbs out of the truck. Knowing what I know now, it's hard to blame him for the way he's been acting.

Evie's words echo in my mind. *Don't give up on him.*

I'm his captain. It's my job to look out for him. I just have to hope he'll let me.

CHAPTER 18

EVIE

TWO DAYS.

It's been two days since Alec told me he was *not* dating Riley. Since he started pinning me with long, pointed looks. Hinting that in the not-so-distant future, probably as soon as we find a minute without Juno and the twins hanging around, he'd like to kiss me.

Unfortunately, all those very exciting developments are tinged with an uneasy awareness lurking in the back of my mind.

Because it's *also* been two days since Devon told me he'd like to come spend Thanksgiving in Harvest Hollow.

Thanksgiving with *me*. And with the daughter he's finally ready to meet.

As I buckle Juno into her carrier on Friday night, I'm no closer to knowing what to do with this information than I was when I first received it. It's so far out of the realm of what I expected, of what Devon has *ever* done before. He does not make trips that do not serve his own interests. He does not prioritize anyone's needs over his own. And since he made it explicitly clear that fatherhood was not his priority, I can't fathom why, when Juno is almost five months old, he would suddenly change his mind.

He did sound different when we talked on Wednesday. Humble. Even a little contrite.

I'm still not convinced it isn't a performance. Some kind of high-level trickery.

But he did just lose his job—one I know he worked hard to get in the first place. Maybe something really has triggered a change in him?

For Juno's sake, I want to give him the benefit of the doubt. But I can't let go of my unease. I don't trust it. I don't trust *him*.

And I really don't like the idea of spending a holiday with just the three of us.

I still don't have a firm move-in date from my landlord, but it should be any day. Definitely within the week, which means I'll be moved in and settled well before Thanksgiving. So at least I won't have to host Devon *here*, at Alec's place.

But does that mean Devon would stay with me? Would he expect to? Would I let him?

"He's missing out, baby girl," I say to Juno as I tuck a blanket around her legs. "But I'm still not sure you won't be better off without him." I make a silly face and squeeze her toes, and Juno smiles, happily kicking her feet. "You're going to be good tonight, yeah? You'll be in a happy mood?" I need her to be, both because after all the Devon stress this week, I could use a really fun evening, and because I really want to make a good impression on Alec's friends.

Once Juno is settled, pacifier in her mouth and blanket tucked around her, I stand and glance down at my sweater, hoping it was the right fashion choice for the evening. I haven't worn it since before Juno was born, but it's black and soft and fitted in all the right places without being too fitted on my slightly different post-pregnancy body.

I haven't seen Alec since this morning, when we stood in this room and talked about kissing.

Only talked, much to my disappointment.

Because he had to go. And I had to go. And Juno was in my arms and the twins were waiting for him and did I really want our first kiss to be on a random Friday morning? But if not then, when?

Is this what romance will be for me now? Snatches of stolen moments? Tiny pockets of time when Juno doesn't need me?

Footsteps across the room draw my attention, and I look up, expecting Alec, but it's the twins who appear on the other side of the room.

Alec mentioned in a text that they were going line dancing tonight, and they are dressed for it. Jeans, boots, shiny silver belt buckles, their hair slicked back in matching styles. For once, I have a hard time telling them apart, not until Carter smiles and I recognize the warmth in his eyes.

"We're heading out," Carter says. "Can you let Alec know?"

"I'm here," Alec says, walking up behind them. "Be safe, all right?"

Carter nods, but Theo doesn't even make eye contact before turning and heading down the hall.

"How's he doing?" I ask once Alec and I are alone. His expression falls, then he takes a minute to fill me in on what he learned during his drive into practice.

"That's a really hard burden to carry," I say, my heart breaking for the twins. "No wonder Theo is struggling."

"He got into it with one of the assistant coaches today," Alec says. "It took Carter and me both to pull him away and calm him down. But—you know what? I don't want to think about the twins right now. Or hockey." He holds my gaze for a long moment. "Hi," he finally says, like we're starting over.

I smile up at him. "Hi."

Alec moves toward me, his eyes moving over my body in a way that makes my skin prickle with delicious awareness. "You look really beautiful," he says, and heat floods my cheeks.

I have never been the girl unraveled by a single compliment, but I've never gotten compliments from Alec Sheridan, so maybe I am now. Maybe I'm the woman flustered and undone by a single word, a single touch.

"Thanks," I say. "You look good too." Alec is wearing dark gray slacks and a navy button-down over a white henley, his sleeves rolled up to his elbows. There's a leather bracelet on his wrist just above his watch and a necklace peeking through the collar of his shirt, and I decide I really, *really* like Alec in jewelry.

Standing this close, it's easy to catch the scent of him, warm and spicy and inviting, and I feel myself leaning closer, yielding to the gravitational pull I'm beginning to expect whenever we're together.

I want to focus on the way it feels to have his gaze on me, to enjoy the tension simmering between us. But in the back of my mind, I can't stop thinking about the fact that I still need to tell Alec about Devon's supposed visit.

We planned to talk tonight, but now that tonight is here, I'm not sure I want to bring it up. Hard to imagine anything feeling more like a first date wet blanket than a conversation about spending the upcoming holiday with an ex.

"Ready to go?" Alec asks, and I nod, hopeful that maybe

he forgot about the Devon conversation we're supposed to have. But luck is not on my side because seconds after we're in my car, Juno secure in her car seat behind us, the Bluetooth connects to my phone and reads two incoming text messages from Devon.

Out loud.

DEVON

Mom sent pictures of Juno. She looks just like you.

Will it just be us for Thanksgiving?

I quickly disconnect the phone in case Devon texts again, but the damage has already been done. When I glance over at Alec, he's sitting stone still, his hands resting on his knees, his eyebrows lifted.

"That...isn't what it sounds like," I quickly say. "I mean, it is. But not really. Not like that." I clear my throat, willing calm into my voice. "Devon wants to come meet Juno. I have to let him because even though the state of New York gave me full custody, taking her out of the state and away from her other parent was contingent upon my willingness to allow visitation should Devon want to make the trip." I grip the steering wheel a little tighter, which is dumb because we aren't even moving. We didn't even make it out of Alec's driveway before the texts came in.

"I did not expect Devon to come," I continue. "Ever. He told me fatherhood was not on his priority list. So all of this is coming out of left field." I reach over and slip my hand into Alec's, giving his fingers a squeeze. "This is what I wanted to talk to you about this morning. I wasn't trying to keep it a secret."

He nods with understanding before taking a slow breath,

then finally asks, "How do you feel about it? About him coming?"

I bite my lip as I consider his question. "I mean, I feel like I'm supposed to want it, you know? If he's willing to step up and be present in his daughter's life, that *should* be a good thing. But I don't trust him. I don't trust that he won't disappoint Juno exactly how he disappointed me. But that makes me feel guilty, because shouldn't he get the chance to try?" I breathe out a sigh. "I don't know. I don't know how to feel."

For a long moment, Alec doesn't say anything. So long that I pull my hand from his and shift into reverse so I can back out of the driveway. I drive in silence until I reach the end of the neighborhood, where I stop just past the security gatehouse because I'm not sure which direction to go to get to Felix's.

"What are you thinking?" I ask, almost afraid to hear Alec's answer.

He looks at me, dark eyes serious. "He just straight-up said that fatherhood wasn't on his priority list?" he says. There's an unspoken question behind his words, but I hear it without him having to ask it. Maybe because I've asked myself the same question a million times.

Why did I marry such a jerk in the first place? And how did I not see this coming?

"We'd talked about kids," I say. It's more answer than he's asking for, but I feel the need to defend myself a little bit, so I keep going. "Only in the vague, somewhere down the road sense. We were both so focused on finishing college and starting our careers, kids were nowhere on the table. But we weren't trying for Juno. She was completely accidental. I found out I was pregnant a few weeks after Devon landed his first official role on Broadway."

"Broadway, huh?"

"He's the trifecta," I say wryly. "Singing, acting, dancing. He's actually pretty talented, as much as it pains me to admit it. My freshman year at Juilliard, I was in the pit at the fall variety show playing with the orchestra, and he was on stage singing 'Dancing through Life' from *Wicked*. He was handsome and charming and the most talented person on stage by a long shot, and I fell hard and fast."

I shift the car into park, ready to just get all of this out in the open and be done with it. I spent a lot of months beating myself up for my marriage to Devon. We were young and impulsive, and I probably should have listened to Megan and everyone else close to me who told me I didn't have to rush into things. But I'm working on having grace with my former self. Hindsight is always twenty/twenty, and I can't truly regret a relationship that brought me Juno.

"Anyway, once I was pregnant, it was easier to see Devon for who he really is. I believe that he loved me, but not nearly as much as he loves himself. Which meant Juno and I were not worth giving up his dreams."

Alec frowns. "It had to be one or the other?"

"For Devon? Yeah. He's not built for concessions or compromise. Babies require you to put someone else's needs above your own, and he wasn't interested in doing that."

Alec finally lifts his eyes to mine. "Except, maybe he is now?"

I lift my shoulders in a shrug. "Maybe? It all feels very confusing to me. None of this truly tracks with what I know of him. But either way, it doesn't change what I said on Wednesday. Devon having a relationship with Juno doesn't mean I will ever want Devon to have a relationship with *me*. Not anymore. And it's very important to me that you know that."

I watch as Alec slowly slides his hands over his thighs, his jaw muscles working like he's really puzzling out what he wants to say. I hold my breath as I wait, because honestly, what else can I do? I can't change the messiness of my situation. I come with baggage. And Alec deserves to know all that going in.

"I don't like what he did to you," Alec finally says without making eye contact. "I can't really wrap my head around walking away like he did." He lifts a hand and runs it through his hair. "You deserve so much better than that, Evie. You and Juno both. You deserve to have someone take care of you. And Juno deserves a father who shows up. Which..." He lets out a humorless laugh. "I guess if that's what Devon is doing, better late than never."

It speaks to Alec's integrity that he's having such a hard time comprehending Devon's actions, but he's being so stoic, so *controlled*, that it still makes me nervous, and I can't keep myself from asking, "Okay, but...what about us?" The question feels way too pointed, but how else can I ask? "Does it impact you wanting to spend time with me?"

Alec shoots me a look, his lips lifting into a tiny grin. "I mean, I don't want to come to Thanksgiving, but..."

I smile, some of the tension finally draining out of my shoulders. "I can't blame you there."

But as I follow Alec's directions and drive the rest of the way to Felix's, a tiny pulse of fear settles low in my gut. Devon already managed to ruin my life once.

I just hope he doesn't try to do it again.

CHAPTER 19

EVIE

"OKAY, I'm going to put you on the spot," Gracie says to me halfway through dinner. Since Felix's dining room table is enormous, all six couples are seated for dinner. Alec introduced me to everyone when we arrived, and it took me a minute to get everyone's names, but I think I have them now. Eli and Bailey, Van and Amelia, Nathan and Summer, Logan and Parker, and of course, Gracie and Felix.

I'm seated between Alec and Bailey and directly across from Gracie.

So far, everything about the evening has been perfect and lovely. Juno fell asleep and settled into her portable crib without so much as a whimper, the conversation has been easy and comfortable, and Alec has basically stayed by my side all night long. A hand on my shoulder. Fingers brushing down my arm. A leg pressed against mine under the table.

Right now, he's turned away from me, talking to Van and Nathan about their fantasy hockey teams, but at Gracie's question, his hand slipped under the table to squeeze my knee, so he must be paying at least partial attention to my conversation too.

I swallow a bite of the most delicious chicken parmesan I've ever had and raise my eyebrows. "Should I be nervous?"

"Not at all," Gracie says. "I just want you to talk about yourself. About your violin. Are you any good?"

When I met Gracie at the symphony concert, Victoria mentioned that I played, but only in passing.

"And don't hold back," Gracie adds. "I need you to legit brag. If you have any qualifications, I want to hear them."

She seems like she's asking for a very particular reason, so I swallow my first inclination, which is to deflect and self-deprecate and tell her what she wants to know. "I went to Juilliard. And I was concertmaster of the Julliard Orchestra my senior year."

"Shut up," Gracie says. "That's amazing. Have you played anywhere since?" It's a valid question. With a résumé like that, I could have gotten an audition at any number of symphonies around the country.

"I was seven months pregnant with Juno at my final concert," I say. "I took a break, for obvious reasons, and I actually didn't play again until just the other night."

"She sounded amazing," Alec says from beside me. So he *was* listening. He grins as he nudges me with his shoulder. "A lot better than she did when she was eleven."

I elbow him in the ribs, and he chuckles.

"Okay, so I'm just throwing this out there," Gracie says. "I have this quartet, and our first violinist is moving at the end of November. It's pretty low-key. We mostly do weddings, the occasional corporate function. But the pay is decent, and we only rehearse if we need to learn new music.

Mostly, we just play standard wedding stuff, which I'm sure is music you already know. Are you interested?"

The thought of having a reason to play again makes my heart ache. Once upon a time, I had *big dreams* when it came to playing the violin. Getting into Juilliard was the first part of that plan. But I wasn't going to stop there. I was going to work my way up through the music scene in the city until I was on stage at Lincoln Center, playing with the New York Phil. It wouldn't even matter if my tiny Manhattan apartment was too cramped and too far from the subway because I would be living my art—my *dream*.

Until it wasn't my dream anymore. Because it couldn't be.

Still. With all my experience, I probably *do* know all the music Gracie's quartet plays, and it would feel so good to make music again. But the idea of committing to anything when Juno is still so young feels really overwhelming. "I don't know," I say. "With Juno, I'm not sure I'd…"

"I could help out with Juno," Alec says. "At least when I'm in town."

"Me too," Summer adds. "I don't usually travel with the team, so I'm around more than Alec is. I'd love to babysit."

"I would too," Bailey says from beside me. "My schedule's a little crazy with school, but if I'm around and not studying, I'd love to watch her."

All the offers of support somehow make me feel both incredibly grateful and equally uncomfortable. I don't like taking advantage of people. I don't like being *needy*. Juno is my responsibility. Other than leaving her with Ruth so I can go to work, I haven't used any babysitters. Maybe because I'm so determined to take care of her on my own. Or because it's hard to imagine leaving in the evenings when we aren't together all day long. I've mostly resigned myself to the fact that I just can't do anything extra until she's older.

At the same time, it feels really good to be at this table, surrounded by people who seem genuinely invested in offering their support. My friends in New York were always more Devon's friends than mine, and it was always a very obvious division. But even though these are also Alec's friends, it doesn't feel like that at all. We just met, but there's still an openness here, a sincerity and sense of inclusion that I haven't experienced since I was a kid hanging out at Megan's house all the time.

Before Juno, whenever I dreamed of my future, it mostly just involved my music. But I'm starting to wonder if my dream was missing something—missing *this*. Community.

It isn't just about Alec, though I won't deny the tiny thrill that shoots through me when I think about being here in a more official *girlfriend* capacity. It's also about how easily Gracie complimented and appreciated my talent. The way everyone is volunteering to help with Juno with selfless ease. The way they all clearly love and support each other.

"Just think about it, yeah?" Gracie says. "We'd love to have you. And the rest of my quartet is so great. We have a lot of fun."

"I definitely will," I say. "Thanks for the invitation."

The conversation shifts onto other topics, and I eat the rest of my dinner mostly just listening. Eventually, Alec stretches his arm across the back of my chair and leans a little closer, his voice soft enough that no one else at the table can hear him. "So, I didn't know you were such a badass at Juilliard."

I chuckle. "I was nothing of the sort."

"With a fancy title like concertmaster? Doesn't that mean you were the best one?"

"Look at you with your orchestra lingo."

"I've done my research," he says. "You got a head start on hockey. I need to catch up."

Juno lets out a tiny cry through the baby monitor sitting on the edge of the table, and we both turn to glance at it, watching the tiny red sound waves dance across the front. As late as it is, I hoped she'd stay down for hours, but in her portable crib, in a strange house, it won't surprise me if she wakes up. But after another moment, she settles back down, and Alec and I breathe out a relieved sigh.

"She's being nice to you tonight," Alec says, and I nod.

"Yeah, she's doing great."

Around us, couples are getting up from the table, carrying plates to the sink and moving into the living room. Alec motions his head toward the couch. "This will go on for a while. Just talking, hanging out. But whenever you're ready to go, we can go. Just say the word."

"As long as Juno keeps sleeping, I think we're good to stay."

He moves his hand forward from my chair to my shoulders. "You should say yes to the quartet," he says. "Take a leap. There are a lot of people here willing to catch you."

I lean into him like a reflex, and my head falls against his chest. He smells so good—clean and woodsy and a little bit spicy. "But they're *your* friends, Alec. I wouldn't want to take advantage."

"They're your friends now too," he says easily. "And they wouldn't have offered if they weren't truly willing to help."

I tilt my head up to look at him. It's nice to feel close to him like this, especially after the discomfort of our conversation in the car. It wasn't quite the wet blanket I feared it would be, but it was close. I credit the fact that we recovered at all to Alec. I'm not sure a guy my age would have responded with so much maturity.

"You're making it all sound very easy," I say. "But I know Juno. Babies are unreliable and unpredictable and total attention hogs. You don't know what you're signing up for."

He smiles, drawing my eyes to his lips, and suddenly, I can't focus on the actual words he's saying. I'm too preoccupied with the curve of his mouth, the dusting of stubble along his jawline...

"You didn't hear anything I just said, did you?"

Alec's words finally penetrate my kiss-hazy mind, and I snap to attention. "What?"

He grins and lifts his hand to my temple, tapping his finger against it. "What's going on up there?"

I bite my lip, thinking about the answer he gave me this morning. I can't know for certain his mind went to the same place mine did, but I'm willing to bet, so I tear a page from his playbook and give him the same answer he gave me.

"I'll never tell," I say.

His eyes turn molten as he lifts a hand to my cheek, his thumb brushing across my jawline, and for a moment, I think he's going to do it. He's going to kiss me right here in a room full of his friends. But then he lifts his gaze and glances around and seems to think better of it.

"Not here," he says, his voice low and sultry. His hand slides back to my hair, that torturous thumb tracing a slow line down the side of my neck. "But soon."

I take in a stuttering breath, relishing the promise in his words. A month ago, I would have argued I wasn't capable of feeling something like this. Of feeling *any* of what Alec has triggered over the past couple of weeks. Pregnancy and childbirth were obviously part of it, but the divorce was too. I stopped thinking about attraction or love or desire. About feeling any kind of connection.

But I'm thinking about it now, and it feels like finding a piece of myself that was lost. Like I'm waking up from a really long nap.

Alec stands and offers me his hand, and I let him pull me to my feet and lead me over to the only remaining empty seat in the living room. I sit down while he retrieves a chair from the dining room table and walks it back, setting it down beside me.

Juno sleeps for another hour while everyone talks. When she finally wakes up, her cry sounding through the monitor, it's Amelia who speaks up first.

"Don't leave," she says, not even lifting her head from Van's shoulder. "Is she hungry? Can you just feed her here? If you leave, then we all leave, and I don't want to get up yet."

Alec stands before I can and moves toward the bedroom door. "I'll grab her and bring her to you," he says.

When he reappears with Juno in his arms, he holds her for a long moment, swaying back and forth a few times just beside my chair, like he isn't quite ready to give her up.

"You seem good at that, Cap," Nathan says.

Alec grins as he finally lowers Juno into my arms.

"You really are a sucker for this baby," I say.

He meets my eye, his hands shifting to either arm of my chair so he's hovering over me, his face as close as it was in the kitchen when we almost kissed. His grin turns mischievous, and my heart skips a beat or two as he leans even closer. "I'm definitely a sucker for something."

He leaves me there, breathless and flustered and completely forgetting that I'm holding a baby who needs my attention. But then he's back with Juno's diaper bag, unzipping it and holding it open so I can retrieve her blanket. Then he's in the kitchen, filling up a cup of water, one of the

217

portable, tall ones with a lid and straw. He returns and holds it out, offering it to me like it's not a monumentally big deal that he just anticipated my needs without me saying them out loud. That he helped without being asked.

That while I'm caring for Juno, he's caring for *me*.

As soon as I see the water, a sharp craving moves through me just like it usually does whenever I start to nurse. I lift my eyebrows in question, and Alec shrugs.

"You once said feeding her makes you thirsty."

I take the water, fighting an inexplicable wave of emotion. He brought me my baby. He remembered how thirsty nursing makes me. He's sharing his friends, making me feel seen and welcome and like I belong here. I can't with this.

I can't experience all of this and not start to fall in love with him.

"Thanks," I say, taking the water.

"It's so sweet," one of the women in the room whispers, but I can't tell which one because I'm still staring at Alec. He maintains eye contact until his phone buzzes. He's standing close enough for me to hear the vibration, so I'm still watching him when he pulls it out of his pocket and frowns at the screen.

He runs a hand through his hair and groans. "Oh no."

"What's wrong?" I ask.

He breathes out a sigh. "It's the twins. They're at the police station."

My stomach sinks. I've spent enough time with the twins over the past week that I'm really starting to care about them. I know Theo gives Alec trouble, but he's always been sweet to me, probably because I don't have anything to do with hockey, and Carter is as good as they come. I hate to think about what this will mean for them. And for Alec, too, who has been trying so hard to figure out what they need.

"What happened?" I ask. "Were they arrested?"

Alec shakes his head. "I'm not sure. Carter is texting, so he still has his phone. That has to be a good sign. Wait…" He pauses, his eyes on his phone, then he sighs again. "Theo was picked up for drunk and disorderly conduct. Carter is asking if we can come down to the station."

"I'll come with you," Summer says. "If charges have been filed, you'll need a legal rep from the team."

"I'll come too," Nathan says. "I can drive, then we'll take you home after so Evie can get herself home."

Alec looks at me. "Is that okay? Sorry. I hate to leave you, but…"

"Don't apologize. It's totally fine. As soon as Juno finishes, I'll head home and meet you there."

He nods and drops a hand onto my shoulder, giving it a light squeeze before he looks at Nathan and Summer. "Okay. Let's go. Actually, wait one sec."

He disappears into the bedroom, returning a few minutes later with Juno's portable crib broken down and packed up in its travel case. He sets it by the door.

"Alec, I could have done that," I say, but he shrugs and offers me a sheepish grin.

"Just one less thing for you to do before you go," he says.

He thought of everything.

He's never been a dad, never had a wife, and still, he anticipates my every need.

In the conversations I had with Devon leading up to our divorce, he always talked about fatherhood like it was some mysterious skillset he lacked and would never acquire.

But maybe it's not so complicated. Maybe fatherhood is just a matter of paying attention, of noticing what your family needs, then stepping up to take care of that need. It's being present. Invested. *Willing.*

Alec looks back and meets my eye one more time before he leaves. "I'll see you at home?"

I nod, and he follows Summer and Nathan out the door, taking a tiny piece of my heart with him as he goes.

CHAPTER 20

ALEC

THE WHOLE TIME we're driving to the police station, I'm wishing I'd tried a little harder to get the twins to come to Felix's. We've had a lot of guys join the Appies when they're young. Fresh out of college, even high school. Last season, Dominic joined the team and didn't get along with anyone. But he settled in. Figured out what it was to be an Appie. But I don't remember anyone causing trouble like Theo.

Now that I have a better sense of what's going on with him, I feel more frustrated than angry. I'm supposed to be looking out for him. But he has to help me out a little. Make choices that reflect an awareness of how seriously he could screw up his career if he messes around.

Still, the kid is only eighteen, and he's hurting. I can't blame him when I'm not sure I would have been able to handle what he's handling when I was his age.

The station is a few blocks away from Felix's place, so we

only drive a couple of minutes before Nathan parks and turns off his Bronco.

"All right, let's do this," I say through a sigh.

"You talk to the twins, let me talk to the police," Summer says.

I nod as we all climb out of the car, then we head inside.

Carter is sitting in a chair against the wall, his head in his hands. He looks up as we enter, and his face relaxes with relief. He stands and steps toward me. "I tried to get him to slow down on the drinks, but he just wouldn't listen. And then the tattoo, and the girls, and…" He shakes his head and lifts the heel of his hand to his forehead. He sucks in a couple of shallow, shaky breaths, his hand trembling.

"Hey, just breathe," I say. "You're all right. We'll figure this out. But let's take it one thing at a time, okay?" I tilt my head, motioning toward the interior of the police station. "They're holding Theo?"

He nods.

"You didn't drink tonight?" I ask.

"No, sir. I was driving. I didn't have a single drink."

"Good. And your dates? Where are they now?"

"I got them an Uber. They're home safe. They already texted to tell me."

"Good." I put a hand on his shoulder. "You did good."

He sniffs and nods. "He's never been arrested before," he says. He takes in another hiccupy breath. "And he wasn't really doing anything bad. Just being a little loud."

A few paces into the police station, it looks like Summer is already talking to an officer.

"That's him," Carter says. "That's the guy who picked him up."

"Did he have alcohol on him?" Nathan asks, and Carter shakes his head.

"There was nothing on him. We'd just left the tattoo place, and he was walking down the middle of the road singing something stupid. I was trying to get him back on the sidewalk when the cop pulled up."

I look over at Nathan. "Does it matter if he wasn't in possession? If he was still visibly drunk?"

"Not sure. It might make it harder to prove, at least."

A few days ago, I might have wanted Theo to suffer a little. To endure the consequences of his own actions. I've talked to him about drinking before, and clearly none of that has registered because he's still making stupid choices—choices he can't really afford as an athlete. But now, I can't stop thinking about what he's up against.

He needs compassion. Not misdemeanor charges.

"Okay," Summer says, stepping up next to Nathan. "Everything's okay."

Carter's eyes widen like he can't quite believe his luck. "They're letting him go?"

"He didn't have alcohol on him, and the arresting officer didn't do a breathalyzer, so it would be tough to make a case against him. He says he mostly picked him up to teach him a lesson and keep him from getting into troub—" Summer's words cut off as her eyes widen. "Ohhhh, no," she says, looking over my shoulder.

We all turn to see Coach Davis standing in the doorway of the police station, a stern expression on his face. He walks toward us, stopping next to Carter. "Does someone want to explain to me why I was called out of bed on a Friday night when *all* of you should be home resting up for our game tomorrow?"

"Coach, we didn't mean—" Carter starts, but I stop him with a firm hand on his shoulder.

"Theo was picked up for underage drinking," I say evenly,

223

"but only because the officer didn't want him to get into any more trouble. No charges have been filed, and they won't be."

Coach frowns. "But he *was* drinking?"

Carter meets my eye, and I give my head a slight shake. "He was, but honestly, Coach, I feel like this is my fault. I should have been watching out for the twins, and I wasn't."

"They're old enough to make their own choices, Alec," Coach Davis says. "And that kid has been causing trouble from the start. I have an entire team to think about, and I can't do that when, over and over again, one player keeps causing problems. He's picking fights with his own team-mates, and now this? What does this do for the Appies image?"

"I understand that. I do. But—" I glance over at Carter, debating how much of his personal business I can justify sharing. "Theo has been through some pretty devastating stuff lately," I say. "He lost his dad a while back, but we've been talking a lot lately. What he needs right now is to play. He needs this team."

Coach studies me closely. At his heart, he's a guy who cares about his team as men as much as he does as players, and since he lost his wife, I'm sure he can imagine the pain of losing a parent. But he's also a firm disciplinarian and maintains a very high bar for the Appies.

He folds his arms over his chest. "Other coaches would healthy scratch a player for less. And they would be justified. Sitting on the sidelines without a jersey on makes an impact."

"I realize that," I say, "but as his captain, I'd like to give him another chance."

He takes a deep breath, his eyes shifting from me, then

over to Carter. "All right. I respect your judgment enough to give you this one. But this is on you, Sheridan."

"Hey! It's like an Appies reunion!"

We all turn and see an officer leading a smiling Theo into the lobby of the station. He gasps. "Is that coach? Coach Davis, what are you doing here? Hey, Carter, did you see Coach?"

On the ice, Theo's struggles seem to make him angry more than anything else, so I'm surprised he's such a happy drunk. But then he makes eye contact with me, and his expression sobers. He looks over to the officer standing beside him. "I don't think my captain is very happy with me right now."

"Your captain just wants you to make better choices." I reach out and shake the officer's hand. "Thanks for picking him up. And sorry for the trouble."

"No problem at all." He looks from me over to Nathan before he grins the slightest bit. "I'm a big fan. Go Appies."

Theo lifts his arms into the air. "Appies!" On the inside of his left arm, a new tattoo has made his skin pink and prickled, the ink slightly raised. It should be wrapped if he only got it tonight, but that's not what has me squinting at the ink, trying to read what it says.

Summer is directly beside me, and I lean toward her. "Does his new tattoo say *Apples*?"

She sucks in a gasp. "Ohhhh, that is one unfortunate typo."

Nathan chuckles. "Let's not point it out until tomorrow."

"Okay, I'm leaving before I regret my decision to give Apples over there another chance," Coach Davis says.

Nathan snickers. "Apples," he repeats. "That nickname might be harder to shake than the tattoo."

"Bye, Coach!" Theo calls.

Coach Davis moves to the door, shooting me a pointed look on his way. "I'm trusting you," he says, and I nod in response, wondering if I've just made a decision I'm going to regret.

———

Carter and Theo's truck is right outside the station, and since Carter didn't have anything to drink, there's no reason why he can't drive us from here. I say goodbye to Nathan and Summer, then climb into the front seat while Theo stretches out in the back. He's snoring in a matter of seconds, and Carter is quiet for most of the ride home. It isn't until we're pulling into the neighborhood that he looks over at me, his expression serious.

"I'll tell him what you said," he says, and I give him what I hope is an encouraging nod.

Evie's car is in the driveway when we get home. I wasn't sure it would be, because it didn't take all that long to retrieve the twins from the police station, so she must have left right after we did.

She was amazing tonight. Funny and likable. She fit right in, something I know I shouldn't take for granted.

Honestly, I think Evie could fit in anywhere. She's got this easy, unassuming confidence. At first, I thought maybe she just doesn't realize how great she is. But after watching her tonight, I think it's more that she doesn't *need* people to like her to feel okay about herself, which allows her to engage with people genuinely. She's happy to talk about herself if the subject comes up, but she'll just as quickly shower compliments and ask questions. She isn't bold like Summer or hilarious like Parker or intense like Gracie. Her confidence is quieter, her humor more understated.

I glance at my watch as we push through the front door. It was after eleven when we left Felix's, and it's almost midnight now, so I doubt Evie will still be up, but that doesn't stop me from hoping. It's a weird sensation, because I just spent the entire evening with her, and it still doesn't feel like enough. Maybe because I had to leave so abruptly. Or maybe because there's an understanding between us now. The promise of a kiss we both want.

Not here. But soon.

Theo is pretty subdued by now, so once the front door closes behind us, Carter waves me away and promises he can handle his brother from here. I pause in the hallway, watching as they stumble their way up the stairs to the bonus room, Carter half-carrying, half-dragging Theo.

"Night, Captain," Carter calls, then the door to the bonus room clicks shut.

I find Evie in the kitchen, pacing back and forth in front of the island.

She turns when I drop my keys on the counter.

"You're still up," I say.

She nods. "I was waiting for you." She looks at the baby monitor sitting next to the sink. "Juno fell asleep on the way home."

She says this like it's very important for me to know. Like it matters that, at least for right now, we won't be interrupted.

"Is Theo okay?"

"Yeah, he's okay. I can tell you the whole story tomorrow, but they didn't press charges. Just picked him up to keep him out of trouble."

She breathes out a sigh. "Good. That's good."

I push my hands into my pockets. There's a nervous energy about her that has me concerned. "Are you okay?"

"Yes! Absolutely. I'm just..." She closes her eyes and swallows before she opens them again, her hands moving to her hips. "The thing is, I don't really feel like I'm at my best right now. My body is tired and a little squishy and it's been a while since I've felt particularly sexy. But somehow, when you look at me, I *do* feel sexy. I feel...*alive*. And desired. Like I'm waking up from a really long sleep." She pauses and props her hands on her hips. I have no idea how she doesn't feel sexy, because she absolutely is. Sexy enough that I was in a police station negotiating with my very intimidating hockey coach twenty minutes ago, and now I'm here and the only thing I can think about is pulling her into my arms.

"You said you'd kiss me *soon*, Alec." She bites her lip. "So I'm just wondering if soon can be right now."

I move around the island, heart pounding as I finally reach her. I lift a hand to her waist, slipping it around to the small of her back as I tug her toward me. I lift my free hand to her cheek, my thumb sliding over her soft skin, across the constellation of freckles on her right cheekbone, then down to her neck, where my fingers tangle in her hair.

"First of all," I say, my voice low. "Everything about you is sexy. Every inch. Every curve." I drop my fingers from her face and find her hand, lifting it to my chest. I slip it inside my coat and press it over my hammering heart. "Do you feel that? That's what you do to me."

She closes her eyes and presses her lips together like she's trying to suppress a smile. Then she lifts her gaze to mine and lets out a shaky breath. "I'm scared, Alec." The tremble in her voice sounds like heartache, the same thing I see in her eyes, and Megan's warning echoes in my head. *She's fragile. Tread carefully.*

"Then we'll go slow," I say.

"I'm too young for you," she whispers, though I can tell her heart isn't really in the protest.

I grin. "I'm too old for you."

"If it doesn't work out, Megan will never speak to us again."

"But if it does work out, we'll make her really happy."

Evie lets out a little chuckle. "True. She already told me that," she says, but then her expression sobers. "Okay, but… Juno is a big deal. If I'm working all day, I won't ever want to leave her at night, which means I can't really date. If we do this, nothing is going to feel normal."

I lean down, brushing my nose against hers. I stop just shy of her lips, close enough to feel the whisper of her exhale on my skin. "Nothing about this has *ever* felt normal," I say. "Not since the minute I saw you standing in Ruth's living room."

She sucks in a breath, then she pushes up on her toes and closes the distance between us.

I wanted it to be her move—her choice—but the minute her lips are on mine, fire explodes through my veins, and it's all I can do to maintain control. But I have to, because I just told her we would go slow. Evie has a lot more at stake than I do. I have to respect that. Respect what she wants, when she wants it.

But Evie isn't holding back, her arms hooking around my neck, tugging me toward her like she can't get close enough. I'm not the tallest of the Appies by any stretch, but I'm just shy of six foot three, and Evie's a solid foot shorter. Plus, I'm in shoes, and she's barefoot, so we're both straining to make this work.

Sliding my hands over her hips, I hoist her up and put her on the counter, all without breaking the kiss.

"That's better," she says, smiling against my lips. "Actually, wait." She slips her hands inside the coat I'm still wearing and slides them up to my shoulders where she pushes the coat off, letting it fall to the floor behind me. *Now* that's better."

She kisses me again, tilting her head, her lips parting in an invitation I happily accept.

My hands slide around her, dipping under the hem of her sweater until they're flat against her skin, warm and soft as silk. Her back arches and she leans into me, pressing close as she deepens the kiss, her tongue brushing against mine. The fact that she's controlling this, guiding me to what she wants is as sexy as it is intoxicating. Right now, in this moment, I'd do anything for her. Anything she wants.

That's the kind of power she has over me.

I keep my palms pressed against Evie's back as our kisses ease into something a little slower, almost lazy. She moves her hands over my body, like she's cataloging every inch of my torso. Over my chest and shoulders, down to my biceps, my forearms. Then she lifts them to my face, brushing her thumbs over the stubble I'll probably shave in the morning. Unless she tells me she likes it. Then I'll keep it just this length forever.

Her hands move to my neck, then up to my scalp where her nails rake through my hair, earning a groan of pleasure that makes her chuckle. I break the kiss and drop my head to her shoulder. "That feels really good."

"You have good hair," she whispers.

"I found a gray one earlier tonight," I say, and she chuckles.

"Old man," she whispers.

"Nerd," I whisper back.

230

She wraps her arms around me, her knees still bracketing my waist, and I relax into the best hug I've gotten in years.

"Why did we wait so long to do this?" she asks.

I lean back and make eye contact. "I mean, technically, it would have been against the law until just a few years ago. So I think we timed things pretty well."

She chuckles and swats at my chest. "I meant, why did we wait until my house is done? Now it's time for me to move out, and it won't be nearly so easy to see each other."

"Your house is done?" This is information I haven't heard yet, and a twinge of disappointment pushes through me. "You didn't tell me."

"I just found out," she says. "My landlord emailed tonight. The new carpet went in yesterday, and the painters touched everything up today. So I can move in as early as tomorrow, assuming you and a few teammates can help me? As much as I love being here, it'll make my life so much easier to be closer to Ruth."

I hate the thought of Evie leaving. But it's probably better if she does. If slow is going to happen, living with Evie will not make that easier.

"We can definitely help," I say. "We have a home game, but it's early, so we'll be done by late afternoon. You don't have much stuff, so I don't think it'll take long."

Before Evie can answer, the baby monitor buzzes to life with Juno's cries.

Evie breathes out a sigh, her head falling against my chest. "This will probably happen a lot."

I cradle her cheeks and lean forward, pressing a quick kiss to her lips. "If it's not Juno interrupting us, it'll be my kids calling me down to the police station."

She grins. "They are kinda like your kids, huh? You're already getting dad skills."

231

I help her off the counter, keeping my hands on her hips, not quite ready to let her go.

"Alec, you're going to spend so much time waiting for me to feed the baby or change the baby or get the baby to sleep."

I shrug. "Some things are worth waiting for."

She kisses me again, her hands still clutching my shirt. "I'll see you in the morning?"

"I have to leave for the Summit pretty early, but I'd love to see you before I go."

"I'll be up," she says. "Juno always is." She finally lets me go and picks up the monitor, turning down the volume as she moves into the family room and toward the stairs. She pauses at the bottom and turns back. "Good night, Alec."

"Good night," I say, then I watch as she disappears up the steps.

I meant what I said. Some things really are worth waiting for, and I don't doubt that about Evie. But something about that response doesn't sit right with me. Because if I'm *with* Evie, it shouldn't always be me waiting for her while she takes care of the baby. I'll be taking care of the baby too.

A twinge of anticipation pushes through my chest. If things work out, if Evie and I end up together long-term, committed, *married*, I'll be a *dad*.

I've thought about it a few times now, and I keep waiting for it to feel overwhelming. Everything I know about babies, I gleaned from having Evie and Juno live here for a couple of weeks. I'm not naive enough to believe that adds up to being an expert. But all my thinking has done is make me want it more. I want to come home to Evie after practice. I want to watch her play her violin and hang out with Juno and be the reason they both smile. I want her to come to my games and wear my jersey and meet me after so I can kiss her senseless.

I want to learn everything there is to learn so I *can* be an expert.

I realize it's early to want all that. I can imagine Nathan lowering a hand on my shoulder and telling me I'm running when I really need to walk, and it would probably be very good advice.

But I'm not sure I can make myself stop. Not when it feels like I've finally found something real.

CHAPTER 21

EVIE

EARLY SATURDAY MORNING, I stand next to Alec's very fancy coffee pot, listening to it whirr and hum as it makes my coffee. It's barely past six, and since I don't have to work today, it feels beyond stupid to be awake. But once I fed Juno and she fell back asleep, I started thinking about Alec, and then I started thinking about *kissing* Alec, and suddenly sleep was the furthest thing from my mind.

I thought I might find him up already—he's proven himself an early riser—but so far, it seems like I'm the only one awake.

Did I spend an extra five minutes taming my hair and brushing my teeth before coming downstairs? Yes. Yes, I did. Am I going to linger in the kitchen and drink my coffee here hoping he'll still show? *Also* yes.

"Good morning."

I let out a little yelp and spin around, one hand flying to

235

my chest. Alec is standing in the doorway, looking sleep rumpled in gray sweatpants and a plain white t-shirt.

His shirt is tucked under itself on one side, making me think he just pulled it on. My eyes snag on the triangle of exposed skin. Pretty sure that last night, my hands dipped under his shirt and touched that exact spot.

The thought makes my cheeks flush with heat, and I force my gaze up to Alec's face.

He offers me a sheepish smile. "I didn't mean to scare you."

"That's okay, I was just…"

Thinking about your body.

Thinking about last night.

Wishing that you would kiss me right this second.

He slowly walks across the kitchen, stopping right in front of me as my words trail off, and I force myself to look at his face. To ignore the way his sweats stretch across his very defined thighs. I used to think dancers had the best quads, but I take it back. Hockey players win.

On the left side of Alec's head, his hair is slightly creased on one side, mussed from sleep. I lift my hand to the spot, running my fingers through his hair to smooth it down. Alec is always so poised and put together, and noticing this tiny imperfection triggers a wave of affection for him that makes my heart crawl into my throat. The vulnerability in his eyes as he looks down at me doesn't help.

"You were just…?" Alec repeats.

I bite my lip, because as fun as this teasing is, a tiny part of me is still afraid last night was a crazy impulsive decision that Alec already regrets.

But then he lifts his hands to my waist, tugging me against him before wrapping me up in a hug. It's a confident gesture, and all my worries evaporate in a matter of seconds.

I melt against him as I breathe in the clean, woodsy scent of his clothes and wrap my arms around his waist. I bury my face in his chest and let out a little chuckle. Because honestly, what is even happening right now? This is *Alec*.

And he's got his arms around *me*.

"I was just thinking I can't believe this is happening," I finally say.

"Me neither." His deep voice vibrates through his chest. "But I'm really glad it is." He presses a quick kiss to my forehead, then lets me go long enough to retrieve two mugs from the cabinet and pour us both some coffee. He adds cream and sugar to mine before handing it over.

"What am I going to do when I don't have you around to make me perfect coffee in the morning?" I take a tentative sip, but there's no need. The healthy dose of cream Alec added brought the temperature down enough to drink without caution.

"Have terrible coffee, probably," he says. He leans down and kisses me on the mouth this time, his lips soft and coffee-warm. "You could always just stay." He kisses me again, sliding one hand up to my face, where his thumb grazes across my cheek until it reaches the side of my bottom lip. "I like you in my house when I wake up."

They might be the sexiest words anyone has said to me in a very long time, mostly because the huskiness in his voice has me thinking about what it would be like to wake up in his bed, not just his house. Rolling over to trail my fingers over his back or tangle them in his hair. Seeing his big body relaxed and vulnerable.

"Don't tempt me. It will be nice to have Ruth just a few doors down, but I'll definitely miss this."

Alec nestles me a little closer, his chin resting on my forehead. "I'm excited for you to be close to Ruth. Anything that's going to make your life easier makes me happy."

The words are so simple and genuine, I'm suddenly struck with how vastly different they are from anything Devon ever said. I knew I was done with Devon when we finalized our divorce, but I'm not sure I truly saw how poorly he treated me. It happened so slowly, over such a long period of time, that the tiny slights, the little ways he made things about himself, they started to feel normal. That's just how our life was. And when Devon was on, when he was treating me well, it was *so well* that it was easy to let all the little things go.

But now, with Alec to compare him to, the contrast is too massive to ignore. Devon was never a man willing to put me first. With Alec, it's second nature.

Realizing as much makes me scared about what my life is going to look like if Devon really does show up. About the patience it will require to navigate Juno's visits with her dad, to moderate whatever kind of relationship he wants to have with her.

I know I shouldn't get ahead of myself, but it would be so much easier if I knew I would be doing it with Alec by my side.

As if sensing the shift in my mood, Alec leans back and moves his hands to my face. He kisses me again, this time with a fervency that takes my breath away. The kiss feels like a promise, and it goes a long way to loosening the ache I've been carrying around in my chest for months.

I dip my hands under the sleeves of Alec's t-shirt and slide them over his biceps, feeling them flex under my touch. He lets out a low sound, something between a growl and a moan, making my blood heat and my skin tingle. It's barely seven o'clock in the morning, and I'm kissing my best

238

friend's older brother like I'm the main character in a freaking romcom.

"I smell coff—*whoa.*"

Alec and I freeze, and I slowly peek my head around his shoulder to see Carter standing in the kitchen doorway, red-faced and chagrined.

"Sorry. I'll just—I didn't mean to interrupt," he says.

"Interrupt what?" Theo appears beside him as he sleepily rubs at his eyes. Considering how hungover he must be after last night, he looks surprisingly lucid.

"It's about time," Theo says as he moves toward the coffee pot.

Alec looks down at me and smiles. "It's less annoying when Juno interrupts us," he says softly.

Alec keeps me cocooned in his embrace while the twins make their way around the kitchen, grabbing coffee and warming up breakfast burritos. He should probably be getting ready too, but I'm not about to suggest it if it'll mean the loss of his arms around me.

Finally, Carter heads back to their room, but Theo lingers. He looks like he wants to say something to Alec, and his hesitation makes me wonder if he's hoping for privacy, but then he finally runs his hand through his shaggy brown hair and clears his throat.

"Carter told me what you said last night." He shuffles his weight from one foot to the other. "What you did."

My curiosity piques. Alec did say he'd tell me the long version of the story, and now I really want to hear it.

"I realize you didn't have to stand up for me with Coach," Theo continues, his eyes looking everywhere but directly at Alec. There is more humility in his posture than I've ever seen before, and my heart goes out to him. "After the way

239

I've been acting, I probably didn't deserve it. So...thanks, I guess."

Alec drops his arms from around my waist and turns to fully face Theo, his hands pushed into the pockets of his sweatpants. "You're my teammate," he says. "We have each other's backs. But my intervention wasn't without conditions."

Theo finally looks up, and Alec takes a step forward, pressing his palms flat against the island in front of him. "There's a counselor who works with the Appies, and you're going to start meeting with him twice a week."

Theo's jaw tightens, and he opens his mouth to protest, but Alec holds up a hand. "It's not your fault, Theo. What happened to your dad. It's not your fault. It's not fair that it happened, and it will never not completely suck. But your dad would want you to play. To live your life. I think somewhere buried deep, you probably know that, even if you don't quite believe it yet. Hearing me say it isn't going to be enough, but I'm guessing talking to a counselor eventually will."

I reach forward and hook a hand around Alec's waist, mostly because I'm so proud of him right now, and this is the only way I can think to show it. He's saying the exact right words, his tone warm and sincere, and he's giving off *strong* dad vibes. Any kid would be lucky to have a father this patient, this gentle.

Juno would be lucky.

The thought sends warmth blooming through my body, and I try to remind myself that we're supposed to take this relationship slow. That means I probably shouldn't fast-forward to imagining a life where Alec is parenting a teenaged Juno.

But it almost feels impossible not to imagine it. Life with

a baby is so frequently governed by survival, by taking care of immediate needs. There isn't a lot of time to sit around and think about what parenting conversations might be like... *fifteen years* down the road. But I'm thinking about it now, and getting this small window into how Alec handles conflict is the best kind of commercial, showing me something I desperately want before I even knew I wanted it.

Theo still looks unsure, though. His shoulders are tense, a nervous energy pulsing beneath his skin, and for a moment, I think he might bolt. Tear out of the kitchen like a frightened calf.

But Alec keeps talking, his tone even and steady. "Maybe you aren't ready to do it for yourself," he says. "And maybe you aren't ready to do it for the team, even though, with my knee crapping out, the Appies really need you. But do it for Carter, man. He's carrying a lot. And he's not really getting to grieve the loss of his dad because he's too busy taking care of you. Cleaning up your messes. Give him a break. Take this on for him."

This, finally, seems to get through to Theo.

His eyes are damp when he looks up, giving Alec the tiniest nod. "I'll do it. Just tell me where to be and when."

He turns and leaves the kitchen, and Alec's shoulders sag as he turns and sinks into me. I wrap my arms around him, my hands sliding up and down his back.

He buries his head in my shoulder, breathing deeply before saying, "I did not know how that was going to go."

"You did great. Truly. You said exactly the right thing."

He looks up to meet my gaze, his expression soft and vulnerable. "You think so?"

"Yeah. I really do."

He leans back against the counter and tucks me into his chest, his arms settling around my shoulders.

"Want to tell me the long version of what happened last night?" I ask him.

We stay wrapped up in each other's arms while he talks through everything that happened at the police station. He breezes a little too quickly through the part where he talks to Coach Davis, but based on what I heard Theo say, I can guess how big of a deal it was that Alec intervened.

I push up on my toes, lifting my hands to his cheeks as I kiss him. "I'm really proud of you," I say. "You earned his trust *and* got him into therapy. Both of those things are pretty big deals."

He breathes out a sigh. "I just hope it works. Because it'll be my neck on the line if it doesn't."

CHAPTER 22

THE DREAM TEAM

FELIX

Dropping this picture here for Wyatt and Camden since they weren't at dinner and didn't see Alec holding a baby like a pro.

<img_1473.jpg>

ELI

Dude's gonna be engaged before the end of the season.

VAN

#dadvibes

I have it on good authority women find men with babies hot

LOGAN

Who cares? He already has a woman.

ELI

Puppies also work.

But I also already have a woman, so…

Project time? We have all this knowledge, we should use it to get Camden and Wyatt women.

CAMDEN

No.

WYATT

Unequivocally no.

VAN

You know that's only going to make us try harder…

CHAPTER 23

EVIE

CONFESSION? I didn't really plan on doing anything for Juno's first Halloween. I bought her a very cute Dalmatian puppy sleeper with a hood and floppy dog ears, and I had every intention of putting it on her to take pictures, but I didn't think I'd take her trick or treating. It's not like *she's* going to eat any of the candy.

But as soon as I get to the Summit, I have zero regrets about our decision to come. Because the Appies are dressed up as firefighters.

Sexy firefighters, I might add. Tight black t-shirts, suspenders, firefighter pants and helmets. And what fire squad doesn't need a Dalmatian puppy? The photo opportunities alone will be worth the effort it took to get Juno ready.

Later, according to the info Alec already gave me, there will be a costume parade down on the ice, but for right now, everyone is gathered in the wide hallway that circles the arena. The space is full of games and snacks and lots of really cute kids holding their parents' hands as they "trick-or-treat" their way around booths set up by Harvest Hollow businesses.

"Oh my gosh!" Parker says as she crosses the concourse to where I'm standing near the door, Juno propped on my hip. "Did you do this on purpose? You brought us a Dalmatian!"

"It was totally by accident," I say. "Alec didn't tell me what the team's costumes would be."

Parker pulls her phone out and snaps a photo of Juno. "Seriously. This is the cutest ever. Are you going to let me put her picture on Instagram? *Please* say yes."

"You absolutely can," I say, but I'm only half paying attention to our conversation because I just spotted *my* sexy firefighter, and he's walking right toward me.

"Hey," Alec says as he reaches us. He leans down and presses a lingering kiss to my lips. "I'm glad you're here," he says, his gaze fixed on mine. A heady rush of pleasure fills my body, pushing out to my fingertips and down to my toes. I'm still not used to this. I still can't believe that Alec Sheridan wants to kiss *me* hello.

He holds out his hands, eyebrows raised as he looks at Juno. "May I?" When I nod, he steals her out of my arms and lifts her in the air. "Hey, Junebug." He smiles a wide, genuine smile. Juno smiles right back—how could she possibly not? —and Parker lifts her phone to take a photo.

"Her costume is perfect," Alec says. "Can I take her over to say hi to the guys?"

"Of course you can," I say, my heart practically bursting out of my chest.

He holds Juno close to his chest as he walks across the concourse to where Nathan, Felix, and a few other Appies are standing. I'm not used to *this*, either. To Alec showing

246

Juno off to his friends. Wanting to hold her, hang out with her.

"Um, was that just a very casual, very public hello kiss?" Parker asks, eyes gleaming.

I grin. There has been *a lot* of kissing over the past week in a lot of different locations. Alec's house. My new house, which he and his teammates helped me move into after the game last weekend. My car. His car. But that actually *was* the first time we've ever kissed in public.

"I love this for you," Parker says. "And for Alec too. But from one Appies girlfriend to another, stay off the internet. Alec has a big following. People will probably have opinions about you, but they're only opinions, and they will usually be based on stuff that isn't true. You just have to ignore it."

I haven't given a lot of thought to Alec's public life, outside of the one Riley-themed rabbit hole Megan and I dove down, mostly because, with Juno, we haven't really spent any time together *in public*. We mostly just hang out at my place because then Juno can go to bed without needing a sitter. But that won't always be the case.

"How do *you* avoid it?" I say. "Isn't it your job to follow everything?"

She shrugs like it's no big deal. "Yeah, but I've learned which comment sections to avoid."

Across the concourse, Alec laughs, looking perfectly comfortable with Juno in his arms. Honestly, with her dark hair, she looks like she could be his. When people find out we're dating, they'll probably assume she is.

Unsurprisingly, that thought doesn't bother me in the slightest. But I *do* wonder if it would bother him.

I look up to see Alec snuggling Juno close, her head dropping onto his shoulder. *Hmm.* I could be wrong, but I'm guessing it wouldn't bother Alec either.

"For real, could the man look any more like a dad right now?" Parker says dryly, and I shoot her another grin.

"He's genuinely so good with her," I say. "It's been really nice having someone around to help."

She holds up her phone. "Okay, be honest. Is this too much of a thirst trap for me to post on the Appies profile?"

She shows me the picture she took of Alec holding Juno up in the air. It's a profile shot, revealing a delicious view of Alec's biceps, the fabric of his black t-shirt stretched tightly across the muscle. But the best part of the photo is the look on Alec's face as he smiles up at Juno. It's genuine and warm, and that, even more than the biceps, is what makes heat pool in my belly. Few things are quite so sexy as a good man trying to be a good father. Of course, Alec isn't a father yet, but potential matters, and he's brimming with it.

"You really think I'm the right person to ask?" I say. "When it comes to Alec, everything is a thirst trap."

Summer joins us just in time to hear my comment. "Everything?" she questions. "Because let me tell you, I've been in the locker room after practice, and those boys are rank."

"True," Parker says. "Nothing smells like hockey smells." She shows the photo of Alec and Juno to Summer. "What do you think? Can I post this?"

Summer studies the photo. "Oh my gosh, is she a Dalmatian? That's the cutest." She hands the phone back to Parker. "But I still wouldn't post it. Not after what happened with Nathan last season. That's an ovary-exploding photo if ever there was one. If it goes viral, it'll be attention for him, but also attention for Juno and Evie. You should send it to Evie, though." She looks at me and grins. "It should absolutely be the wallpaper on your phone."

Parker nods. "Okay, good. That's what my instincts were telling me. That just means I have to get a photo of Juno with the entire team. The Dalmatian/firefighter thing is too cute not to."

"What happened with Nathan last season?" I ask before the conversation can move on.

"Just a few adoring fans who got a little *too* adoring," Parker says. "Summer had to pretend to be Nathan's girlfriend to create a buffer."

"Shut up," I say. "Is that how you ended up getting together?"

"What can I say?" Summer says, pulling her dark hair over her shoulder. "We're a walking romance trope."

Our conversation ends abruptly when Alec returns with Juno, but he makes no move to give her back. Instead, he tilts his head toward the growing party behind us. "Want to walk around a little?"

I say goodbye to my friends and follow Alec into the crowd of people moving their way through the Summit concourse. More than a few people take notice of Juno in Alec's arms, their gazes quickly darting to me, but Alec is an expert at ignoring them, and since he doesn't look like he's wanting to engage, most people just let us walk on by. Eventually, a few fans stop us and ask for selfies, so Alec gives Juno back to me and spends a few minutes chatting and taking photos. It's fun watching him in action, seeing how charming and genuine he is as he interacts with fans.

We make our way around the arena, talking, laughing, eating a few of the apple cider donuts Harvest Hollow is apparently famous for. When we've almost made a full circle around the Summit, we run into Malik and Ruth.

"Well, hello there," Ruth says as she reaches up to give me a hug. She looks at Juno. "Aren't you the cutest little

Dalmatian I've ever seen." She holds out her hands, and I happily hand Juno over.

Alec talks to Malik for another minute or so, but when he glances over and sees Juno in Ruth's arms, his gaze narrows the slightest bit, his expression turning shrewd.

"Hey, Ruth, do you mind keeping her for us? Just for a few minutes?"

"You can take more than a few," Ruth says. She points to a line of padded benches against the wall. "I'll be right here enjoying my favorite baby girl."

Alec grips my hand and tugs me toward a shadowy hallway that leads to an access door for a concessions area. There's a small recess at the end of the hall, and he pulls us inside so we're completely hidden from view.

He spins me so my back is flat against the wall, his eyes flashing with hunger before he leans down and delivers a bone-melting kiss. He moves with intention and confidence and barely banked passion, and he completely steals my breath.

I lift my hands, hooking them around his suspenders and pull him even closer. His lips part as he deepens the kiss, his palms moving up to my face, cradling my cheeks like I'm something precious, like he's holding something truly valuable in his hands. His thumbs brush across my cheek, featherlight and soft, then his teeth graze across my bottom lip, lightly nipping until I suck in a breath.

He finally breaks the kiss, but he keeps his face close, his forehead pressed against mine.

"I've been wanting to do that all night," Alec says, his voice low and raspy.

I swallow, but I'm not capable of words just yet. Instead, I let out a strangled sort of "Mmm," and Alec chuckles.

"You okay?" he asks, his tone a little too cocky. Like he

knows he just unraveled me and he's proud of himself for doing it.

Well. Two can play at this game.

I grab his elbows and spin him around so now he's against the wall, then I push up on my toes and brush my nose along the curve of his neck. I breathe in his woodsy, delicious scent as I press a slow line of kisses up the side of his jaw. When I finally reach his mouth, I kiss him again, except this time, I'm in control.

He yields willingly, letting me set the pace, the position, the pressure. His hands grip my waist, his fingers pressing into my skin with gentle pressure while I explore his mouth with mine. When I finally pull back, *he's* the one who's left breathless.

I lift an eyebrow and give him a playful smirk. "Are *you* okay?"

He grins. "Never been better."

He wraps his arms around me, and I settle into his chest, reveling in the solid safety of his embrace.

The first night he kissed me, Alec told me that nothing about our relationship has ever felt normal. It's only been a week since then, but it still feels true. We haven't even been on an actual date, but we're seeing each other as frequently as possible, getting to know each other through snatches of time and stolen moments. Kisses while we watch a movie at my place after Juno goes to bed. Late night text conversations when I can't sleep and he's on the road, traveling to or from a game. But it still feels like we're progressing, learning about what we like and don't like, growing more comfortable, more familiar with each other.

"So, I have a question for you," Alec says.

"Okay."

His tongue darts out to lick his lips, my gaze tracing the

movement before I force my eyes back to his. "I know it's kinda fast, but we *have* known each other a really long time. And I just think…I would really like to call you my girl-friend." A hint of vulnerability passes over his expression. "Is that okay with you?"

I can't keep a cheesy grin from breaking out across my face. "I think that's a wonderful idea."

He leans down and presses a quick kiss to my lips. "Really?"

"Really."

"Okay. It's official, then." He grins, looking boyish and totally adorable. "Are you going to tell Megan, or should I?"

I reach up and pat him on the chest. "Honey, I've talked to your sister every night this week."

He nods. "So you're saying she knows?"

"She knows."

"But she doesn't know it's official," he says. "Let me be the one to tell her that." He pulls out his phone. "Here. Come here." He hooks a hand around my neck and tugs me up for one more kiss, using his free hand to take a selfie. The results are a little shadowy, since we're standing in a mostly dark corridor, but it's clear enough to see that it's me and Alec, and we're definitely kissing.

He sends the photo to his sister, reading out loud as he types, "Meet my girlfriend…"

"Cute. I love it."

"There. Sent," he says, pocketing his phone, but it's already buzzing with what I'm sure is Megan's response. He pulls it back out and looks at the screen, then smiles and holds it up for me.

Megan's message has no words, just a long row of heart eyes and celebration emojis.

"All right," Alec says, reaching for my hand. "Let's go get Juno."

Ruth is sitting right where she said she'd be, but she's no longer holding Juno. When she sees us coming, she points across the concourse. "The tall one has her," she says.

We look to see Nathan standing near the opposite wall, Juno fast asleep in his arms.

"He looks like a pro," Alec says, admiration in his tone.

"Want me to take her back?" I ask Nathan as soon as we approach, and the grumpy glare he gives me is answer enough. I raise my hands in an exaggerated gesture. *"Fine!* You can keep her."

He does keep her, and it's a good thing because now I need to pee. I squeeze my boyfriend's hand—*boyfriend!*—and tell him I'll be right back, then I dart off to the bathroom.

I check my own phone on my way back, sure that Megan texted me too, and find a message just as enthusiastic as the one she sent Alec. All the heart eyes. All the fireworks. Followed by one more message with actual words.

MEGAN

I have never been so happy for either of you.
Truly. Best news ever.

When I find Alec and Nathan exactly where I left them, Juno still sleeping peacefully, I cross the concourse and sit down next to Ruth. We chat about her kids and their plans to visit for the holidays and joke about trash pick-up on our street and how hard it is to predict when the truck will actually come through.

I don't take Juno back until it's time for the costume parade, when Alec and Nathan both have to head down to the ice to help supervise.

253

I sit inside the arena with Summer and Parker and watch as the athletes carefully shepherd skaters of all skill levels around the ice. Princesses and hockey players parade through the arena, along with astronauts and ghosts and fifty other costumes I can't identify—and twenty-two well-muscled firefighters.

Honestly, the addition of their hockey skates only sharpens the appeal.

The stands are by no means full, but scattered groups of parents and onlookers sit all over. Behind us, a group of dads are talking loudly enough that when they mention Alec's name, I immediately perk up.

"He oughta just quit," one guy says. "He's older than half the guys out here anyway, and he's not half as fast as he used to be. What's he trying to prove?"

"You're claiming you're faster?" another guy answers, and they all chuckle.

"Nah, but I'm not getting paid to play," the original guy says. "I'm just saying. The Williamson twins are better. Mark my words. They'll drop him down to third line before the end of the year."

The conversation goes on, eventually shifting to other players on the team, but I can't fully quell the pulsing discomfort their comments triggered. They don't know anything about Alec. Not really. They don't know how much he's hurting, how hard he's fighting to keep playing, to be what his team needs him to be.

"Ignore it," Parker says softly. "They just like to hear themselves talk."

Behind us, one of the guys mentions Nathan's name.

"Actually, let's go sit somewhere closer," Summer says, standing up. Parker and I exchange a quick glance, but Summer's tone was just commanding enough that we don't question before we stand and follow behind her. As we file out of the row, Summer glares at the men, silencing them with what I imagine is her very tough courtroom face.

Actually, I'm not even sure Summer does the kind of law that requires courtrooms. But if she did, she'd use that face, and it would be very intimidating.

It clearly was to the men, because they're all completely silent until we're several rows away and out of earshot.

"Think they realized who you are?" Parker asks.

"I don't care if they didn't," Summer says. "They deserved a withering look either way."

Our new location is much better for observing the costume parade, which is now fully in swing. "Well, this is probably the cutest thing I've ever seen," I say as I settle into my new seat.

"Cuter than my boyfriend snuggling your baby to sleep?" Summer says. "Because that definitely wins for me."

"Did I tell you about the time Alec sang Juno to sleep in the middle of the night—*shirtless*?"

"Oh geez," Summer says. "Did you immediately marry him?"

I laugh. "I thought about it." I tap a spot on my chest. "He has an Appies tattoo right here. The team logo."

"Really?" Parker asks. "I didn't know that."

"Sexy," Summer says. "I love a good tattoo." She's quiet for a beat before she laughs and says, "Poor Apples."

Thinking about Theo draws my eye back to the ice. The twins are with Alec, the three of them hovering around a pair of girls, who can't be more than seven or eight, wearing twin Appies hockey uniforms. The girls are not great skaters, but every time one of the guys tries to help, they get their hand swatted away. Finally, Theo runs off the ice and returns with a hockey stick. He crouches down in front of the girls and shows them how to hold onto the stick, then

255

he slowly skates backward, pulling them forward around the rink.

Alec watches him for a second, then he looks into the stands, finding my gaze in the crowd. He smiles, and I know exactly what he's thinking.

It's not like one conversation fixed everything for Theo. I know Alec isn't naive enough to think it did. But this still feels like progress. Right now, at least for this moment, it feels like Theo is going to be okay.

I return Alec's smile and lift Juno's arm up in a pretend wave. He winks and waves back before turning his attention to the kids, and I find myself thinking about how recent it was that *I* wasn't okay. There was so much stress and sadness and disappointment in the months leading up to and immediately after Juno's birth. Of course, there was joy too. But I was mostly just surviving. Getting through one day at a time. Learning how to be a mom and a single parent.

But then I came to Harvest Hollow, and things started to change. Happiness snuck up on me. I've found friends, a job I love, a man who kisses me like his singular purpose in life is to melt me into the floor but who also looks at my daughter like she's worth his time and effort. Like she matters too.

I'm not just okay. I'm *more* than okay.

I'm really, truly happy.

I just have to hope that this time, the happiness lasts.

CHAPTER 24

ALEC

"WHAT DO you think it would cost to get just the bottom of the L removed?" Theo asks, holding his arm up as he studies his new tattoo.

Even though it's past lunchtime, they're sitting on the opposite side of my kitchen island eating piles of pancakes, sausage, bacon, eggs. Breakfast is pretty much the only category of food either twin is comfortable cooking, but they're buying their own groceries, they mostly clean up after themselves, and when they do cook, they're usually willing to share, so I can't complain.

"Just embrace it," Carter says. "The team isn't giving up your nickname. Just be the apple guy."

Theo rolls his eyes. "I can't be the *apple* guy. I'm a defenseman. I'm supposed to be tough."

"I'm tough, and I like apples," I say dryly, and Carter chuckles.

It's only been a few weeks since Theo and I had our

257

reckoning, but our relationship is already improving. He's still dealing with some anger issues, mostly on the ice, but he hasn't been out drinking again, and he hasn't missed a therapy appointment yet.

It helps that I've done my level best to keep him busy enough that he doesn't have a choice. When we're traveling with the team, he's my roommate. When we're in Harvest Hollow, he's either at my house with his brother, or he's out with me. The other guys are stepping up too. On the way home from our last away game, Nathan had a long conversation with Theo, likely about losing his own dad. And Dominic, who's an explosive skater, has been working with both twins in the weight room, sharing the workouts he created to increase his power on lateral starts.

It's clear the team is rallying around them as much as they can. There are still no guarantees. Theo has to keep putting in the work. But it's at least easier to see the light at the end of the tunnel.

It's also been nice seeing his relationship with his brother improve. Only incrementally—it takes a long time to break habits. But it's been enough to notice, and I know Carter has noticed too.

We're back at the Summit for a home game tonight, our last one before Thanksgiving, and for the first time, Evie and Juno are coming to watch. Megan and my parents are also on their way into town—we're all spending the holiday together at my place—so this is the perfect game for Evie to attend, since there will be plenty of people she trusts to help with Juno.

Evie's ex-husband, Devon, will *also* be at my house for Thanksgiving, but I'm choosing to ignore how uncomfortable this makes me. Mostly because Evie doesn't need to worry about my feelings when she already has so much on her mind. She just needs my support. My steadiness. My trust that Devon's presence doesn't have anything to do with *my* relationship with Evie.

He's coming for Juno, and that's a good thing.

Doesn't mean I like it. Doesn't mean I don't *really* want to punch the guy. But I'm willing to pretend I don't for Evie's sake.

Just for the record, though. If we're talking hours logged in Juno's company, I've got the man beat by a mile. And I don't plan on that changing any time soon.

I stand and reach for my suit coat draped over the back of my chair. "Are you guys riding with me to the Summit?"

"Nah," Carter says. "Our bones aren't nearly as rickety as yours. We don't need the extra warmup time, so we'll drive over in a bit."

I ignore the jab because Carter isn't wrong. I spend at least thirty extra minutes before every game applying heat and stretching with one of the trainers just to make sure I'm as loose as possible before hitting the ice.

I nod and grab my keys from the counter. "Sounds good. See you over there."

As soon as I'm in my truck, I return a missed call from my mom, learning that their plane has landed in Asheville and they're working on picking up their rental car, then I call Evie.

She answers on the first ring. "Hi."

"Hey. How's it going?"

She breathes out a sound that makes my blood heat. "Mmm. I just took an amazingly long nap, and I'm still in bed, so I would say it's going pretty well."

I'm momentarily distracted by the imagery her words bring to mind. Evie in her bed, lounging on her pillows, her dark hair falling onto her shoulders. I almost ask her for a picture. We've seen less of each other the past few weeks—we had four away games in a row, which kept us on the road for almost ten days—and I'm hungry for the sight of her. But I'll see her tonight, and then we'll have three uninterrupted days together.

Well. Uninterrupted by hockey. I'm sure Juno will stick to her regular schedule.

Evie yawns. "Juno woke up super early, which was super annoying," she says, "but then she tired herself out rolling in circles around the living room. So when she napped, I napped."

"Sounds like a good strategy. Did she really roll in circles?"

"Like she was circumnavigating the globe," Evie says. "She rolls up and a little to the left every time, so it takes about nine rolls to get back to where she started."

I chuckle at Evie's description. One thing I did not expect when we started dating was how much Juno would change. Every day she's doing something different. Reaching some new milestone.

I'd never even really thought about babies having milestones before Juno. Now, I have a chart of them saved on my phone.

"I swear, she's going to start sitting up on her own any day now, and I'm not even a little ready for it," Evie says. "What's up with you? How are you?"

"On my way to the Summit."

"Have you heard from your family yet?"

"Yeah, they're all good. Landed and on the ground and getting a rental car."

Evie grumbles. "I wish they'd just let me come pick them up."

"It would have been a tight fit in your Honda. They're

fine. They don't mind getting a car," I say. "Will you still meet them at my house before the game?"

"Yeah, but I'll work that out with Megan. You just focus on you. We'll figure out everything else."

"But you know where to pick up the tickets? My mom has asked me at least three times."

"Alec," she gently chides. "We'll be fine. Stop worrying."

I force myself to take a deep breath. It's been a long time since Evie has seen me play in person, and she's never seen me play as an Appie. Even though I know she doesn't care about my stats, I still want to play my best. With my family watching too, I'd love to have a game that's better than my current average, because right now, I'm playing my worst season on record.

Every game, my minutes played gets lower and lower, a combination of me changing myself out faster, whenever my knee starts to hurt, and Coach Davis shuffling defensive pairs, switching us up, looking for better chemistry, more effective combinations.

I don't like to think about what it all means, so I'm mostly just *not*, instead channeling all my energy into the parts of my job I *can* control. Working with Theo. Keeping team morale up. Babying my knee.

"I'm done worrying," I say to Evie. "I just want everyone to have a good time."

"We will. We'll be watching you. That's all that matters."

We talk for a few more minutes, then say goodbye as I turn into the Summit parking lot and pull into my usual spot. A few spaces down, Felix is standing next to his Audi, and he lifts his hand in a wave.

In between the parking lot and the Summit, a crowd of fans lines the sidewalk. We're still hours away from puck drop, but this is a home game, and fans have learned that if they come early, we'll usually stop on our way inside to sign autographs or take pictures.

Felix reaches my side. "You ready for this?" he asks, motioning to the crowd.

I shoot him a look. "Are we ever really ready for this?"

Parker is outside, filming our progress toward the stadium, and she waves, giving us each a thumbs up to let us know she has the content she needs. The videos she makes highlighting the team walking into the arena are always a hit, something that's led a lot of guys to get flashier and flashier with their game-day suits. Last home game, Dumbo wore Appies turquoise from head to toe—pants, dress shirt, suit, even his shoes.

Felix and I spend the next few minutes making our way down the line, signing posters, jerseys, and hats, and posing for at least a dozen different selfies.

"How are you?" I say to a little girl holding a team poster. "Want me to sign that for you?"

She nods, then hands it over. "You're my second-favorite Appie," she says as she pushes her glasses up her nose.

"Yeah? Just your second? Who's got the top spot?" I drop to a knee in front of her so I can talk to her eye-to-eye while I sign.

Her gaze shifts past me and pauses on Felix. "Jamison's my favorite because I'm a goalie and he's a goalie, but every good goalie needs solid defensemen, so I decided you should be a favorite too."

I lift my eyebrows as I hand the poster back to her. "Well, I appreciate that."

"You guys weren't really vibing at your last game, though. Jamison let some shots through, but you didn't have his back like you should have," the little girl says.

It's weird to hear criticism coming from someone so small, but she's not exactly wrong. Our last game ended with one of our ugliest losses of the season. It takes a whole team to win or lose a game, and our offense was weaker than usual, with Eli and Logan spending way too much time in the penalty box, but Felix *was* left on his own more than he should have been.

Felix moves up beside me as I stand, and I can tell by his amused expression he heard every word of the little girl's critique.

"The last shot in the third period?" she goes on. "For real. Where were you? Were you even watching the puck?"

"Okay, Bree. That's enough." A hand drops on her shoulder, and I look up to meet the gaze of a guy who I assume is her father.

"Sorry," he says. "She's really into the sport. We're all big fans."

"We appreciate it," I say, then I look down at Bree, mostly amused but still slightly discomfited by her honest critique. "We'll try to play better for you today, all right?"

As soon as we're inside the Summit and away from the crowd, Felix gives me a good-natured shove. "Yeah, Sheridan. Why'd you leave me hanging? Were you even watching the puck?"

I chuckle. "She's got a future, I think." We're quiet as we continue down the hall, but the little girl's question is pinging around my brain.

Were you even watching the puck?

I look over at Felix. "Was she right about the shot at the end of the third period? Was my game off?"

"You saw the score. We were *all* off," Felix says.

"I know. But did I really not have your back?"

Felix's steps slow as we approach the locker room. "Come

on, man. Are you seriously letting a six-year-old get inside your head?"

"Should I?" I ask, suddenly intent on getting an honest answer. I'm aware of my own stats, so I'm not claiming things haven't been different this season. But when I'm on the ice, *I'm on*. My play hasn't suffered. At least, I didn't think it had. "Was she right?" I ask again.

Before Felix can answer, Coach Davis appears at the end of the hall. "Sheridan." He tilts his head toward his office. "Come talk to me a minute."

I look back at Felix. His expression is unreadable, but he drops a hand on my shoulder, giving it a quick squeeze before moving past me and pushing into the locker room.

Tension coils in my gut as I walk toward Coach's office. It's not unusual for him to pull me aside and talk about one thing or another, but after the comment from the little girl outside and my brief conversation with Felix, there's a sense of foreboding to this meeting that I've never felt before.

I lower myself into a chair across from his desk. "What's up, Coach?"

He clasps his hands in front of him and gives me a long look. "You've done good work with Theo the past few weeks."

I nod. "Thank you. He's a good defender. And it seems like he's made some good progress in therapy."

Coach nods, then breathes out a sigh. "Alec, there's no easy way to say this." He pulls off his hat, then rubs a hand over his hair before putting it back on again. "I'm pulling you from our special teams. Power plays and penalty kills."

I lean forward. "What?"

"And I'm starting Carter with Nathan tonight."

The tension from earlier morphs into a sinking ball of

dread. "Coach, if it's my knee, I'll play through the pain. Get another shot of cortisone. You can't—"

He holds up a hand, silencing my protests. "It's already done. The decision is made."

I slump back into my chair and work to slow my breathing. I probably should have seen this coming. Except, I *did* see it coming. I've been watching my stats. I've just been choosing not to do anything about it. Choosing to focus on Evie and Juno instead.

"I know how hard you've been taking care of your knee," Coach says. "And you're still a valuable part of this team. But Alec, be objective for a minute. Even outside of your injury, do you really feel like you've been playing with your whole heart?"

I swallow my first impulse, which is to bark back, *I thought I had been.* At this point, it won't be productive to argue with Coach. And after the look Felix gave me when I asked him to be honest, I'm beginning to think my first impulse isn't actually the truth.

"Alec, look at me," Coach Davis says, and I slowly raise my gaze to meet his. "It's okay to ask yourself if this is still what you want. And it's okay to admit it if it isn't. We all know the schedule is crap. That it's hard on families, hard on bodies. You've put a lot into this team. And I will be honored to coach you through your very last game whether it's this season or five seasons from now. There is no ultimatum in this conversation. But my priority is to win games. And the decisions I'm making are what I think will give us the best shot."

I'm in the locker room applying heat to my knee when Nathan drops down beside me, stick and tape in hand.

"Is Evie coming tonight?" he asks as he lines up the tape with careful precision.

I readjust the heating pad. "Yeah. Bringing Juno and everything. Plus, my whole family is in town."

He nods. "That's got to feel good. I don't remember the last time you had family in the stands."

I grab my own stick from where it's leaning against my stall and work on peeling off the tape so I can replace it. "Yeah, it's nice. Not sure how much they'll get to see me play, but I guess I'll take what I can get." The words come out biting, and Nathan looks up sharply. I frown and shake my head. "Sorry. That wasn't—I shouldn't be barking at you."

"It sucks, man," he says, and I know from his tone he's already been told about the changes to tonight's lineup.

"It's the right call though," I say, meeting Nathan's eye. "You've noticed too?"

He's quiet for too long, eyes on his stick, so I lean forward, elbows propped on my knees.

"Just be straight with me, man."

"You've been off," he says. "But I'm not sure it's just your knee."

"What does that mean?"

He taps the side of his head. "It seems like it's more up here."

I think of Coach's question. Do you really feel like you've been playing with your whole heart?

A sense of panic swirls in my gut, slowly clawing its way up my throat. It's not like I've been unaware of the realities of my injury, my age, the looming possibility of retirement sometime in the future. But in a matter of minutes, I've been

266

confronted with a very different reality than what I thought I was living.

How did I miss it?

How did I miss my teammates thinking I've been letting them down?

I think about the time I've spent texting Evie from the road. How quickly I hurry from the Summit after a game because I want to get over to see her.

I've been distracted. Ignoring the signs. And my team has suffered for it.

I'm the captain of this team.

And I've let everyone down.

I pull the heating pad off my knee and toss it onto the bench before heading over to where Eric is waiting to help me stretch.

"How's it feeling?" the trainer asks as I lay down on the table.

"Pretty good," I say, though the words feel a little more hollow than they should. "Better than a week ago."

My phone buzzes with a text, and I pull it out, holding it over my head while Eric maneuvers my right knee up to my chest.

"Hey, I need you to focus, man," Eric says.

"Yep, just one sec," I say, quickly pulling up the message. It's from Evie—a picture of her and Juno, both decked out in Appies gear. Evie is wearing her Appies jersey—*my* Appies jersey—and she's smiling wide, her eyes the same bright blue as Juno's.

I'm still studying the picture when a second one pops up, this one of my entire family. Mom, Dad, Megan, and Evie right in the middle, Juno in her arms.

A text comes in immediately after the second photo.

> I hope you're feeling great and that your knee is kind to you. Juno and I will be cheering for you.

At the end of her message, there's a single red heart that makes *my* heart push against my ribcage with new pressure. I want Evie to be proud of me as much as I want to be what my team needs. And I've been trying.

But what if I just can't do it anymore?

I drop my phone onto my chest and focus on the stretches Eric is working me through, willing the ligaments in my knee to loosen.

Critics might say my game is off because I'm distracting myself with Evie, losing my focus.

Others might say I'm just getting old. Or they might look at the latest scans of my knee and say it's a wonder I'm still playing at all.

But it doesn't really matter what the reasons are.

What matters is that the time I've been dreading is finally here.

CHAPTER 25

EVIE

I'M nervous when I drive over to Alec's house to meet his family before the game. Not because of Megan, obviously, since she and I talk so frequently. But I haven't seen or spoken to Alec's parents since he and I started dating.

I know they've always loved me. But that doesn't mean they'll think I'm right for Alec.

To be fair, Megan has insisted at least twenty times that my worry is unfounded, and her mother and father are thrilled for me and Alec.

But I'll feel better once I've seen them and can judge for myself.

Megan is waiting for me on the front porch when I pull into the driveway, her smile wide, her arm waving with way too much enthusiasm. She meets me at the car, bouncing on her toes while I lift Juno out of her car seat. Juno has outgrown her infant carrier now, so once she's out of the car, I drop her right into Megan's arms.

269

"Oh my gosh!" Megan sing-songs. "She's so big! Oh Juno, you love your Auntie Megan, don't you? Yes, you do!"

Alec's mom is waiting for me at the front door.

She has a few more wrinkles than she did the last time I saw her, but she's still as lovely as she's always been, with warm brown eyes and a smile that reminds me of Alec. She pulls me into the warmest hug, then looks me right in the eye, her hands pressed against either cheek. "I knew giving you that cinnamon roll recipe was a good idea," she says.

Alec's father is a little more reserved when he says hello, but he still shakes my hand and pats me on the shoulder. "If my son's phone calls to me the past few weeks are any indication, you're good enough for him, and that's good enough for me."

"See?" Megan says. "I told you there was nothing to worry about."

She's right. At least, when it comes to her family.

But there's still one storm cloud looming over my holiday plans.

Devon is still coming to dinner.

He's supposed to arrive sometime tomorrow night, just in time for Thanksgiving on Thursday. We haven't talked too much about his plans. I gave him Alec's address, and he knows we're eating with the entire Sheridan family.

What he doesn't know is that Alec and I are together.

I can't decide if it was a mistake not to tell him, but I was afraid it might influence his decision to come. And for Juno's sake, I didn't want that to happen.

I'll just tell him about Alec as soon as he gets here, when it's too late for him to change his plans. Hopefully, as soon as he meets Juno, he'll fall as much in love with her as the rest of us are, and nothing else will matter.

It should be easy if she's in her Appies gear because my

baby is the cutest thing on the planet in Appies turquoise and gray.

By the time the five of us finally make it to the Summit for the game, the arena is buzzing with energy and excitement, and I eat it up. It's been years since I've done this, and I can't wait to get inside the arena—and not just to see Alec play, though he's definitely the biggest part of my excitement. But it also just feels good to be back at a game.

"Just like old times, huh?" Megan says, giving my arm a squeeze.

I point at Juno, who is strapped to my chest in her sling, facing outward. "Really? Just like old times?"

Megan rolls her eyes and laughs. "Okay, fine. The baby is new." Juno's diaper bag slips off her shoulder, dropping onto her elbow, and Megan grunts. "Oof," she says as she shifts it back up. "What did you pack in here?"

"A bottle for Juno, a water bottle for me, two extra baby outfits, a full day's worth of diapers and wipes, a blanket, and three different teething toys," I say without missing a beat.

"You're seriously gonna need all that during one hockey game?"

"I hope not," I say. "But I'm prepared for every possible contingency."

Once we arrive at our seats, I introduce Alec's family to Gracie and Bailey, who are sitting nearby, then turn my attention to warmups. Most of the guys warm up without their helmets on, so it's easy to spot Alec skating a wide loop around the Appies' half of the ice. I wait for him to look up, to search for me in the stands, but he keeps his focus down. Which is totally fine. This is not a moment I need to be about me. But something about the set of his shoulders has me worried. I could be wrong, but he looks like something is bothering him.

Then again, it's not like I'm familiar with Alec's warmup routine. This could be totally normal.

Megan's dad passes a bucket of popcorn down the row, and Megan takes a big handful before offering some to me. I do the same, careful not to drop any in Juno's hair while I watch Alec work on his stick handling.

"Have you and Alec said I love you yet?" Megan asks in between bites like it's *not* a monumentally enormous question.

I practically choke on my popcorn. "Seriously? You're just tossing out that question like it's no big deal?"

"Why not? I'm curious."

"It hasn't even been *a month*," I say.

"Yes, it has been. You kissed him before the Halloween thing, and that was definitely a month ago."

"It was *three* weeks ago," I correct. "And that is way too soon to be saying any I love yous."

"You guys are no fun," Megan says. "You've basically known each other forever. You should just say it already. I bet you already feel it."

It's possible she's right, but if she is, I'm definitely not telling *her* before I tell her brother.

Eventually, Parker drops into the seat beside me, and we chat for the last few minutes of warmups. The entire time, something niggles in the back of my brain. A quiet discomfort telling me that all is not right with the world. Is it Alec? Was there really something bothering him during warmups?

I look down to check on Juno and find her perfectly content, pacifier in her mouth and noise-cancelling headphones snug on her ears. Yesterday, Alec brought over a pair in Appies turquoise and gray, tiny logos centered on each earpiece. He had them made just for her, and I'm so glad he

272

did because it's really loud in here, and I wouldn't have thought to get her any.

She seems fine, so what else could it be?

When my phone buzzes from the outside pocket of my diaper bag, I scramble for it, already expecting bad news. Which is weird. I'm not the kind of person who usually gets premonitions.

But sure enough, the text on my phone is definitely bad news. It even came with its own warning label. *Hey, Evie. Bad news.*

DEVON

Hey, Evie. Bad news. I've got to go to California for a few days, so I can't come for Thanksgiving. But this is big. Could even be huge. I wish I could see you and Juno, but I can't miss this opportunity. I'll let you know more soon.

I read the text once, then again, then a third time.

He's not coming.

For weeks, I've been preparing my mind, thinking through how co-parenting is going to look, making room to let him back in, at least in part, because I wanted Juno to know her father.

And he's not. freaking. coming.

I force a breath out through my nose and hand my phone to Megan, my eyes locked on the Zamboni driver as he moves from one side of the ice to the other.

Beside me, I hear Megan swear under her breath before her arm wraps around my shoulders. "You okay?"

I breathe out a disbelieving laugh. "Honestly, I don't know why I ever believed him. This is Devon we're talking about. *Of course* he isn't coming. I should have known from the start."

"No," Megan says, her tone firm. "There is no *you should have* in this situation. He told you he was coming. That he wanted to meet his daughter. You had every reason to believe him."

I shoot her a knowing look. "Did I, though?"

"Okay, so maybe he doesn't have the best track record." She holds my gaze for a long moment. "Break down the feelings for me. Sad? Angry? Annoyed? What do you have going on?"

I take a deep breath and wrap my arms a little tighter around Juno, grateful that she's too little to know the disappointment of her father not coming.

"Is it terrible that I mostly just feel relieved?" I look over at Megan. "I was trying to rally and be optimistic for Juno's sake, but I don't want her to have a father who makes empty promises. He'll just keep breaking her heart, Megan. Even if he came this time. Would there be a next? Would he ever decide to prioritize her over his own selfish desires?"

"I don't know," she says, giving my shoulders another squeeze. "But it's your job to protect her, and if you don't think you can trust him, it's okay to keep him at a distance until he's earned the right to be present."

"If he ever earns it," I say. But after this, I'm not sure I want to give him the chance. I can't live the rest of our lives with the possibility of his involvement looming over us. He either wants to be Juno's father or he doesn't. End of story.

Our conversation slows as the overhead lights in the arena dim, and turquoise strobe lights flash across the ice. The national anthem plays, the teams are introduced, and then it's game on.

Only, Alec *isn't* on the ice.

I scoot forward in my seat, anxious to find him, and

Megan does the same. "Did he *not* start? I don't remember the last time he didn't start."

A few more minutes pass before a line change finally brings Alec onto the ice. I practically hold my breath as I watch him play. He's playing well, but something feels different. When I moved into my new house, Alec transferred his sports subscription package to me so I could continue watching his games. I have been *diligent*, watching every Appies game he's played since we started dating, so I've gotten used to the way he moves on the ice. It's why I was so excited to finally come see him play in person.

But tonight, there's a physicality and a roughness to his game that I haven't seen before. Even as a defenseman, he's not the kind of player who will ever throw the first punch. When he was in college, he spent very little time in the penalty box relative to other players, and when I dug up his stats on his Appies seasons, the same held true. He uses his speed and his ability to read the game more than he uses his body. But he's using his body tonight.

A lot.

He looks like a tightly coiled spring ready to explode if someone touches him the wrong way. If I didn't know him so well, I might not notice anything. But there's definitely something off.

"Um, what has gotten into him?" Megan says at the end of the first period.

I bite my lip. "I don't know. I don't think I've ever seen him play like this."

She glances at the scoreboard. "I mean, they're killing it, so maybe it's not a bad thing?"

Van's wife, Amelia turns in her seat and looks up at me. "Alec's really on fire tonight."

I nod and smile, and we chat for a few minutes about the

game, but I can't quite shake the tension spreading up my shoulders, making my neck feel tight.

We're two minutes into the second period before Alec is back in, this time paired with Theo as his defensive partner.

I cross my fingers for Alec as the game shifts from one defensive zone to the other. It's hard to follow all the action when I'm semi-distracted by Juno, so I happily surrender her when Alec's mom asks if she can hold her for a while.

I've just moved back to my seat and gotten Juno's sling off when Megan gasps, and I turn my eyes back to the ice. "What is it? What happened?"

"He was hit," she says. "I think Alec was hit with the puck."

At first, I can't find Alec on the ice for all the players surrounding him, but then they move out of the way, and I finally see his face.

His *bleeding* face.

"Oh gosh, Megan. He's bleeding. Is he bleeding?"

She wraps an arm around me. "He's bleeding. But he's okay. He's still on his feet."

We watch in silence as he crosses the ice and heads into the tunnel. Play continues without him, but I have zero interest in watching the game.

"I have to get to him," I say, spinning in my seat, looking toward the aisle.

Parker lifts her hands, gently placing them on my arms and stopping my momentum. "You can't get to him," she says gently. "But I'm sure he's okay." She drops her hands and pulls her phone out of her pocket. "I'm going to text one of the trainers and see if he can get me an update from the medical team."

I force myself to take a deep breath while we wait for a response.

Parker smiles warmly. "It's not his first injury," she says, her voice infused with a measure of calm I wish I could steal and have for myself.

"Definitely not," Megan adds.

I think of the bruises and scars I've noticed on Alec's body over the past few weeks. Some he's had a story for, others he hasn't been able to identify at all. That's how many there are. *Not* very many on his face, though, which is lucky because he has *such a pretty face.*

I force another calming breath. "Does this feeling ever go away? This...worry?"

Parker's eyes turn sympathetic. I'm not sure how long she and Logan have been together, but she has to know exactly what this is like. "Not really," she says gently. "But you do get a little more used to it."

Down on the ice, the Appies score, and I look down to see that it was Logan who made the goal. I feel bad for keeping Parker's attention off the game, but she waves away my concern. "He's done it before, and he'll do it again." Her phone pings with an incoming message, and she looks down. "Okay. Eleven stitches on his left cheek, but otherwise, he's totally fine."

I sink back into my chair while Megan relays the information down to her parents, but barely another moment passes before a cheer erupts in the arena because Alec is back on the ice.

With eleven stitches in his freaking face.

Megan laughs, but I only shake my head. "What is he doing? Is he for real going to keep playing? With stitches?"

Parker shrugs. "Hockey players are a different breed. He wouldn't be the first one to do it."

I watch the rest of the game with my heart in my throat. With two minutes to go, the Appies are up by two—they're all playing like machines—and I start to relax. Alec has been in more minutes of the third period than the first two combined, and I have to wonder if the coach sees what I see. That he's literally managing to be everywhere at once. He's blocking, he's passing, he's reading the game with expert eyes. I don't know what came over him. If it's having his family in the stands, if it's having *me* in the stands. With less than a minute left, Alec sprints after the puck, pulling up in front of the boards before sending it over to Theo, but then his body twists and contorts, and he's down, flat on his back. He drops his stick and lifts his gloved hands to his knee.

I gasp, shooting to my feet. "It's his knee," I say to Megan, but it's stupid to even say it out loud because *of course* it's his knee. Even someone who doesn't know his history would guess. Juno is in my arms now, and I clutch her against me as I watch the trainers gathering around Alec. The refs have stopped play, and his teammates are hovering nearby. Nathan is closest to him, and since I can't see Alec's face, I watch Nathan's, looking for any clues as to what's going on.

A minute later, Alec is lifted to his feet and Nathan and Van move in beside him, bracing him between them as they move off the ice.

"Okay, now I really do have to get to him," I say.

"I'll come too," Megan says. "*Can* we get to him? Will they let us back?"

I look over to Parker, who is still sitting on my other side. "I can get you downstairs, at least," she says. "But it'll be up to the medical staff to get you closer than that."

CHAPTER 26

EVIE

MEGAN'S PARENTS end up coming with us, so Parker leads all four of us into the lower levels of the Summit. Juno is front-facing in her sling by this point, something I'm grateful for because she is a very good security blanket. As long as I have to worry about her, I can't let my panic over Alec's injury consume me. The game is over by the time we make it downstairs, so when Parker takes us to a family room, where players can meet friends and loved ones after the game, it's already starting to fill up.

"Okay, Eric says you can come back," Parker says. She looks at the four of us. "Well, not all of you, probably."

Alec's mom steps up beside me. "Evie, honey, give me Juno, and you go be with Alec. We'll take the baby home and get her to bed so you can focus on him."

"And drive him home," Megan says. "If it's his knee, he might not be able to drive."

"Are you sure?" I say, my hands lifting to Juno's back. I

279

hate the thought of sending her home without me, but since I nursed her in between periods, she never used the bottle I packed. And there's a portable crib at Alec's that he purchased so she'd always have a place to nap at his house. There's no reason why Megan and her parents can't handle getting Juno to bed without me.

"We can totally handle it," Megan says. "Just promise you'll text me updates."

I unstrap Juno and kiss her on the forehead before handing her over to Alec's family. I give Megan my car keys, then I follow Parker down the hall to where a man in an Appies polo is waiting outside a room labeled *Medical Suite*.

"This is Eric, one of the Appies trainers," Parker says to me. "He'll help you from here."

I reach up and give her a quick hug of thanks before she disappears down the hall. Then I turn my full attention to Eric.

"He's totally fine," he says when we make eye contact. "Just a little grouchy."

I nod as I follow him into the suite. Alec is on a table in the middle of the room. In any other situation, I might flush to see Alec in nothing but a tiny pair of compression shorts, but given the moment, my eyes barely skate over the dips and curves of his muscles, only logging the many ways he's battered and broken.

His knee is propped up on the table, wrapped in ice, and the left side of his face is puffy and bruised to a mottled, deep blue, a line of stitches stretching downward through the center of the bruise. There's another grapefruit-sized bruise on his torso, this one wrapping around his ribs to his back.

My heart clenches at the sight of him like this. He's played a lot of games since we started officially dating, but I've never seen him this torn up.

Behind me, the door finally clicks shut, and Alec opens his eyes, noticing me for the first time. His expression shifts into something soft as he takes me in, then he lifts a hand, stretching it toward me in invitation.

I glance at Eric, who nods his permission, and I dart forward, slipping Alec's hand into mine.

"You're here," he says, giving my hand a quick squeeze.

"Of course I'm here." I lift his fingers to my lips and press a kiss against his knuckles.

"You're brave," he says. "I smell terrible."

"Like you just played a hockey game," I say, because he really does smell pungent. "But it's nothing I can't handle."

He leans his head back and closes his eyes. "Where's Juno?"

"Your family took her home," I say. "Which means you're my ride, so I hope you don't have big plans."

"Assuming I can even drive," he says with a slight edge to his voice.

I squeeze his fingers. "What happened?"

He tilts his head to look at me, lifting one arm and tucking it behind his head. "I heard a pop," he says. "The doctor's checking the x-ray now, but I'll need an MRI to really see what's going on."

There's a distance to his voice that worries me—like he's here, but he's not really *here*. Not that I would expect anything different when his entire career could be on the line.

There are so many things I want to know. How he's feeling. How long his recovery might be. If he'll need another surgery. If he's scared, frustrated, angry. I want to know if something happened before the game. Why he didn't start. Why he was skating like he was legitimately out for blood.

But I don't ask him any of those questions.

I doubt he's in the right headspace to answer me honestly, and we aren't alone anyway. Right now, my job is to just be here. Be whatever support he needs.

"You played quite a game out there," I say, and he huffs out a strangled laugh.

"A lot of good it did me."

"But it *did* do good. The Appies won, you had two assists, you were a machine—"

"Until I wasn't," he says sharply, cutting me off. "And now I'm out for how long? For surgery, recovery. And for what? To keep playing when every day, there are stronger, faster, *younger* players who deserve my spot on the team more than I do."

"Don't talk like that," I say gently. I lift my hand to the good side of his face. "You're such an asset to this team."

He closes his eyes, his jaw tensing. "But I'm not," he says. "Tonight, I played like I should always play, and my body couldn't handle it. *I* couldn't handle it."

"But it's not your fault. Your knee—"

"Evie," Alec says gently. He lifts his hand to mine, pressing a kiss to the center of my palm before tugging it away. He winces as he shifts and props himself up on his elbow. "Thank you for trying to make me feel better. But you have to leave this alone. Words can't fix it. Nothing can."

My heart squeezes, hating the pain etched along his brow, hating that I really *can't* take this away from him. "I know. I'm sorry. I wasn't trying to fix anything. It's just hard to see you hurting."

Eric returns and adjusts the ice packs on Alec's knee. When he pulls them away, the swelling and redness is visible even to my untrained eye.

"Listen," Alec says, reaching for my hand. "I still need to shower and talk to Dr. Samuelson, so I'm going to be a while.

If you find Nathan, he can get my keys for you. Just take my truck. I'll have one of the guys drive me home."

"I don't want to leave you here," I say, my words laced with a panic I wish I didn't feel. Logically, I know it's probably not helping him to have me hovering, worrying. But it doesn't feel right to just walk away either.

He squeezes my fingers, pulling them up to his lips. "I just have to figure this out," he says. "And you've got a lot to think about right now. With Thanksgiving and Megan visiting and Devon coming. I don't want you to get wrapped up in worrying about me."

I'm not sure what Alec is implying because none of those things he just mentioned are as important to me as he is. And one of them isn't an issue at all.

"Devon isn't coming," I hear myself say.

It's a *stupid* thing to say. Totally irrelevant to the moment. But my brain must have its own agenda because those are the words that come out of my mouth.

"What?" Alec says.

For the first time tonight, his eyes are locked on mine and he's fully present, concern etched in his expression.

"He's not coming," I repeat. "He's going to California instead."

Alec breathes out a sigh, then leans his head back, tilting his face away from me. "I'm really sorry, Evie," he says. "Juno deserves better." He winces and shifts one more time, letting out a low groan as he tries to readjust his knee. Just in the few minutes I've been standing here, it seems like his pain has gotten worse.

Before I can say anything else, the trainer, Eric, moves back into the room with an older man I assume is Dr. Samuelson. I take a few steps backward, making room for them, then move all the way to the door.

The doctor is talking to Alec now, but his back is to me, and he's talking quietly enough that I can't hear what he's saying.

I hate to leave, but it also doesn't feel right to stay. I watch as the doctor steps back, then all three men turn to look at me. Alec says something to Eric that I can't hear, then Eric nods before he walks toward me.

"Come on," he says. "I'll get his keys for you."

I cast one final glance at Alec, who is sitting up now, his attention focused on the doctor, then I turn and follow Eric into the hallway.

"You'll have to be patient with him," Eric says, as if sensing my disquietude. "He's in a lot of pain, but an injury like that is a pretty significant mental blow too."

"I'm sure." I swallow against the knot of emotion in my throat, wishing I could run back into the room and throw my arms around Alec, tell him he's going to be okay. That I'll make him okay just by sheer force of will. "Eric, will he ever play again?"

Eric frowns, glancing at the med suite door like he's considering how much he should say out loud. "We won't know anything for sure until after the MRI," he says, "but I doubt he'll be back on the ice anytime soon. With everything that knee has already been through..."

"Maybe not at all?" I finish for him.

He holds my gaze. "Either way, if he's rehabbing to come back or...dealing with early retirement, he's going to need a lot of support." He motions down the hall toward the family room. "If you want to wait in there, I'll bring you his keys. It'll just take a minute."

Gracie and Summer come over to greet me as soon as I step into the room. I give them both hugs and tell them what little I know about Alec's condition, but I'm too anxious to talk much beyond that. As soon as Eric shows up with Alec's keys, I say goodbye, promising to text updates, then make my way out to the player parking lot.

I sit behind the steering wheel in Alec's truck for a long moment, but I can't bring myself to start the engine. I know Alec told me to go, and maybe it was right for me to leave him to his doctor's care. But that doesn't mean I have to leave him altogether.

It's a risk. I don't want to be pushy. But I do want him to know he can count on me. That I'll listen whenever he's ready to talk.

Eventually, I start the truck, if only to keep warm. It's late November, and the temperature has to be close to forty degrees outside, but I stay warm enough with the heat on.

Eventually, the Appies players start to leave the Summit, one or two at a time as they head to their cars. Fans stand behind a barrier at the edge of the sidewalk, and a few of the guys go over to sign autographs and say hello. But as the flow of players leaving for the night slows and eventually stops, the fans give up, and they leave too.

I'm just starting to wonder if Alec left through a different door when he finally emerges from the Summit, flanked by Nathan and Felix with Theo and Carter directly behind them.

I quickly climb out of the truck, heart pounding in my chest, and stand outside the driver side door.

Alec's knee is braced, his gait stilted and slow, but he's at least walking on his own, which has to be a good sign. Nathan and Felix stay close to Alec, hovering like they're worried he might need steadying. Alec does okay until they reach the three steps that lead off the sidewalk into the parking lot. Here, he reaches for Felix's shoulder, using him as a crutch as he maneuvers his way down to flat ground.

As soon as they reach the pavement, Alec looks up and finally spots me standing beside his truck.

His expression softens as he slowly makes his way forward, his friends staying close until he's right in front of me.

"You've got him from here?" Nathan asks me, and I nod.

"We can help," Theo says, eyes on his captain. "Drive his truck. Whatever we need to do."

I hope Alec realizes that his friends are here because of how much he means to them. There are so many people in his life who will stand by him through this, no matter what happens.

Alec looks at me. "It's all right," he says without breaking eye contact. "Evie's got me." The twins nod and head to their truck parked on the other side of the lot.

"We'll see you at home," Carter calls.

Nathan and Felix leave next, but not before each of them moves up to Alec and gives him a hug. Not one of those half bro hug things guys do. *Real hugs.*

As soon as his friends have moved away, Alec closes the distance between us and melts into me, pulling me against his chest. I wrap my arms around his middle, bracing myself as some of his weight shifts onto me.

"You're still here," he says into my hair.

He's freshly showered, and he smells incredible, *familiar,* but I'm too distracted by the relief coursing through me to fully appreciate it. I rub my hands up and down his back. "Of course I'm still here. Would you have left *me?*"

He huffs out a laugh that I feel more than I hear, his chest lifting once. "Fair point," he says. When I look up and make eye contact, his lips lift the slightest bit. It's not quite a smile, but it's the closest thing I've seen tonight, so I'm calling it a win.

"I'm not going to make you talk about it," I say, holding his gaze. "Not tonight. Not unless you want to. I just wanted to be here."

He leans down and kisses me, warm and slow. "Thank you," he says softly.

He's quiet on the way home, leaning back in his seat, eyes closed, one hand lifted to his forehead. His jaw is clenched, and I wonder what kind of pain he must be in. He has to be medicated, but it doesn't look like it's doing him much good.

Because I told him I wouldn't, I don't ask him any more questions about how he's feeling, so we end up making the entire drive in silence.

Inside, Alec's parents have already gone to bed, and the rest of the house is dark. The light is on in the twins' room, but otherwise, there's no sign of anyone else being awake. I walk with Alec to his bedroom door. "I'm going to go check on Juno, then I'll come back and help you get settled."

I disappear before he can protest—because he might—and go in search of Megan.

She's sitting in the living room, reading by lamplight with Juno's baby monitor sitting on the side table beside her. She smiles when she sees me. "Hey! You're back! I tried to get my parents to stay up, thinking Alec might need the morale boost, but then I remembered they're actually grandparents and that might be elder abuse, so I let them go to bed."

"I think that's pretty much all Alec wants to do anyway. How's Juno?"

"Sound asleep," Megan says. "She drank her whole bottle and went straight to sleep like a champ."

"Perfect. Thank you for taking care of her."

"Do you want to just leave her here tonight? Her portable crib is in the guest room I picked for myself. She's welcome to stay in there with me."

I look at my watch. I hate to wake her up just to drive her home when she's already asleep. And she *has* been sleeping longer and longer lately. Now that she's had a bottle, she might even sleep through till morning. If she does, and I don't pump before then, I'll be miserable by the time she wakes up, but I don't have my pump with me, and I'd rather stay here and risk being uncomfortable than leave and have her wake up when I'm not here to feed her.

"If she stays, I stay," I say. "She might sleep all night, but she might not, and since she's out of bottles, I'm all she's got."

"Sleepover?" Megan asks, hope in her eyes. "Just like old times?"

"Fine. But I have to go check on Alec first."

I find him sitting on the edge of his bed, phone in his hand. He looks up as I enter the room and tosses the phone onto the comforter behind him. His injured knee is still braced, his leg extended out in front of him, but he makes room for me anyway, pulling me into the space between his knees so he can wrap his arms around me. He drops his head onto my chest, and I lift my hands to his hair, slowly massaging my fingers into his scalp.

"What do you need?" I ask. "Drugs? Water? Something to eat?"

"Just you," he says simply, and my heart squeezes in my chest.

"See, the trouble is, I'm not made of calories, and you just burned about a billion in your game. Let me fix you something to eat before you sleep."

His arms tighten around my waist. "I'm too full of painkillers to eat," he says. "I'll just have a big breakfast in the morning."

288

"Let me help you get settled, then." I take a step back and study him. "The brace stays on while you sleep?"

He nods. "But I can sleep in these." He pats the top of his thigh.

"Good. That's easy. Shoes off, then."

It takes a few more minutes of Alec begrudgingly allowing my assistance before his coat is off, his teeth are brushed, and he's finally situated in bed, his knee propped up on two extra pillows.

"I don't want to wake Juno this late, so I'm staying here tonight," I say. "I'll be here in the morning."

He reaches for my hand, tugging me closer, so I sit down on the edge of the bed beside him.

His thumb runs across the tops of my knuckles as he tucks my hand against his chest, then puts his own hand over mine, like he's holding me in place. "Stay with me?" he asks, his eyelids heavy, almost half-closed. "Just to sleep. I just...don't feel like being alone."

I lean down and kiss him because it feels impossible to do anything else. "Okay," I whisper against his lips. "Just give me a quick sec."

In a matter of minutes, I've found a pair of Alec's pajama bottoms to replace my jeans, washed my face with the hand soap in his bathroom—a decision I will possibly regret in the morning—and claimed a spare toothbrush from his bathroom drawer to brush my teeth.

Luckily, since it's Thanksgiving week and I knew Megan and her parents would be in town, Victoria isn't expecting me to work tomorrow, so staying over really shouldn't be a big deal. But since I left Megan with Juno's baby monitor and an expectation that I'd be sleeping upstairs in her room, I have to at least let her know my plans have changed.

> Slight change of plans. I'm staying with Alec tonight. If Juno wakes up, will you bring her to me?

MEGAN

> Sure. But if I walk into my brother's bedroom holding your baby and find you touching each other AT ALL, I might throw up in Juno's hair. Just remember that when you pick your spot on the bed.

EVIE

> Noted.

> Thanks for watching her for me.

MEGAN

> Thanks for watching out for Alec. I'm glad he has you.

"Who are you texting over there?" Alec asks.

"Just Megan," I say as I drop my phone on his nightstand. "She's got Juno in her room with her, but she says she'll bring her to me if she wakes up."

Alec lifts his arm in invitation, and I shimmy up the bed until I'm cradled in the curve of his shoulder, my head on his chest.

He lifts his head enough to kiss my forehead. "I'm sorry to make things harder on you," he says.

"Yeah, this is pretty horrible," I say, as I snuggle a little deeper into his mattress. "A real strain."

We've been quiet so long, I'm wondering if Alec has fallen asleep when his voice cuts through the stillness. "Can I make a confession?" he says, his voice barely above a whisper.

"Mmhmm," I say sleepily.

He takes a long, slow breath. "I'm really glad Devon isn't

coming for Thanksgiving. Is that bad? Because I'm also *sad* he isn't coming. At least for Juno. Does that make sense?"

I lift my head and prop my chin on his chest. A streetlight outside filters in through the blinds, making it just bright enough for me to see the outline of Alec's profile, but there's no way to see his expression.

"It makes sense," I say. "It's exactly how I feel too."

I drop my head again, nestling into Alec, and listen as his breathing slows and steadies.

I have a lot of things to be happy about right now. Megan and her parents are here. Juno is healthy and happy. Alec and I are together.

But ever since I read Devon's text, a knot of uncertainty has rooted itself into my gut. I don't want to live with a question mark hovering over us all the time. Will Devon come? Will he not? Will he finally decide to grace us with his presence? It's not fair to me, and it isn't fair to Juno, but it isn't fair to Alec either.

Devon shouldn't get to just show up when it's convenient for him and claim his place as Juno's father. Juno deserves a father *now*, one who knows how important she is.

Once I'm sure Alec is fully asleep, I push myself up and carefully reach across him to grab my phone from his nightstand, making sure not to touch one of the many places on his body where he's bruised.

With phone in hand, I lean back onto the pillows beside him and pull up Devon's text.

I take a steadying breath, then type out a reply I should have sent him a long time ago.

I can't live with the uncertainty of your involvement hovering over us. You're either here for her, engaged and present and connected, or you aren't. Juno doesn't need a father who only shows up when it's convenient. I won't put her through it, Dev. I won't let you break her heart. Please. Don't come. Not now. Not in a few weeks. Just let us move on.

CHAPTER 27

ALEC

I WISH I could say I was a charming and gracious host over the holidays.

Unfortunately for my family, I was nothing of the sort.

It started on Wednesday, the day after the game, when I had Nathan pick me up and drive me to the hospital for an MRI. I know it hurt Evie's feelings that I didn't want her to take me. But here's the thing about Evie.

She sees me.

From the very beginning of our relationship, she looked me right in the eye and told me I was more than a hockey player, that my value didn't just stem from my stats on the ice. I know she's right. *Of course* I know she's right. And I really do love her hope and optimism.

But I just wanted to be angry for a minute.

And Nathan was the one to let me do that.

The next few days went by in a similar haze of anger and frustration. A Thanksgiving meal I tried and failed to properly appreciate. A consultation with Dr. Samuelson and the best orthopedic surgeon in North Carolina. And then, the Friday after Thanksgiving, a surgery to repair both my ACL and my MCL, as well as a torn meniscus.

Now, two weeks post-surgery, the fog of my frustration has cleared enough for me to recognize a few things.

One, I don't deserve my family because they came all the way to North Carolina to see me, and I couldn't get out of my own head enough to appreciate and enjoy their visit.

Two, I definitely don't deserve Evie because she still hasn't given up on me, even though I've given her more than enough reason to do so.

And three. My knee is never going to be the same.

On the kitchen island in front of me sit two different plans for my physical therapy over the next three months.

One is designed to prepare me for hockey. I'd be out for the rest of this season, but with a lot of work through the off season, I could probably be back in commission by the start of next.

The other is designed to prepare me for life *after* hockey. And it's the one Dr. Samuelson thinks I should embrace.

I shift the individual sheets of paper forward and back on the cool countertop, staring at them until the words blur. Like this, it seems like such a simple choice. One plan or the other. Option A. Option B. But nothing about giving up hockey is simple.

Dr. Samuelson made it clear that even though the surgery was successful and it's probable I could rehabilitate to the point of being a sufficient player in the AHL, I will never play with the same speed and power I had before.

Meanwhile, the Appies are on a winning streak, in large part due to Theo and Carter, who are developing into truly outstanding defensemen.

I'm proud of them.

Most of the time.

But I don't love the idea of doing all the work of PT and rehabilitation just to play third line to a bunch of guys fifteen years my junior. There's something to be said for quitting while I'm still ahead.

"Morning, Captain," Theo says as he strolls into the kitchen. It's already two in the afternoon, but I don't correct him. They had an away game yesterday and drove home after. I doubt they were back at the Summit before three in the morning.

"Hey. Carter still sleeping?"

"I assume so," Theo says. "I haven't seen him."

After Evie and Juno moved out, freeing up the upstairs bedrooms, Theo and Carter moved out of the bonus room over the garage and claimed their own rooms. According to them, it's the first time in their lives they haven't been room-mates, so I'm sure they're loving having their own space.

"What are you looking at?" Theo asks. He pulls a bowl out of the cabinet, then rummages around in the pantry, emerging with a box of cereal.

"Plans for PT," I say, my eyes drifting back to the paper.

"Ah," Theo says. "A lot of guys are wondering what you're going to do."

I look up. "Yeah?"

He nods. "If you'll come back. You think you will?"

I blow out a breath. "That is the question."

He carries his cereal to a barstool at the opposite end of the island and sits down. "What does Evie think?"

The question sends a wave of uncomfortable guilt washing over me. I don't know what Evie thinks because I haven't talked to her about it.

We've talked about other things. A lot about Juno.

About her work. But whenever she tries to steer the conversation to hockey, I find a way to talk about something else.

I know she's frustrated with me. That she senses me shutting her down. Shutting her *out*. But I don't know how to stop. Whenever I think about walking away, figuring out a life that exists outside of the Appies organization, I'm filled with a cold sense of dread, a fear that I'll never be able to do anything else. I'm not worried as much about the financial piece of it. I've planned well and have decent savings. I just don't know what I'll do with myself.

"I don't know what Evie thinks," I finally answer. "I haven't talked to her about it."

Theo stares at me over his cereal bowl. "Why not?"

Because she'll tell me what I already know. She'll tell me it's okay to let myself walk away.

When I don't immediately answer, Theo shakes his head in disbelief. "I mean, if you..." His words cut off, like he's struggling to figure out what to say. Or maybe *how* to say it. "Can I just talk to you like you're my age for a second? Like you're not my team captain?"

I'm not, technically, his captain. Not anymore. The alternate captains have been rotating the position, but I appreciate Theo still offering me the respect.

"Go ahead," I say. "Say whatever you want."

He's quiet for a long moment before he says, "It's just a game."

I lift my eyebrows.

"If you come back, it'll be for, what, two, maybe three more seasons? Four, if you're lucky? But all of us will be done by the time we're forty," he continues. "Probably sooner. And then what?" He holds up a finger and points at me. "But see, you already figured out what comes next for you. You already have something else to live for." He shrugs. "Why not just go do that now?"

I already have something else to live for.

It's a very simple distillation, but it rings true in a way that nothing else I've thought over the past two weeks has.

"When's Juno's birthday?" Theo asks.

"What? Uh, late May, I think. The 29th."

"So right in the middle of playoffs. If you play four more seasons, she'll be five by the time you retire. Wonder how many of her birthdays you'd miss for games."

His words hit like a gut punch. Juno's little now, but she won't always be little. Eventually, she'll be old enough to have expectations, hopes. To look out the window and wonder if her dad will be home in time for her party.

It's exactly what Evie didn't want for her daughter. A dad who isn't around.

Theo stands and carries his empty bowl to the sink. He looks at me and grins. "That one got you, didn't it?"

I scowl. "What is that therapist teaching you?"

"The true meaning of life, Captain. And I have you to thank for that." He's halfway across the living room on his way to the stairs when he turns and adds, "Spoiler alert. The answer isn't hockey."

I make the fifteen-minute drive to Evie's house in just shy of eleven minutes only to arrive and realize it's not even three p.m. and she doesn't get off work until five.

I debate leaving and coming back, but then I look down and see Ruth's house and come up with a new plan instead. I park and climb out of my truck, taking it easy as I walk down the sidewalk to Ruth's. I can walk without crutches now, but my knee is still braced, so I have to keep all of my movements slow and intentional.

Before I knock on Ruth's door, I send Evie a quick text, not wanting to overstep or make assumptions when it comes to Juno.

> **ALEC**
> Hey. I've got a free afternoon. Can I go grab Juno early for you? I'll just hang out with her at your house until you get home.

> **EVIE**
> Of course! That actually works great—I was supposed to get her at four anyway because Ruth has an appointment, but I'm behind here, so leaving early was going to be tough.

> **ALEC**
> I'm on it. Take your time.

> **EVIE**
> Thank you!

Ruth answers the door on the first knock, Juno tucked into her hip. She smiles wide when she sees me.

"Hi, Ruth," I say. "I'm here to pick up Juno. Evie said you have an appointment."

Ruth glances at her watch. "Come on in," she says. "You're early, so I haven't packed up her stuff, but it should only take a minute."

She hands me Juno, then bustles around the room, adding diapers and bottles and jars of baby food into the bag.

"Is Juno eating solid food?" I ask.

"Just started," Ruth says. "So far, she loves the bananas but hates the peas."

Something like hurt tiptoes up my spine. Evie didn't tell me. Juno started solid food, and Evie didn't mention it.

It's not like I have a right to know. But before my injury, she was constantly sharing her notes about milestones, her debates about how long is too long and how soon is too soon. The fact that she hasn't shared this is on me.

Because I've been checked out. Wrapped up in feeling sorry for myself.

Once Juno's belongings are in her bag and she's bundled up for the short walk home, I thank Ruth and make my way up the hill to Evie's house.

It's not until we're inside and unpacked and sitting on Evie's couch that I realize all the times I've ever taken care of Juno, Evie has always been with me. But this time, I'm alone.

Ruth at least told me she just had a bottle, so she doesn't need to eat. Maybe we can just hang out? Roll around in circles?

I put Juno on the floor in front of me, flat on her back. "Okay, Juno. You want to roll?"

She stares up at me like I've completely lost my mind.

"Not in the mood for rolls, huh? Maybe we can watch some TV?"

I scoop Juno back up and settle on the couch, extending my braced knee so it's resting on the coffee table.

She rubs her eyes like she's sleepy, so I grab her pacifier, giving it to her before tucking her against my chest. To my surprise, she settles right down and eventually falls asleep.

I hold her for a long time, even after I know Evie would have insisted I move her to her crib. But sitting here with Juno, holding her like this, feels like the perfect time to be honest with myself.

It's time for my hockey career to end.

I wait for the wave of dread that's been chasing me all week, but with my hand on Juno's back, feeling the steady rise and fall of her breaths, the dread never comes.

I think I've known all along it was time to be done, even before my injury. I just wanted to believe I had more time. I was managing the pain, but managing the pain came at a cost, and when I pushed myself as hard as I should have been pushing, it was too much.

I can't keep doing that to my team. Make them accommodate, make up for my limitations.

Especially not when Theo was right.

I really do have something else worth living for.

After another few minutes, my knee starts to feel stiff, so I carefully stand and carry Juno back to her crib. When she's settled and quiet and I'm sure she isn't going to wake up, I head back to the living room where I spend a few minutes doing a few easy stretches to loosen up my knee.

It's almost five, which means Evie should be getting home any minute, so I sit back down and reach for the remote, hoping there's a hockey game on to help me pass the time. Not that I mind waiting. I owe Evie an apology and a long conversation. I'll wait all night if I have to.

Half an hour later, footsteps sound on the porch, and I sit up, turning off the TV as I do. I expect her to just walk in, but then someone knocks instead.

I stand and open the front door, finding a man I don't recognize on Evie's porch. He has dark hair, light eyes, and a mouth that looks familiar, though I can't immediately place where I've seen it before.

Until he smiles and holds out his hand.

That smile is *Juno's* smile.

Which means this guy is Evie's ex.

"Hey. You must be Alec. I'm Devon." He shoots me a devilish grin, eyebrows dancing. "Thanks for holding my spot for me."

300

CHAPTER 28

EVIE

IT'S ALMOST five-thirty when I finally pack up and leave Victoria's for the day. I never would have stayed so late had Alec not texted and told me he had Juno, but the timing couldn't have been more perfect.

This afternoon, Victoria and I finally added strings to the Georg Winterling. And because she is the most incredible boss on the entire planet, she let me be the one to give it a test run.

Or test *play*, in this case.

It sounded incredible. Amazing. Unlike any violin I've ever played before.

I can't wait to tell Alec about it. I can't wait to *see* Alec.

I've been worried about him the past couple of weeks. The days right around Thanksgiving and his surgery were admittedly terrible. Managing his pain, dealing with the frustration of not knowing what will happen next with hockey.

But things are slowly getting better. Luckily, it hasn't

been hard to be patient because even at his worst, Alec is never anything but sweet with me. But I can still tell he's put some walls up. He won't talk to me about hockey. He won't talk to me about his plans. About how he wants to handle his physical therapy. He just closes off and shuts down.

Still, I'm confident we'll get there.

I pull into my driveway, hopeful and anxious to see Alec, but then I freeze, hand still on the ignition, when I see a man sitting on my front porch.

I swear under my breath as I turn off the car, a riot of emotions at war in my chest.

I told Devon not to come. To leave us alone and let us be.

And he's here anyway. He has some nerve showing up like this, no text, no warning.

But *nerve* is pretty much Devon's trademark.

I sigh as I grab my purse off the front seat and slowly make my way up the front walk.

Devon stands as I approach. The porch light casts his face in shadows, but it's easy to see he's still the same Devon. Same charming smile. Same devil-may-care vibe.

I stop in front of him, arms folded over my chest. "Devon, I told you not to come."

"I know. You did. I'm sorry for just showing up like this. I should have let you know I was coming." He looks me up and down. "You look good, Evie. Back to your old self."

I'm nothing like my old self. Mostly because I see him for exactly who he is. He's saying all the right words, getting the apologies just right, because he *always* says all the right words. Especially when he wants something.

Which has to be my endgame here.

I have to figure out what he wants. What does *he* think he's going to get out of this visit?

If his motives are anything but sincere, I'll kick him back

to New York so fast his head will spin. I'm sure Alec would love to help me.

Oh gosh. Alec.

I look up the porch steps to the front door. "How long have you been here?" I ask Devon.

His jaw flexes, and a flash of uncertainty passes over his expression. "Not long. Twenty minutes or so. Your *boyfriend* refused to let me inside."

A million emotions pass through me at once. Gratitude for Alec, because I know he must have recognized I would want to introduce Juno to Devon on my own terms. Also worry for Alec, because I can only imagine what Devon said to him.

"I'm glad he refused," I say. "He knows this is my house. I'm the one who gets to decide how welcome you are."

"That's why I waited," Devon said. "I'm sorry for sounding so defensive. It's still hard for me to imagine you with someone else." He takes a step closer and reaches for my hand with a familiarity that makes my skin crawl.

I yank my hand back.

Devon slips his hands into his pockets, undeterred. "Can I come in, Evie? Can we have a real conversation?" He glances toward the house. "In private?"

I almost ask how he knows about me and Alec, but I haven't exactly kept it a secret. Even though Parker didn't post the thirst trap picture of Alec and Juno, she did post another of all three of us. After we walked through the party together, touching, kissing each other hello and goodbye, there was all kinds of online chatter about our relationship. At least according to Parker. I doubt very seriously that Devon follows the Appies, but someone in our shared circle probably does. It's easy to imagine a mutual friend finding out and giving him the heads up.

"Did you drive here, Devon?"

He shakes his head. "I got a rideshare from the airport."

I almost groan out loud because that does not make this situation easier. "Okay. Then, can you take a walk around the block for me? Just…give me a few minutes?"

"Evie, I've been sitting in the cold for almost an hour. It's forty degrees out here."

I love how his *twenty minutes* turned into an hour in the three minutes we've been standing here talking.

"Please, Devon? Or take my car. Go drive up and down Maple Street. It's pretty this time of year. The Christmas lights are up."

"Fine," he says through a grumble. "I'll go for a drive." He holds out his hand, and I give him my keys. I wait on the porch until he's backed out of the driveway, then I open the front door and step inside.

Alec is sitting in the living room, but he stands as soon as he sees me come in. "Are you okay?" he asks, moving toward me and pulling me into his arms. "What did he say to you? Is he still here?"

His hands slide up and down my arms like he's checking me over, making sure I'm whole and okay.

"I'm fine," I say. "He's going for a drive. But he'll be back in a few minutes."

Understanding passes over Alec's expression. "You had him leave so I would have time to go."

I sigh. "I don't want you to go. But I think it will be easier to have the conversation I need to have with him alone."

He runs a hand through his hair. "I'm sure you're right, even if I really don't like it." He huffs out a humorless laugh. "Do you know what he said to me when I opened the door?"

I cringe because I can only imagine what it was. "Tell me."

"He said, 'Hey man, I'm Devon. Nice to meet you. Thanks for holding my spot."

I gasp. "He did not."

"He did," Alec says. "And I didn't punch him."

"I kinda wish you had," I say.

It suddenly occurs to me that I haven't seen Juno yet. "Where's Juno?"

"Still sleeping," Alec says. "She fell asleep around four."

I nod. "Yikes. Okay. That means she'll probably wake up any minute." I groan. "I would really love for her to be asleep. At least until I figure out what he wants."

"Hey," Alec says, reaching out and putting his hands on my shoulders. "What if I just stay? I'll stay in Juno's room. Have a bottle at the ready. If she wakes up, I can feed her and keep her until you're ready for her."

My heart thumps against my ribs. This man is so good. *So. incredibly. good.*

"Why would you do that?" I ask. "When he was such a jerk to you, why would you—"

"Because I'm in love with you," he says, cutting me off.

I suck in a breath as his words land.

"Because I love you, and I'd rather be here supporting you than running away to prevent my own discomfort."

I lunge into him, wrapping my arms around his neck as I press my lips to his. "I love you too," I say. "So much." His arms loop around my waist, and I melt into his solid warmth, pressing into his chest as I kiss him again and again. "Juno started solid foods," I say in between kisses, and Alec chuckles.

"What?"

I lean back and look at him. "I didn't tell you because I was mad that you weren't talking to me about hockey. I

305

thought if you had secrets from me, then I should have secrets from you."

His expression softens. "I didn't have any secrets, Evie. I just didn't know what to do."

I bite my lip. "I know. I just wanted you to talk to me about it."

"I want to," he says. "I do. But probably not right now because Devon just pulled into your driveway."

I breathe out a sigh, glancing over my shoulder and out the front window. Sure enough, my car is back, and Devon is making his way up the front walk.

I turn back to Alec. "As much as I love that you offered, I really do think this conversation will be easier without you here. I need him to be honest with me, and I'm not sure he will be, even if you're in the other room."

He nods. "Okay. As long as you're sure you'll be okay."

"I will be."

Devon's knock sounds through the house.

"Will you come back?" I ask Alec.

"I will," he says, leaning down to press another kiss to my lips. "But I might be a minute. I think I need to go to the Summit."

"What? Why?" I ask as Devon knocks one more time.

"Because it's time for me to say goodbye."

———

I barely keep myself from giggling at the way Alec uses his looming height and broad shoulders to intimidate Devon as he passes him on the front porch. The man does *not* yield his space. He just walks straight forward, trusting that Devon will sidestep out of the way.

It was a territorial move, with more alpha energy than I've

ever seen from Alec before, and I'll be honest. I'm definitely a fan.

"Come on in," I say to Devon, pulling the door open and stepping to the side.

He steps into the living room and looks around. "Nice place."

"Thanks. It's perfect for us. More room than we had in Manhattan."

He chuckles. "That's not hard to do." He sits down on the far end of the couch, probably hoping I'll sit down next to him, but I pick the overstuffed chair I always sit in to nurse Juno. It has low arms, which makes it really comfortable, but right now I pick it simply because it puts me as far away from Devon as possible.

"So," he says, rubbing his hands over his thighs. "How have you been?"

"Good," I answer honestly. "Great, actually."

He tilts his head to the side, like he can't quite believe my answer. "Really?"

"Does that surprise you?" I ask.

He rubs a hand across his jaw, eyes down, and I get the distinct impression that he's considering his next move. Like this is a chess game, and he's trying to figure out how to get my pieces where he wants them. It's baffling to me how I never saw this before when it's so obvious to me now.

Devon stands and shifts to the other end of the couch so he's closer to me, then he leans forward, giving me a soft smile. "Look, I'm nervous about how this is going to come out, so I'm just going to say it. Spit it out and get it over with. Evie"—he clears his throat—"I miss you. I think I was premature in ending things the way I did."

The line is so far from what I expect, I choke on my own spit and spend the next thirty seconds coughing up my left

307

lung. When I finally regain my composure, I look at Devon and say, "I'm sorry, what?"

"I miss you, baby," he says, his words soft. "I miss *us*."

I narrow my eyes. It's not lost on me that so far, Devon hasn't said a single word about Juno. Hasn't asked where she is or if he can meet her.

"You miss *us*?" I ask because this man cannot be serious right now.

"We had some good times, Evie. You know we did."

I lift a hand and pinch the bridge of my nose. "Are you serious right now? You want to have this conversation without even mentioning your daughter's name? Without even asking about her?"

Devon seems to realize he's miscalculated because he leans back and taps his fingers on his thigh—a nervous tell I remember from when we were together. "I mean, obviously, if we were together, she would be around."

"She isn't a puppy, Devon. She won't just be *around*. She's your daughter—one you haven't even met—and she should have been the first thing you asked about when you walked through the front door."

"Even before you? I thought putting you first was the right call."

"Even before me," I say. "You and I are divorced. I'm not your concern anymore. But she should be. I thought that's why you were here. Why you were coming in the first place."

"I'm here for you," he says sharply, but I don't believe it even for a second. There's something else going on here. I just have to figure out what it is.

"What happened in California?" I ask.

He looks up and meets my gaze. "What?"

"You said something big could be happening. That's why you didn't come to Thanksgiving. What was it?"

He waves a dismissive hand. "It didn't pan out. I met a director. They went a different direction." He says this last part with so much condescension, I have to fight to control my eye roll.

"So you aren't working, then? You haven't worked since you lost your *Great Gatsby* role?"

"I didn't think you'd heard about that," he says, and the first crack in his very shiny exterior starts to show.

"Megan ran into Gina on campus," I say. "Gina told Megan, and Megan told me. Are you working anywhere else?" I repeat the question because I'm starting to get an inkling of what might be going on.

"I've done a few things. Contract work. I'm not sure why this matters right now."

"It matters if you need money," I say.

"You clearly don't," Devon mutters, and the final puzzle pieces of my theory click into place. I think back on the conversation I had with Devon's mother, Karen, just after Juno was born. She promised me she wouldn't leave me hanging, that she would help support me and Juno as long as I needed it. It's the only reason I haven't made a big deal out of Devon's lack of paying child support. I may not be getting it directly from Devon, but I'm getting it, and I respect Devon's mother too much to cause trouble just for the sake of causing trouble. I don't love Devon anymore, but she still does. And it was a big deal that she was willing to help when she had no obligation to do so.

But Karen was also generous with her support of Devon and me *before* Juno. When he was in between roles and our finances were tight, she'd send us a little cash to help us make rent or a grocery delivery when our pantry was a little too empty for comfort.

Maybe Karen decided she couldn't do both. She couldn't pay Devon's child support *and* pay to support Devon.

"Look," Devon says, leaning forward. "We both know my mother is the only reason you can be down here, living the life you want. I'm willing to overlook the fact that you've been dating someone else, but it's time for us to make things right, Evie. We can be a real family. The three of us."

"Or what?" I say. I feel the threat in his words even if he hasn't said anything explicit, but I'm too over him to let him get away with passive-aggressive implications.

His jaw tenses, and he lets out a derisive laugh. "Or maybe you won't be getting any more money from my mom."

"Is that a threat?" I say, my voice cold.

He rolls his eyes. "You can't think she likes that you're down here hooking up with a hockey player. Leaving her granddaughter alone with him—"

"Stop," I say, surprised by the coldness in my own voice. "Do not talk about him that way. Right now, he's the closest thing to a father that Juno has, and that's on you."

"So you get to have it all, then. Date the guy you want, live on my parent's dime, while I'm..." His words cut off, like he realizes he was about to say too much. He drops back onto the sofa with a huff.

Without saying another word, I stand and move to my purse and pull out my phone. I sit back down and dial Devon's mom. He looks at me, frowning as the phone rings.

When his mom answers the call, he rolls his eyes.

"Hi, Karen. How are you?" I ask.

"Good, dear. How are you? I loved the last pictures of Juno you sent."

"Good. I'm glad." I eye Devon. "Listen, I just wanted to make sure that I was being honest with you about every-thing. I really appreciate that you're lending your support while I'm doing my apprenticeship. It means so much to me, but I don't want you to think I'm taking advantage, so I want to be fully transparent and let you know that I'm dating someone."

"Oh, that's wonderful news," Karen says. "I'm so happy for you."

"Things are getting pretty serious, so if we end up getting married and my financial situation changes, I'd love to have a conversation with you about it."

Devon's muscles are tense, like he's just waiting for me to out him to his mom, but Karen's words are as gentle and loving as I expected them to be. "Oh, well, we can cross that bridge when we come to it. Maybe after, if you no longer need the help, we could start a trust for Juno. Save for her future education expenses."

"That would be amazing. And no matter what, Karen, you will always be a part of Juno's life. I promise."

"You can never have too many people loving you," Karen says. "That's what I always say."

"I absolutely agree. Listen, I've got to run, but maybe we can do a video call in the morning so you can say hi to Juno."

"Oh, I'd love that," she says, her voice full of a warmth and sincerity that I hope Devon hears all the way down to his bones. "We love you, Evie. Kiss Juno for me."

I hang up the call and look right at Devon. "I'm sorry, what were you saying about your mom?"

He frowns and scoffs, all the feigned affection from before, his talk of wanting to be a "real family" completely gone. But he's also lost his fight. I called his bluff and took away his leverage. He has nothing to hold over me now, and he knows it. "It's really great for you," he says, his words hollow. "That you've won my parents over and have their support. Meanwhile, I'm in New York, and they won't help

311

me with *anything*. I can't find work, I can't pay rent...you know how hard it is to live in that city, Evie. I'm drowning."

A tiny shred of compassion unfurls in my chest. I do know how hard it is to make it in New York. But it's not nearly enough to negate the *ick* of Devon coming down here in the first place, pretending to want a family just to have access to his mother's generosity.

"I want things to work out for you, Devon," I say. "I do. And I'm sorry you're struggling. But you can't use my heart as a pawn in whatever game you're playing. And you definitely can't use Juno's." I stand, making a decision I hope I won't regret. "Stay here a second," I say as I leave the room.

I cross through my kitchen and back to the bedrooms where I find Juno awake in her crib, feet kicking. She smiles when she sees me appear.

"Hi, baby girl," I say as I reach in and pick her up. I carry her back to the living room and sit down on the couch across from Devon, keeping Juno tucked onto my lap.

"She has your mouth," I say. "And my eyes. She loves bananas and sweet potatoes and pears and she gets really cranky when she's sleepy, but if there is anything exciting happening in the house, she does not want to miss it. She'll fight sleep for hours if she thinks she might miss the party."

Devon smiles. "Sounds like me."

I watch him for a long moment while he looks over at Juno, emotions playing over his face.

"She's the best thing I've ever done, Devon," I say softly. "The best thing *we've* ever done."

Juno squirms in my arms, wanting to stand, and I let her, her chubby legs bouncing as she lifts her hands to my face. I kiss her palm, and it makes her smile.

Devon lets out a little laugh. But then he's quiet for a

long moment before he finally says, "I'm not built for it, Evie. I know that makes me terrible. But...I'd just disappoint her."

A part of me wants to tell Devon to step up. To trust that any sacrifice he makes for Juno will feel worth it ten times over. No parent ever fully feels equipped. But you learn. You try. You figure it out as you go. But I know Devon too well. If I pushed him, he might try. But how long would it last?

That last sentence was probably the truest thing he's ever said to me. It's selfish and unfair and disappointing on several levels, but I don't want to put myself or Juno in a position where we'll ever be resented.

Devon glances down at his phone. "My ride is almost here."

So that's it, then. He doesn't want to hold her. Isn't moved by seeing her. He just...*isn't cut out for it.*

I wonder how long he would have lasted had I actually been willing to take him back.

A car horn sounds outside, and Devon stands. "So Alec— he's Megan's older brother?" he says as he moves toward the door.

I follow behind him, Juno propped on my hip. "Yeah."

"Isn't he like...ten years older than us?"

"Nine years," I correct.

Devon nods. "I thought he might break me in half."

I fight a smile, though I'm not sad about the imagery that pops into my brain. "He probably wanted to."

He swallows, Adam's apple bobbing in his throat, and I recognize the effort he's making here. I have to at least give him credit for that. "He's good with her?" he asks. "He'll be a good dad?"

My heart squeezes in my chest as I think about Alec and how gentle he is with Juno. How invested he is in making

313

sure we're both happy. "Yeah. He definitely will be. He already is."

Devon lifts a hand like he's going to brush it over Juno's hair, but then he seems to change his mind, letting his hand fall back to his side.

"I'm sorry," he says simply. The words are soft, almost too soft for me to hear. I can't even begin to categorize the many, *many* things he could be apologizing for, but I'm not sure I actually want to.

I'm ready to move on from this part of my life. No anger. No animosity.

"I know you are," I say. And then I watch him climb into a car and drive out of my life for good.

———————

I sit in my quiet living room for a long time thinking about what happened. Considering the fact that Devon came down here to lie, to try to manipulate me into a relationship just to get access to his mother's money, I was probably too kind. But he's the one who has to live with himself for trying something so low.

And I really don't want to carry around bitterness and animosity toward him. Not anymore.

It helps that I have the love of a man who is Devon's polar opposite.

A man I wish would hurry along whatever it is he's doing, because I have a desperate need to be in his arms, safe and whole and fully, unquestionably happy.

Except...*wait.*

He said he was going to the Summit to say goodbye.

I was so distracted by Devon's knocking that I didn't even process what that means.

314

Alec is done playing hockey.

I reach for my phone, tapping it against my palm as I debate what to do.

Alec has his location shared with me, so I pull it up and check. Sure enough, he's still at the Summit. Two weeks post-surgery, I know he's not skating. Is he just sitting? Alone?

He's probably fine if he is, but when an idea pops into my head, I cross my fingers and run with it, hoping against hope that I'm making the right call.

CHAPTER 29

ALEC

WHEN I HEAR a door open somewhere behind me in the upper seats of the Summit, I don't turn around. I'm sure it's Evie. She's the only person who knows I'm here.

But it isn't Evie.

It's Nathan.

He doesn't say a word, just files into the row I'm occupying and sits down.

Footsteps echo on the other side of me, and I spin to see Eli moving in on the other side, followed by Felix and Camden. When I look back at Nathan, Van and Logan are sitting down on his opposite side.

Nobody says anything. They just sit and look down at the ice, just like I've been for the last two hours.

A surge of emotion makes my chest tight.

My team. *My brothers.* I didn't know how much I wanted them to be here until they showed up.

I lean forward and prop my elbows on my knees. The rink

lights are on, thanks to Javi, the facilities manager who let me into the Summit earlier, and the ice is pristine and smooth. I don't often see it from this angle, and it's a beautiful sight.

Nathan drops a hand onto my back. "It looks good from up here."

"Yeah, it does," I agree.

Another few moments pass before Eli clears his throat. "So, my mom just had a really bad flare up and we aren't sure why. The past few days have included a lot of doctor's appointments, but no real answers. It's wearing on all of us."

"Sorry, man," Camden says, and a few guys nod their support.

Nathan leans forward. "Uh, Blake just busted up his shoulder playing flag football," he says, talking about his little brother, who is a top draft prospect for the NHL. "He'll be out for six weeks, and he's beating himself up for it, worried it's going to impact his prospects. It sucks, because it actually might."

"Nah, he'll be all right," Logan says, reaching over to give Nathan a good-natured punch in the arm. "His stats are too good."

"My father-in-law still hates me," Van says, and we all chuckle.

"Coach does not hate you," Eli says.

"Then why do his eyes frown every time he looks at me?" Van asks.

"His eyes frown?" I ask, and Van sits up, mimicking Coach Davis's favorite expression, brows furrowed, lips pursed. I roll my eyes. "He looks at all of us like that," I say. Except, Coach won't look at *me* like that anymore. Van must sense my thoughts, because he reaches behind Nathan and gives my shoulder a squeeze.

318

Nathan lifts a thumb and points it at Camden. "Pretty sure this guy is still heartbroken."

"I'm not heartbroken," Camden says.

"Yeah, you are," the rest of us all say in unison.

Camden mumbles something under his breath, then a few beats of silence pass before Felix clears his throat.

"Gracie and I have been trying for a baby," he says. "It's only been a few months, which, I realize isn't that long, but we keep striking out, and Gracie is really focused, and it's making sex feel weird and a little like work."

"That's rough, man," Eli says.

A few other guys echo Eli's comment, and Camden reaches over and claps Felix on the back.

"Okay, if I say this out loud," Logan says, "you have to swear you'll never say anything to Parker."

We all sit up a little taller and look toward Logan.

His jaw tenses before he finally admits, "Please don't tell Parker, but I really, *really* hate the color pink."

We all laugh, and a little more of the tension in my shoulders drains away.

"Dude, why do you keep buying her so much pink stuff?" Van asks.

"Because *she* loves it," Logan says. "That's all the reason I need."

I know what my teammates are doing. Normalizing the struggle. Being vulnerable with me so that if I need to, I can do the same thing with them.

Nathan nudges my leg with his. "Come on, man. You're up."

I take a long, slow breath, then finally say, "Evie's ex showed up at her house tonight, and I made him sit outside in the cold for half an hour while we waited for Evie to get home."

319

Nathan scoffs. "If anybody deserved it, he did."

"Also," I say, hating that I finally have to say these words to my teammates. "I'm never going to play hockey again."

For a long moment, nobody says a word. It's not like I expected my teammates to be anything but supportive. But it still feels like I'm failing somehow. Like if I'd just played a little differently that last game, taken care of myself a little better, maybe my knee could have made it a few more seasons.

"Hey, do you guys remember that time Alec scored a hat trick?" Van asks. "Three goals from a defenseman. How often does that ever happen?"

Nathan chuckles. "He was on fire that night."

"Remember when we accidentally left him sleeping on the bus in Chicago, and when he finally woke up, he had to climb the bus lot fence and hitchhike to the arena?"

"That was crazy," I say. "I was so late to the game, I missed warmups."

"Coach was totally freaking out," Van says, and I wonder if he's finding particular satisfaction in remembering his father-in-law so close to unraveling.

"What about the time he broke that guy's nose?" Logan said. "Was that last season?"

"It was the only fight he ever started," Nathan says.

"What did that guy even do?" Eli asks.

"He made fun of Felix," I say. "And he pissed me off."

"Really?" Felix asks. "Your only fight was over me?"

"A man's gotta protect his goalie," I say.

A general murmur of assent moves down the line, then we're quiet again. The silence feels good this time. Better than it did before when the weight of my confession was still pressing down on me.

"It was a good run, Cap," Felix says.

"Yeah, it was," Eli adds.

"The team isn't the same without you," Logan says.

Van nods his head in agreement. "It never will be."

"Best defensive partner I've ever played with," Nathan adds.

I look down the row when I hear the clink of glass. Camden is passing out bottles of my favorite Dark Horse Brewery IPA. When everyone has a beer, he lifts his and points it toward me. "To Captain."

The toast is echoed down the line from these men, these teammates who have meant more to me over the past few years than anyone in the world.

I came to the Summit to say goodbye, and I did, in my own way, before they showed up. But having them beside me has made something that was mostly just bitter feel bittersweet.

It *has* been a good run. Because every day that I've spent on the ice, these men have been beside me.

"Did you really make her ex sit outside?" Van asks after a long swig of beer. "It's December, man. That's cold."

"Literally," Camden adds.

"The guy knocked on Evie's door, looked me dead in the eye and said, 'Thanks for saving my spot.'"

A chorus of *ohhhs* sounds down the row.

"See? I was totally justified."

"What did he want?" Eli asks.

"No clue," I say. "To meet his kid, probably. For all I know, he's still there."

"He's not," Nathan says. "He's gone."

I sit up and look toward Nathan. "You talked to Evie?"

He eyes me. "I mean, we're here. She was the one who suggested we come."

I sink back into my seat.

Of course this was her doing. I shouldn't be surprised. One of the things I love about Evie is her emotional IQ. She's always been good at reading me. At sensing what I need, sometimes before I realize I need it myself.

A sudden restless energy pulses through me. It's late. Already after ten, and Evie has to work in the morning. But I need to see her. Talk to her. Make sure she's okay after talking to Devon.

"I think I need to go," I say, my fingers drumming on my thigh. I look around at my friends. "I should, right?"

"Yes!" they all say at once.

I stand and look back at the six of them one last time.

"Thanks, guys," I say. I can only hope they understand the true depth of my gratitude.

"Get your ugly face out of here," Felix says, and I smile.

Then I turn and leave the arena as quickly as my knee will allow.

CHAPTER 30

ALEC

EVIE'S PORCH light is still on when I pull into her driveway, and there's a light on in the living room. I told her I'd come back, so I skip knocking and just use the lock code to let myself in. I leave my shoes at the door and tiptoe into the living room.

Evie is stretched out on the couch. Her glasses are on, and a book is resting open on her chest. She looks so incredibly beautiful, and I take a minute to just look at her.

Somehow, over the past couple of months, this woman has worked her way into my heart, and I don't have a single doubt in my mind.

From now on, I'm living for her.

For us.

I kneel beside Evie on my good knee and lift a hand to her face. She leans into the touch, then her eyes slowly flutter open.

"Hey," I whisper, and she smiles.

"You're here."

"Sorry it took me so long."

She sits up, shifting to the side to make room for me. It's a tight fit, squeezing my six-feet-three inches onto her couch, but having her nestled against me is worth a little discomfort.

Once we're settled, her head resting on my chest and my arms wrapped around her back, Evie asks, "Are you okay?"

"Yeah," I say softly. "I'm really good, actually."

She takes a deep breath and relaxes into me. "I'm so glad." We settle into a peaceful silence for a few moments. I have more to say, but now that we're together, Evie in my arms, I want a second to just savor being with her. Holding her like this.

Eventually, Evie lifts her head, propping it on my chest so she can look at me. "I have to show you something."

My arms tighten around her. "Don't get up."

She leans up and kisses me. "I'll be quick."

She climbs over me and disappears into the back of the house, returning a few moments later with a notebook in her hands. I sit up, swinging my legs over to sit normally, and she plops down beside me.

"I found this when I was unpacking," she says. "It's my journal from my freshman year of high school." She reaches over and flips to the back few pages. "I won't put you through the agony of reading the entire thing—I was a tiny bit dramatic when I was fourteen—but I do think you'll get a kick out of this."

Scribbled on the inside back cover of the journal are at least a dozen different variations of the name *Evie Sheridan*.

I lift my eyebrows. Megan mentioned once that Evie had a crush on me growing up, but I never gave it much thought. It hits differently to see actual evidence of it. I lift my hand and run a finger over the largest, swirliest signature, then grin at Evie.

"I mean, it has a nice ring to it," I say, and Evie chuckles.

"I never thought it would actually be my reality," she says, her expression turning serious. "And even though Devon put me through so much heartbreak, I can't regret him. One, because he gave me Juno, and two, because that heartbreak led me to you."

I run a hand over my face. "Are you okay? After his visit? Did he upset you at all?"

She smiles, her expression serene enough that I know she's telling me the truth when she says, "He really didn't, actually. But also, he isn't going to be a part of our lives."

I don't miss the way she says *our lives*.

She gives me a condensed version of Devon's visit. His hope to get back together. His less-than-pure motives. Her insistence that he at least look at Juno. He earns back a tiny shred of respect when Evie mentions that he asked about me, hoped I would be a good father to Juno, but I can't say I'm sad the guy won't be around.

And maybe it's selfish to think it, but I'm glad I'll get to be the only father Juno knows.

At least, I hope I will be.

I look at the notebook for a long time, at the evidence of a future I never dreamed of but now can't imagine living without. Eventually, she tugs the notebook out of my hands and climbs onto my lap. I slide my hands up to her hips and give them a squeeze. "Thank you for sending my teammates to the Summit."

Her expression softens. "Did I guess right? That when you said you were saying goodbye, that means no more hockey?"

I nod. "No more hockey."

"Are you feeling okay? About retiring?"

"Better than I was, for sure," I say. "Thanks to you."

She leans down and kisses me, and I'm tempted to give in, forget about words and surrender to the taste of her, the weight of her body as she leans against me. But there's one more thing I need to say, so I pull back, lifting my hands to her face and gently pushing her back. "I have to say one more thing."

"Okay," she says, curiosity filling her big blue eyes.

"I just..." I lick my lips. "Evie, I want to be Juno's dad. And I know it's early still, and I don't want to pressure you or rush into things. But I want you to know that's where I see this going. I'm all in here, all right? With you. But with her too. And not just because of you. It's not like I see her as necessary because you guys are a package deal. I really want to be a father. I want to be *her* father."

Tears well in Evie's eyes. "I would really love that," she says. "It's what I want too."

I grin. "Okay. Now you can kiss me."

She does kiss me. That night, and the next morning, and every day after that.

She kisses me the day I go in to talk to the Appies management and let them know my knee is never going to let me play professional hockey again, and I'm finally ready to own that truth.

She kisses me the day of her first symphony concert with the Harvest Hollow Symphony, in which she plays the very rare and apparently expensive violin she and Victoria took months to painstakingly restore.

She kisses me on the day we both take an emergency trip to New York when my dad scares us all by having a stroke. And when we learn the stroke was mild, and the most he'll endure is a few missed pickleball tournaments.

And she kisses me when, after my retirement from the Appies is official, I offer to take over Juno's full-time childcare.

Best full-time gig I've ever had, honestly. It means I'm with Juno when she takes her first steps and says her first word. It is *not* Dada, much to my disappointment, but it *is* puck, which, despite Evie's protests, I think is almost as good. Though, having your baby girl saying *puck, puck, puck, puck, puck* while you walk through the grocery store does tend to turn a few heads.

Lucky for me, Evie also kisses me when I screw up. Turns out, I'm not always perfect at this whole relationship thing, no matter how hard I try. But Evie has had her own share of missteps too.

Even though loving each other is mostly amazing, I'm not going to lie and say it isn't punctuated with short bursts of intensity, of arguments and sadness, even disappointment. But those moments just serve as reminders to focus, to connect, to look at each other and remember that what we have with each other is worth it.

And it *is* worth it.

When I look at my girls, with their matching blue eyes and big smiles, when I think of everything we've been through, of how good it feels to love them, I don't have a single doubt in the world.

EPILOGUE

EVIE

THE ENERGY in the Summit is absolutely electric. Even though the season is technically over, the Appies just won the Calder Cup for the second year running, and tonight, they're having a celebration in their home arena. It's a tribute to their fans and, much to my delight, to their former captain. They're retiring Alec's jersey number as part of tonight's proceedings, honoring him in a way that has already moved my tender-hearted boyfriend to tears more than once.

And it hasn't even happened yet.

Alec has been at the Summit all day, doing who knows what with the rest of the team, so I'm only with Megan when I arrive at the arena. After a long debate with Alec, I decided to leave my very squirmy thirteen-month-old with Ruth for the night. I would love to have her here with me, but she just started walking and is basically trouble on legs. Two *adorably*

329

squishy legs. But still. I'd rather not miss half the event because I'm chasing her up and down the arena stairs.

Unfortunately, after his dad's stroke, Alec's parents weren't able to make the trip to be here with us. But Parker promised me the entire thing would be live-streamed on the Appies' social media platforms, and my little brother Brady agreed to drive over to their retirement villa in White Plains to make sure the tech part of participating didn't overwhelm them.

He already checked in and gave me a thumbs up that all is set and ready to stream.

My family will also be watching, which makes my heart happy, even if I do wish they could be here in person. They'd initially planned to make the trip, but since Alec and I were just in New York for Brady's high school graduation, they decided to save their travel points and come back this summer when they can stay for a couple of weeks and really enjoy the mountains.

Parker meets the three of us at the VIP entrance to tonight's event with a huge smile on her face. "Hi. Are you excited? I'm so excited!" She squeezes my hands. "I'm so glad you're here."

I'm not even a little surprised to see Parker so out of her mind with excitement. This is exactly the kind of thing her social-media savvy brain loves. She talks the entire time she's walking with us to the seating she has reserved just for us, hinting at the many things the evening will include. Some sort of special shoot-out. A Texas-themed performance from Carter and Theo I can't wait to see. And lots of audience-participation things I'm sure the fans are going to love.

"So the jersey retirement ceremony is happening at the end of the night," Parker says when we finally reach our seats. "And that's when you two need to be down on the ice with Alec. When you see the Summit staff rolling out the walkway to cover the ice, that's your cue to move. Got it?"

We nod in unison, and Parker smiles. "Good," she says. But then she gets this weird look on her face, like she's fighting back emotion before she adds, "I'm so excited for you guys, Evie. It's going to be so great."

Nerves coil in my belly as Parker turns and leaves. *What* is going to be so great? The jersey retirement? Or...does Parker know something I don't?

Megan must be asking herself the same question because as soon as Parker is out of earshot, she turns and grips my arm. "Evie, do you think Alec is going to propose tonight?"

I bite my lip as my eyes dart around the arena. He *might* propose. Our relationship has definitely progressed to the point where it wouldn't surprise me. We talk about Juno like she's ours, I refer to him as her dad whenever we're out and about and we meet new people. And Alec is constantly trying to get her to say *Dada*. At this point, an actual proposal will feel more like a formality. We both know this is the future we want. The *family* we want.

Still. My romantic heart has been excited about the actual event. Anticipating when and how Alec might ask.

A tiny thread of disappointment unfurls in my chest. I'm not sure the Summit and a sea of hockey fans is the location I would have picked.

"Hey," Megan says when I don't answer. "Are you disappointed? What's with the face?" She frowns. "Oh gosh. Please tell me you'll say yes if he asks."

"What? Of course I'll say yes. Are you crazy? I just... never thought he'd go for a big public proposal." As much as Alec shines in the spotlight, as good as he is at talking to people, our relationship has always been something we've kept private. Partly because of Juno. Alec has a *big* online following, and we decided to be very intentional about how much of our personal lives we share in his feed. But also because this thing we've built together has just felt so special, I think we've both had the impulse to hold it close. Cherish the magic of it without really needing it to be a big thing we celebrate with *everyone*.

At least, I thought that's how we both felt.

Megan loops her arm through mine. "Come on. Don't stress. Just trust him. He loves you, and he knows you. I'm sure whatever happens tonight, it's going to be amazing."

And it *is* amazing. Entertaining and hilarious and a true celebration of the magic that is the Appies. The team really is special, largely because of the relationship they have with their fans, and everything about tonight is geared to celebrate that support. Like one giant hockey-themed thank-you card. Alec is dressed out with his team, and it feels good to see him in uniform one last time. He looks so happy, his smile wide as he interacts with teammates and fans.

Finally, it's time for the jersey retirement ceremony. When members of the Summit staff start rolling out the walkway Parker mentioned, Megan and I jump up from our seats. Parker is waiting for us as soon as we step into the concourse, and she hurries us down to the tunnel, where we find Alec already waiting. He's changed out of his Appies uniform and is wearing my favorite of his gameday suits— navy blue with a pale pink pinstripe—and he looks good enough to make me cry. There's a band around his arm, marked with a Captain's C and his jersey number, forty-four.

I step up beside him and slip my hand into his, reminding myself that this moment is about him, and if he does propose at some point in the next half hour, I will be happy about it, and I will say yes.

"Hi," I say as I squeeze his fingers. "Fancy seeing you here."

He looks down at me and smiles. "Hi," he says, but then his eyes narrow as he studies me. "What's wrong? Why do you look nervous?"

I scoff. "What? I'm not nervous. I'm totally fine."

He looks over at Megan, who is standing on his other side. "Why is she nervous?"

Megan grimaces in my direction, then, like the total traitor she is, says, "Because Parker made it seem like there was something big happening tonight, besides all this jersey stuff, and Evie is worried you're going to propose in front of all these people."

If I could shoot actual daggers out of my eyes at Megan, I would, but when I look up at Alec, he only looks amused.

"It would be totally fine if you *did* propose," I say, suddenly feeling *very* sheepish. "If that's the plan."

He lifts his hands to my shoulders, giving them a gentle squeeze. "Have you no faith in me?"

I breathe out a sigh of relief. "So that *isn't* the plan?"

"I mean, not in the next half hour. What I'm planning in the future is an entirely different story, but don't think I'm giving you any spoilers."

I bite my lip, suddenly feeling so overwhelmingly proud to be standing next to him. I lean up and kiss him softly. "I really love you. And I'm so, so proud of you."

Seconds later, the event announcer calls Alec's name, and the three of us walk onto the ice to an eruption of cheers and applause. Alec waves to the crowd, then we stand in a small line in the center of the arena, and the entire Appies team moves into a line behind us. They tap their sticks on the ground as the cheers around the arena grow louder and louder. I'm suddenly extra glad I didn't bring Juno with me tonight, and not just because the noise would overwhelm her. Mostly, I'm just glad that right now, I get to watch Alec's face as he takes in the crowd. As he hears them cheer.

Finally, the lights in the arena dim, and a video compilation of all of Alec's best moments on the ice plays on the jumbotron. By the time it finishes, all three of us are crying, some more stoically than others.

The tears continue as Coach Davis and several of Alec's teammates pass around a microphone to pay tribute. Some comments are funny, some are a little more serious, but all demonstrate just how much Alec means to the Appies organization.

When Theo takes the microphone, I'm not sure exactly what to expect. But then he runs a hand through his hair and looks right at Alec. "When I first came to the Appies," he says, "I was already a pretty good defender. But that's about all I had going for me. In every other way, I was lost. Until my captain found me. Thanks, man."

It's the simplest tribute, but if the tears in Alec's eyes are any indication, it's the one that impacts him the most. At the end of the ceremony, we all watch as Alec's jersey is lifted into the rafters of the Summit, guaranteeing that no other Appie will ever wear the number forty-four.

After lots of hugs and handshakes and interviews and photo ops, Alec makes Megan drive my car back to his house so he can drive me home, just the two of us.

"You realize you're stranding yourself at my house, right?" I ask.

He only grins. "I did think of that."

I narrow my eyes, noticing the gleam in his expression. Something is happening here. Something more than just Alec driving me home.

"What's happening?" I ask, and Alec grins as he slows his truck to a stop.

"Close your eyes for me?" he asks.

"Why are we stopped a block away from my house?"

"Evie," Alec says, a smile in his voice. "Just close them. I promise it'll be worth it."

I breathe out an exaggerated sigh. "Fine, fine. They're closed!"

"You aren't peeking?"

"If you didn't want me to peek, you should have gotten a blindfold."

"Excuse me for being slightly preoccupied by everything else that was happening tonight," he says dryly. "Please? No peeking."

I turn my head to face him, eyes squeezed shut. "No peeking. I promise."

"Okay. Give me just a second," he says.

The truck starts moving again, and we drive for a few seconds before he makes a turn and parks in what I'm guessing is my driveway, but with my eyes closed, I can't actually be sure.

"Don't move," he says before jumping out. Seconds later, my door opens, and his hand slips around my waist. "Okay. Just hang onto me."

I do just that as he leads me over grass, the sidewalk, then finally up a set of steps. "Is this my house?" I ask.

"No questions," Alec says.

A light spring breeze brushes across my face, and the wind chimes hanging by my door play their familiar song. "It *is* my house!" I say.

"Just a few more steps," he says as I awkwardly shuffle behind him. "Okay, now sit."

I do as he asks, and then...I'm swinging.

My eyes pop open.

I'm on a porch swing…on my own front porch.

Alec sits down beside me. "Remember when you first moved in?" he asks. "You mentioned the house had a porch swing in all the pictures. You were sad it didn't have one."

"You remembered that?" I say. "I barely remember that."

"I decided right then I'd get you one." He gives me a sheepish grin. "I just had to wait until it wouldn't scare you off."

"You wouldn't have scared me off with a porch swing," I say. "Never."

"I don't know. Felt like a pretty big gesture for a first date."

I roll my eyes. "I was so far gone for you by date one, I promise it wouldn't have mattered."

He picks up my hand and tugs me closer, wrapping an arm around my shoulder as we gently swing forward, then back.

"What about an engagement ring?" he says gently. "Would I scare you off with that?"

I sit up, flailing with the motion of the swing and practically dumping myself out. As soon as I'm steady, thanks to Alec putting down his feet and holding us stationary, I fix him with my most intimidating look. "Alec Sheridan, so help me, if you are only proposing right now because of what happened at the Summit, I will…" My words trail off because I have no idea what I will do. "I don't know," I finally finish. "But it won't be good."

He grins. "I swear on my retired jersey number that I was always planning on proposing tonight."

I bite my lip. "Really?"

He nods. "I've had the ring in my suit pocket all night long."

"And you were never planning on asking me during the ceremony?"

"Absolutely not," he says. "Though I do know what Parker was thinking of if she made you think something big was happening."

"Really?"

He nods. "It's a job. The Appies want to hire me as a player development coordinator."

My eyes widen. "Really?"

"I would mostly be focused on helping players transition into professional hockey, filling the gaps in their training both on and off the ice."

"So, just like what you did for Theo and Carter."

"Partly. And more stuff too. The best news is I wouldn't have to travel with the team. So my schedule would be a lot more flexible than it was when I was playing. Assuming I actually take the job."

I lean forward and press a quick kiss to his lips. "Why wouldn't you take it?"

"Because I wouldn't be able to keep Juno," he says.

"Okay, but...do you *want* to do it? Would it make you happy?"

He shrugs. "Probably, yeah. But that's not the only part of the equation here. I like Juno being with one of us. And I love her being with me. When I think about the time I'd miss out on, that just makes me sad."

He has no idea how much it means that we're even having this conversation. That he's giving our daughter's needs equal weight against his career goals.

"Alec," I say, a surge of love for this man pushing against my ribs. "We can figure out the childcare stuff. But remember, once we get married, you won't just be with Juno during the day. We'll be together all the time. Nights, weekends. Whenever you aren't working. We'll be a family."

He closes his eyes for a brief second, then leans forward and kisses me. "I really like the sound of that."

"Besides, my apprenticeship is over in July, and then everything will shift for me. I have no idea if Victoria will even offer me a job. Maybe I'll be home with Juno for a while. I would love that, actually."

His expression turns thoughtful. "I bet the Appies would give me flexible hours at least through July. Something part-time, so Juno wouldn't have to be with Ruth five days a week."

I grin. "I love that you're thinking like this. And we can absolutely sort out all the details. But can we go back to talking about the ring that you're hiding on your person somewhere? Because I am seconds away from going on a scavenger hunt to find it."

"A scavenger hunt?" Alec says, eyes dancing. "That actu-ally sounds like a good idea."

It's possible I take an intentionally long time exploring Alec's body in search of pockets. You'd think I have zero clue how suits are constructed based on my search across biceps and abdominal muscles, glutes and thighs. But how else can I make sure he doesn't have a secret ring-concealing pocket stitched on somewhere?

"You're killing me here, Evie," Alec finally says.

With one final smirk, I dip my hand into his left pants pocket, the only one I haven't yet searched, and pull out a tiny velvet bag. Alec drops to one knee—the good one—in front of the porch swing, then tugs the bag from my hands and pulls out the ring.

"Promise me you'll tell me if you don't like it," he says.

"Megan helped me pick it out, and she swore you would, but I want it to be perfect, so if it isn't, just tell me."

I force myself to ignore the fact that Megan already *knew* he was planning to propose when she pulled that little stunt at the Summit because the ring is right in front of me, and it really *is* perfect. If that's because of her influence, I can absolutely forgive her.

I hold out my hand and let Alec slide the ring onto my finger.

"Marry me, Evie?" he says simply. "I can't think of anything I want more than to be your husband and Juno's dad."

I pull him to his feet and kiss him long and slow before murmuring a quiet yes into his ear.

If I could go back and tell fourteen-year-old Evie Thomas that all those scribbles in her journal were more prophecy than daydream, I think she'd probably laugh.

Alec Sheridan. Her best friend's much older, far too sexy, much too perfect brother? *Never.*

But maybe it's better that I had no idea what was coming. Half the magic of falling in love with Alec was how unbelievable it all seemed. How perfectly improbable.

I expect that at some point, I'll grow used to this new reality in which I get to love someone so good and honest and lovely. But a part of me hopes I never do. I hope I spend every day feeling a little hint of the marvel. That I never stop seeing the magic of Alec Sheridan.

"You know," I say, after a kiss that almost unravels me, "we should probably go pick up our daughter."

Alec nuzzles his nose into my neck, his lips pressing a trail of kisses across my skin. "You know she's already asleep. Ruth won't care if we take a few more minutes."

My breath catches at how easily he says this, and not

because I know exactly how he'd like to spend those minutes. I said *our daughter,* and he didn't even pause. That's just how he thinks of her.

I slip my hand into Alec's and tug him toward the front door. "In that case, we'd better take advantage."

As soon as we're inside, Alec presses me up against the closed front door, hands tangling in my hair as he kisses me with an intensity he kept banked when we were sitting on the front porch, out where any of my neighbors might have seen.

"Promise me you'll always kiss me like that," I say, a little breathless. "Even when we're fighting for alone time. When Juno is old enough to climb into bed with us or when I'm pregnant again and the size of a house. Don't ever stop kissing me just like that."

Fire flashes in Alec's eyes before he leans in one more time. "I've never been so happy to make a promise," he says.

And then his lips fall on mine, and he proves every single word.

For a Bonus Epilogue,
visit www.jennyproctor.com/alecbonus

340

ACKNOWLEDGMENTS

There was something so bittersweet about finishing this book, knowing it was my final book in the Appies series. I have loved getting to know the Appies, loved creating a shared world with Emma St. Clair, and I'm so sad that this is my final contribution! (I think? I've learned to never say never!) As always, I'm endlessly grateful to Emma for being an extraordinary critique partner and for having the vision to ask me, all those many months ago, if I wanted to write a hockey series with her. You make my writing life so much more fun than it would be without you. I will never forget the cruise that gave me the last twenty thousand words of this book and all the hockey we watched in the middle of the ocean.

Of course, I must ever acknowledge my sister and brilliant editor Emily, who edited this book in an unbelievable twenty-four hours because that's how much time I had and, amazingly so, she loved me enough to make it work.

To all my other cheerleaders and friends and family who support me in this work, thank you, thank you, thank you. I'm so lucky. I love you all.

I also want to say a little something about hockey. Here's the truth, guys. I didn't know anything about hockey when I started writing this series. I did a lot of research. I watched a lot of videos and scrolled through a lot of message boards and Reddit posts looking for insights. I'm sure I didn't always get it right. But as I researched and read and studied...something unexpected started to happen. I started to develop a real and genuine interest in hockey. Not just because I needed info for my books. But because, you guys, it's really fun to watch. Since I'm a Carolina girl through and through, I started watching the Hurricanes play, and as I followed their team and learned about their players, my understanding of the game deepened tenfold. Suddenly, (weirdly?) I can name their roster. Talk about player stats. About division and league rankings. I watch as many of their games as I can and watch recaps of the ones I miss. My husband has no idea what happened to me, but he claims the sports talk is sexy, so he's not complaining. (Just wait...I'll make him a hockey fan yet!) I don't mention this because I want anyone comparing my hockey knowledge from the first book to my hockey knowledge in the third book (please don't...spare me the embarrassment!) I mention it for one very simple reason: it's just a lot of fun.

I've had to research a lot of different things over the years. I've written characters who are musicians and athletes, who run dog rescues or have YouTube channels. I've written accountants and fashion designers and farmers and teachers and white water kayakers. But I'm one hundred percent positive that even when I'm done writing hockey books, I won't ever be done watching hockey games. And that makes me so happy. So thanks to all who play and watch and contribute to the world of hockey. I'm glad you exist, and I'm so happy to be among you. Go Canes.

ABOUT THE AUTHOR

Jenny Proctor is an award-winning author of more than fourteen romantic comedies and an Amazon bestseller.

She began her career in publishing in 2013; her writing has been a constant since then and is now her full-time focus, but in the past, she spent several years as the owner and managing editor of Midnight Owl Editors and as the chair of the Storymakers Conference.

Wired for relationships, Jenny loves public speaking, teaching, and building lasting connections.

Jenny was born in the mountains of Western North Carolina, a place she considers one of the loveliest on earth. She loves to hike with her family and spend time outdoors, but she also adores lounging around her home, reading great books or watching great movies and, when she's lucky, eating delicious food she did not have to prepare herself.

Jenny currently resides with her husband and children in the Charleston, South Carolina area. To learn more, find Jenny online at www.jennyproctor.com.

ALSO BY JENNY PROCTOR

The Some Kind of Love Series

Love Redesigned

Love Unexpected

Love Off-Limits

Love in Bloom

How to Kiss a Hawthorne Brother Series

How to Kiss Your Best Friend

How to Kiss Your Grumpy Boss

How to Kiss Your Enemy

How to Kiss a Movie Star

The Oakley Island Romcom Series

Eloise and the Grump Next Door

Merritt and Her Childhood Crush

Sadie and the Badboy Billionaire

The Appies Hockey Romance Series

Absolutely Not in Love

Romancing the Grump

Other Novels

The Christmas Letters

Her Last First Date

Just One Chance

Love at First Note

Wrong For You

Mountains Between Us

The House at Rose Creek